Shadows Beyond The
Ghost Town

By the same author

"The Half Widow"

Available at;

Flipkart.com

Infibeam.com

Amazon.in

Junglee.com

Power-Publishers.com

Crossword.com

And as e-book on

Smashwords.com

Instamojo.com

Shadows Beyond The
Ghost Town

SHAFI AHMAD

PARTRIDGE
A Penguin Random House Company

To order additional copies of this book, contact
Partridge India
000 800 10062 62
www.partridgepublishing.com/india
orders.india@partridgepublishing.com

CONTENTS

Remembering
The un named
The un identified
Buried in mass graves

Arundhati Roy

Democracy is the Free world's whore, willing to dress up, dress down, willing to satisfy a whole range of taste, available to be used and abused at will."

George Orwell

In a time of universal deceit, telling the truth is a revolutionary act.

Bob Wadgar

We need to stand up when others tell us to sit down, and we need to speak out when others tell to be silent.

Author's note and acknowledgements

During the book release function of my debut novel "The Half Widow", I informed the audience that my next novel shall be titled as "The watch Tower". However, during my Hajj pilgrimage the title "Shadows Beyond The Ghost Town" was proposed in a dream at the holy city Makah. After reading my earlier novel "The Half Widow" my teenaged niece Mehak Maqbool said, "Now I understood the story behind violence in my land." The youngsters of her age understood the story behind violence but not many stories conceived in the womb of the conflict; stories of deceit, exploitation and brutality.

With hand on my heart, I do not take offence to the Kashmiri Pandit lady, who, through 'flipkart.com' advocated banning my novel "The Half widow". Pain is pain. It only makes one scream. It can't be divided into compartments of religion, caste or sex. It can't even be quantified as less or more.

Giving the story of pain, shape of a book is a daunting task which can't be completed without help from luminaries, friends and well wishers. My friends Dr.Jowhar Quddussi and Dr.A.R.Khan have extended me support and guidance all through my attempts. I owe them gratitude. My thanks are due to columnist and writer Z.G.Muhammad for giving valuable suggestions in shaping this book. Dr.Ishaq Wani deserves special thanks for reading this script word by word, line by line. Gemma Ramos Publishing Service Associate and Mark Mentoz the Publishing Consultant at Partridge Publishing have been of great support.

I owe gratitude to all those who encouraged me after going through my earlier book.

Shafi Ahmad

The war is on

The war is on. The youth who returned from across the border are in direct confrontation with the armed forces. The sound of blasts, both grenades and IEDs, is audible time and again. The bullets fired from rifles and the ammunition from rocket propelled guns are a rage and these ricocheted the atmosphere. The citadel of pro-India political leadership has crumbled and the civilian governance is like ricks spread in various places unable to wield any authority. The semblance of government control is visible through forces personnel who roam in groups with guns dangling down their shoulders. Due to recurring attacks they have forgotten sauntering and instead move around in ready to fire position. They retaliate the attacks by local gun men and sometimes go pro active to thwart any possible attack on their camps or convoys. They look at every local individual as a suspect who may take out a gun or hand grenade and throw at them. They walk over cautious. The new development has made them standoffish towards the local populace who, in turn, rankle cavorting on the success of Mujahidin. The newspapers and electronic media are abuzz with news reports of armed skirmishes in the length and breadth of the state.

And the war is on!

Sun was doing a hide and seeks behind the moving clouds which made the atmosphere more or less pleasant. The blue patches of sky looked elegant and the slight grey clouds, doing rounds, did not look too dark. So there was hardly any apprehension of an immediate rainfall. Salt tea in the morning and afternoon and rice meals for lunch and dinner are religiously followed by the people in Kashmir, as if it is written in some holy scriptures. Kashmiris don't change the menu but for few who have gained access to outside world or who are health conscious and do not like to be obese. In the afternoon when people were preparing to take the salt tea, around twenty vehicles plied on the road in a long queue. The caravan consisted of small, medium and bigger vehicles.

Bigger vehicle, the Shaktiman.

Medium, the one tonner.

Smaller, the Gypsy.

The olive green vehicles belonged to the army and these plied comparatively faster on the potholed road, a speed faster for such a rough surfaced road. Potholed road had willow and *kikar* trees lined just few feet from the edge of the road. The tree branches extended up to the edge of the road at places and made the road a bit darker, hindering the passage of sunlight under the shade of such trees. One army soldier stood atop the smaller and medium sized vehicles while two stood on bigger vehicles. These soldiers, peeping out of the vehicles, wore helmets and held bigger guns in front of them, the muzzles resting over the vehicle body shaft. The soldiers standing on the front exposed themselves to the heat and dust rising from the broken patches of roads. In order to stay safe from rising dust they hung black coloured cloth around their head, neck and face which loosely went over their shoulders. In a way they resembled women of Kashmir who like to cover their heads and shoulders with cloth. This earned the nick name of *Mache* (insane women) for the soldiers. They stood in alert position and moved their eyes around to thwart any attack by the militants. The back of the open vehicles had loosely fitted mesh so that no grenade finds its way into the vehicle. Hurling of grenade by the militants had become order of the day for months together. The militants would throw grenades into the moving vehicles and then they would disappear into the nearby fields giving the soldiers no chance to react or catch them. Occasionally, these grenades missed the target and detonated on the ground which resulted in civilian casualties. There were instances when grenades caused damage to the forces personnel and they retaliated by firing on the passersby, causing civilian casualties. Such causalities found their entries into 'cross firing' incidents between militants and security personnel.

In war zones armed forces used mesh over the vehicles as camouflage to deceive the enemy. In civilian area people used mesh as dividing line between two teams to play volley ball or badminton. But now the armed forces were forced to devise an intelligent use of the mesh. The army and other security establishment had devised a way to prevent such deadly attacks by hanging the mesh on the back side of their vehicles. The caravan of these vehicles stopped on the main road and the soldiers took position on the higher platues to guard the entourage.

Hardly any civilian was visible on the road. The moment large convoy passed, the civilians, if any, moving on the road, took alternative routes to save themselves from the possible wrath of soldiers. Some entered the houses nearby while others retreated. There had been many incidents when civilians were sloshed by the forces personnel holding sceptre in one hand and the gun in other.

Suspicion at peak!

Fear psychosis!

As dust settled, the door of the black flag car in the middle of the caravan was opened and a grey moustached officer alighted. A ring of soldiers was thrown around him. The officers from other vehicles also alighted and joined the senior officer. Ajay Ranawat read his name plate and a gold national emblem over three gold stars in a triangular formation as insignia gave his recognition as the brigadier. The emblem, officially Ashok Chakra, is called *Patul* (idol) by Kashmiris. Others who joined him included Colonel Sandeep and Major Salvan. They were identified as colonel and major by their insignia of gold national emblem over two gold stars and gold national emblem respectively. The names could be identified by the name plates tucked to their shirts on left side.

The officers then moved towards the apple orchard where a couple of soldiers made way by cutting down the barbed wire fencing. Few soldiers walked in front and few on either side of the trio of officers. The group walked deep into the orchard and found the back of it having a down wards sloping ground. The area was minutely surveyed. Before leaving, the brigadier gave his nod and Major Salvan stood in attention to acknowledge his acceptance.

The senior army officers were on travel from the morning and they kept surveying some spots which were to be turned into additional camps necessitated due to recurring militant attacks. The brigadier was himself on survey to keep him fully satisfied with the proper choice for the new camps. The survey was not confined to Arwanpora area only. At other places similar exercise had been performed by the respective officers. In city area hotels, school buildings and parts of hospitals had been occupied. Even cinema halls were not spared after they became non-functional due to ban imposed by militants on running movies which were declared un-Islamic.

The three officers walked with the colonel and the major flanking the senior officer. The brigadier and the major were tall and well built around six feet in height. In his late fifties, sharp nosed brigadier had broad shoulders and protruding cheek bones. He held his dark blue army cap on his head. The major in his early thirties was also stout bodied. He held a revolver in his holster tucked to his back on his left side near the hip. The colonel was around six inches shorter in height. His pear shaped nose occupied larger space over his round face which gave him a bit awkward look. He was stout bodied but looked like a gunny bag walking. At places he lagged few steps behind and had to increase his speed time and again to keep pace with his officer. He wore a military hat.

"So major this place is ok," Brig. Ranawat stared at Major Salvan.

"Sir,"

"Be aware, this Arwanpora is a big area spread over more than fifteen kilometres and big and small ten villages. Highly infested with militants, some of them dreaded ones,"

"Sir, you are right," Col. Sandeep intervened.

"You just stretch your arms and you will hit the nose of a militant or lift your foot it will rub the ass of an extremist,"

"Sir," Major responded.

"Or you throw a stone it will hit the head of an *atankwadi* (terrorist),"

Both colonel and the major nodded their heads.

"So you need to be careful . . . . one more thing some of these villages consist of affluent villagers while some are poor peasants and daily wage workers. Entering into their hearts to get more information about presence of militants will depend on your intelligence and wit,"

"I won't let you down, Sir,"

"I like your confidence,"

"Thanks, Sir,"

"And be assured we are at your back . . . . so be strong."

The caravan left the spot after survey.

These people did not talk to anyone or did not think it necessary to call any person. As the caravan left the civilian movement started. Those who had taken refuge in nearby houses came out and resumed their pedestrian walk. Some tried to know asking questions through their eye movement. All pouted.

The purpose of the visit remained ambiguous.

The utterances Delphic.

And whispers continued!

Ama Ganaie and his family got suspicious as to why have such a big military contingent entered their apple orchard and what were they looking for in his orchard. He also came out from his home and tried to ascertain the reason of their entry. Nobody knew and nobody had any answers. He himself went into the orchard, walked the whole periphery for any clues. Army presence in the area panicked all who heard about it. The panic was justified as they could label anybody as a militant and finish him off. Like a needle which always points in the north direction, forces personnel's eyes pointed towards the Kashmiri youth treating everyone as a militant.

During his movement in the orchard, Ama's mental machine explored all possibilities. Stretching and bending his hands, time and again, he engaged himself in soliloquy.

Would army take over my whole orchard and set up their camp?

Lest they have dumped some ammunition and will involve me showing recoveries from my estate.

In such case will my sons be safe.

God save my young daughters.

However, Ama Ganaie in his early fifties gathered courage, tried to look fearless and walked with confidence in all directions. He was dressed in white Shalwar Kameez with an open buttoned black short coat. Instead of chapels he wore a sports shoe so as to move freely within his orchard. In the apple orchard he found crisscrossed prints of army boots and imagined that more than twenty persons have roamed the whole area. In between he looked at the fruit trees lest some damage has been done to the sprout or the branches but found all intact. He entered the entrance area of his hut, checked the locks on the doors and found everything in place. No damage had been done. Coming out of the orchard he set the broken barbed wire right by connecting the two limbs and twisting the same for strengthening. He then had a final overview of the orchard and then a glimpse of the road where one loaded truck moved slowly negotiating the potholes. The truck raised some dust and smoke and Ama moved towards his home back.

Finding no replies, he returned back to his home.

"What was the issue?" asked his wife.

"I don't know. They called none so nobody knows their purpose of visit," he replied.

"What do you think could be the cause?"

"*Pushar Khodayas. Yi tohund mansha aasi ti bani* (Have faith in Allah. Whatever is His wish will happen)."

The servant brought a samovar of tea and all sat around to sip.

Rags to riches

'Amsons Construction Pvt Ltd' read the multicoloured board hanging outside the wall of the big house in the Arwanpora village. The big house was situated near road edge which had broken black topped surface. The ruts and potholes on the road surface made it very difficult to traverse in a vehicle. But all kinds of vehicles plied over it. The big trucks, passenger buses, Ambassador Cars and even the horse driven carts called Tonga. The ruts and potholes of the road were source of nuisance, particularly during the rains, when water collected in the ditches would raise a splash of muddy water. The quantity and distance of the splash depended on the speed of the vehicle. More the speed more would be the thrust of water splash. This muddy water splash drenched the passersby and ruined their clothes. In return the drivers would be labelled as 'blind' by these pedestrians whose clothes got soiled and spoiled. In addition, the mud would be thrust on the walls on the road edges. Such incidents had collected thick layers of mud on these walls. So was the case with the big house where from 'Amsons Constructions' board hung.

This board has its own history, though unrecorded. This house was not big always. Around twenty five years back it was just a mud brick hut with thatched roof and some land on the back side.

Gulam Ahmad Ganaie started his career around thirty years back when he invited the overseer of the Public Works Department (PWD) for a cup of tea. The overseer was on the tour to the area making estimates in the beginning of the financial year. The department had to identify the bad patches of important roads for annual repairs with quarry muck and some metal so that ruts and potholes don't get bigger and be a cause of worry for the drivers. The overseer visited the area, recorded the important measurements in his diary. Some works supervisors and road coolies accompanied him. Since this took them some time to walk on foot, it was cumbersome and made the overseer tired. Moreover, the passenger bus plied on the road at definite timings and hardly any other vehicle passed on the road which could take the overseer to his destination. Gulam Ahmad Ganaie was known as Ama Ganaie by one and all. When Ama Ganaie saw the overseer passing by, with three more people from his department who looked tired and hungry, he called out.

"*Bob Jee myon hai bozukh chai dama che.*" (Babu Jee, listen to me. Better have a cup of tea)

Overseer was known as Bob Jee those days and was the senior most engineer of the area in his jurisdiction because his superiors would hardly find any time to visit these areas and, as such, he was 'all in all' in the area. Calling the overseer as Bob Jee has its own history. In past education among Kashmiri Muslims was scant and hardly few families opted for it. The reason being that Kashmiri Muslims were a subjugated lot who remained under slavery of various non Kashmiri rulers. They used all types of tyranny against them. These rulers were mostly non Muslims, however even the Muslim rulers were not benevolent towards them. There were hardly any avenues of education and they remained discouraged. Against that Kashmiri Pandits had all facilities.

The government jobs in these circumstances were in a way 'reserved' for the Pandits and a very few Muslim families enjoyed the fruits of education and jobs in government. The Kashmiri Pandits liked to be called Bob Jee as a mark of respect and may be some Kashmiri Pandit had served as an overseer in the area sometime whom people called Bob Jee. This title, as such, remained glued to every overseer later on.

The overseer was in his mid forties with a protruding belly over a medium frame. Wearing sky blue shirt and black pants he dropped the shirt out of pants so as to conceal his flaccid drooping belly. In between, he tried to lift his pants to its original position above the hips as it slipped down his belly button. He placed his handkerchief over the neck under his shirt collar to save it from getting blackened due to drooping sweat beads down his medulla.

His accomplices were in mid forties. One of them wore shirt and pants while others had the official Khaki dress prescribed and arranged for the road workers by the department itself.

Ama Ganaie had complete information about the status of the overseer. He knew, when he invited him for a cup of tea, he was making a long time investment.

His assessment was absolutely right!

Overseer and his departmental colleagues agreed readily and entered the mud brick house where Ama Ganaie spread a woollen rug and placed the only pillow, available in his house, against the wall where the overseer sat. Ama Ganaie asked his wife to prepare tea for the guests. In the room the introduction began. In about thirty minutes, Ama Ganaie was introduced to the overseer as a farmer who cultivates food grains and vegetables, sufficient for his own family's consumption, from his own fields. In addition, he owns a cow which gives sufficient milk to feed his family. And thanks to God half a *seer* is extra to be distributed to the neighbours who are in need. Newly born calf pranced here and there as it occasionally went nearer to mother cow that used her long tongue to lick its forehead. In one corner of the courtyard a coop housed half a dozen local hens. These hen roamed full day in the courtyard picking some grains and insects. These laid eggs at regular intervals and one would be slaughtered if some important and very close relative entered as guest for the night. By this conversation it could be inferred that serving tea to the overseer would in no case be a burden over the family as they were well off as per local standards of economic condition.

On the back of the hut was a ten feet by ten feet square covered area under which was placed an earthen hearth. After every use it would be painted with white clay which used to be brought by women of the village from a particular spot as far as three miles. A particular day would be fixed by the women of the village who would go in a group to fetch a basket of white clay from the particular spot. The kitchen area had a platform made of timber logs which had space for at least two earthen pots which stored drinking water. The water would be brought from the local spring. The local spring had clean water and the residents ensured that it remained free from any pollution or dirt. The water was free from dust and impurities and so clear that even a coin lying at the bottom would be visible. Nobody roiled.

The older generation was conscious of its duties towards the environment!

The storage in the earthen pots had two advantages. One, copperware was costly so uncommon among the lower strata of the people and second, earthen pitcher kept the water suitable for drinking serving as a natural refrigerator.

As soon as Ama Ganaie asked his wife to prepare tea for the guest, she swung into action. Put some rejection wood into the hearth, some dried grass in and soon it was burning. In very short time Ama Ganaie's wife prepared salt tea, boiled half dozen eggs and baked corn flour thin breads. She spread some local ghee over the bread a kind of special attention and respect for the special guest. Ama Ganaie was helped by the road coolies in serving tea to the guest. A cloth sheet locally known as *dastarkhwan* was spread. Ama's family used to take tea in earthen cups but he had bought three chinaware cups from the market around Hazratbal shrine when he and his wife visited the sacred place last time on the *Urs-Nabi*, birthday of Holy Prophet (SAW).

Large gathering of people assembled in the shrine on such auspicious days, prayed and had a glimpse of Holy Relic kept in glass container attached to silver strings. The head Molvi of the shrine attired in long robe with chain stitch borders and green turban over his head extended his arm holding the relic from various balconies over the second story of the marbled shrine. Couple of his close associates held his arm which usually trembled while holding the relic.

Reverence and respect for the Holy Prophet!

The large number of people assembled and having a glimpse of the Holy Relic recited religious verses. After every Namaz the people had a glimpse of the Holy Relic. After that, before leaving the place they made some purchases in the nearby marketplace especially local snacks *Monji and Porat.*

The shopkeepers arranged various merchandise knowing that good sales are expected on such days. The goods included eatables, clothes, utensils, crockery, brassware and photographs of various shrines and bigger mosques. Like others Ama Ganaie and his wife made some purchases.

They had an argument whether purchase of chinaware cups was unnecessary waste of money but Ama Ganaie proved a person with far sight.

"*Yi wutchta kar legi bakar yim pyala. Nabi Sabni badi doh lajaeth ladaie asi kath kiti chi.*' (Remember you did not agree this purchase on Prophet's (SAW) birthday. See how important it became)

Ama quibbled as he tried to impress his wife with his far sight and intelligence.

The guest was hungry and the bread prepared by Ama's wife was crisp and relishing. The overseer ate two boiled eggs and took four cups of tea. Ama and the employees pestered on the overseer to have more but he thanked tapping his belly to show that his stomach was full now.

Ama Ganaie had a watch which his father in law brought from Makah when he visited the place few years back on Hajj. He had brought Zam Zam water and local dates for all others but a watch for his only son in law. Ama always tried to show off the wrist watch and stretched his arm time and again to know the time. Although he had hardly any work to do which required punctuality but brandishing a wrist watch that too brought from Hajj gave him a special place in the village. As overseer finished his tea and asked for leave, Ama Ganaie requested him to stay back for the night. The overseer thanked saying he had lot of estimates to prepare so can't stay but promised to do so in near future.

"*Bob Jee wuni chu oud ganta busi yinus*"(there is still half an hour for the bus to arrive). Ama Ganaie showed off his wrist watch. He, in fact, was searching for a pretext to show off his only luxury 'The Watch' to the overseer.

"I know but we will walk another mile and take measurements till the bus arrives," the overseer looked at his own wrist watch.

He got up, so did others with him. Ama Ganaie walked side by side to the overseer till all came out of the premises of Ama Ganaie. On the road, overseer shook hands with Ama Ganaie and left.

Ama Ganaie watched them walk on the metalled road till they were off the sight beyond a curve on the road. The overseer took out his note book and pen and the accompanying persons stretched the measuring tape to know the size of the damaged portion of the road. They would then show it to the overseer who wrote in his note book. The process went on like that.

Around ten days passed, Ama Ganaie got a message from the overseer through the PWD works supervisor. The overseer wanted to meet him at the headquarters which was about fifteen miles away. Ama Ganaie waited for the passenger bus in the morning which was scheduled to arrive in around fifteen minutes. He kept looking at his wrist watch time and again and other passengers envied him having a wrist watch. Seconds became minutes and minutes became hours. Finally the bus arrived. Few people alighted, few more boarded including Ama Ganaie.

Ama Ganaie was dressed in an off colour Shalwar Kameez and black waist coat, locally known a *wasket* which he used to wear when he travelled to the city on some important work or the auspicious religious day to the shrine. After every visit he would fold it neatly and keep in a wooden box, locally called as *sandook*, till next occasion. All important papers found the safety in the wooden trunk.

The revenue papers of the land holdings.

Ama's papers relating to his wedlock.

His state subject certificate.

And some paper currency.

Very few people had the luxury of having extra dress to be used for the city visit. Ama Ganaie was one among them.

Ama Ganaie reached the overseer's official residence before office time. As a gift he had taken a sack of special walnuts for the overseer. These walnuts were from Ama's personal trees. *Burzul doon* (soft walnut) was a special gift for the overseer. The two sat in the private room of the residence where the servant, a departmental employee, served sugar tea locally known as Lipton tea. The private room in fact was overseer's bed room where very few people had access. The room was equipped with a timber cot, one chair and some furnishing on the floor. In addition to this one more room was used as a drawing cum office room where Bob Jee received all guests and did his paper work. A low lying wide wooden table was kept in this room over which overseer wrote on papers. Couple of books, pencil, graph sheets, wooden scale and eraser found their place on this 8 inch high table. Since the overseer worked mostly while seated on the floor, it would be comfortable for him to use the low height table.

The departmental employee was a privileged person as the Bob Jee kept him at his residence and, as such, had not to work on the road. In addition, he would relish the dishes that were prepared in the residence and even some contractors, who used to visit the overseer for their bills, paid some tips to this man also. Many others envied, rather hated, him as they also desired to be privileged to be part of overseer's residence.

"Let us come to the actual point," said the overseer "can you invest some money for the time being?"

"What for and how much?"

"We need to repair the road passing through your village. There are ruts and potholes. We need to fill them with quarry muck and some metal," overseer continued "you know Rajab Khan used to do this work annually but he seems to have grown bigger. He tells incredulous stories about expenditure incurred on various items. So I decided to change the contractor. Secondly, you were so nice to serve us the tea and snacks that day."

"Bob jee, what you are saying. That is my duty. Work has got nothing to do with that."

"I have already talked to the Assistant and DEE Sahib. I have their consent. Bills will be passed as soon as work is eighty percent completed. No worry on that issue." Bob jee tried to convince Ama lest he feels the pinch of late payments which could create financial problems for him.

Ama Ganaie left the place after some time and straight away went to the quarry owner. He somehow turned out to be known to Haji Sahib, Ama's father in law. Due to this proximity, quarry owner promised to send the quarry metal and wait till bills are passed. From next day quarry metal was dumped along the road near bigger potholes and stacked on the road edges. Not more than five days passed when message was sent to the overseer to issue road roller for the work. This message created ripples in the office because none expected execution of work on such a faster pace. The DEE Sahib and the Assistant Sahib wanted to visit and see for themselves the quantum and pace of work.

The day when the officers were scheduled to visit, Ama's wife was asked to roast a local fowl, prepare some quality corn flour bread and salt tea. Couple of local employees helped her in preparing dough. Crisp local fowl, known as *Koshur Kokur*, turned out to be delicious. Thin corn flour bread prepared on local hot *tawa* and baked along edges over embers made it the novelty. Local ghee was spread over the surface. The salt tea mixed with pure cow milk is amazing.

All relished the chicken and tea but still Ama Ganaie smirked and was pretending to have 'failed in his duty to serve better'.

"Had it been conveyed that Sahibs are visiting, I would have slaughtered a sheep," he continued to flatter as words wheezed out of his throat.

"No problem . . . . next time . . . . but I think you have dumped more quantity of metal than required . . . ." the Assistant Engineer wanted to convey to his officer a subtle message. The DEE Sahib received the message well that more than sufficient quantity has been dumped at site and he should not raise any objection later on about availability of funds for the work or the quantum of excess work executed.

The officers, before leaving the place, decided to allot the road roller to Ama who started filling of ditches with metal and consolidation with the road roller. The work continued for some days with labourers filling the ruts and potholes and sprinkling water over it with hand held sprinklers. The roller operator then moved his heavy roller over the surface for proper consolidation.

The movement of road roller was a delight to watch particularly for the children of the area. And during the process of execution of work, children lined up to watch the show. They yearned to sit beside the operator while the roller was on move to the extent that if they were asked their aim in life their innocent reply would be 'to have a ride on the road roller'. Only a couple of children had the privilege to do so. They were somehow related to Ama Ganaie. Their request was paid heed by the operator on the instructions of Ama. And incidentally they felt elevated after riding the roller as their schoolmates envied them. Interestingly, some children bribed the operator with walnuts, eggs and fresh fruits so that he allowed them the luxury of a ride.

In a very short period of time, against the expectations, the road surface was repaired and brought to fine shape. The drivers plying their vehicles on this particular stretch of road praised the staff and the contractor for the good work.

Ama was a semi literate person who had studied up to 5th primary and himself wrote in Urdu. But he wrote Urdu without the dots locally known as *Aamezi*. Not all people were able to read the alphabets which actually were in Urdu but due to absence of required dots would become difficult for others to read. He had kept his accounts in the same language recorded in a note book. Daily entries were made in the note book of every penny spent on this first engineering work. The accounts were precise to the extent that cigarette pack for the works supervisor, walnuts for the overseer, chicken and bread for officers, tobacco for the roller driver and the like got a mention in the accounts book.

Then came the day when overseer prepared the bills and the cheques were issued by the officer. Ama Ganaie went to the treasury to get the government cheque cashed and he expressed honesty of highest order. No big denomination currency notes were issued those days in the banks. And small amount currency notes made a huge thing to carry along. Ama Ganaie devised his own way of carrying large amount of cash. He wrapped the cash bundles in his Pheran and straightway took the money to the overseer's official residence.

"Bob Jee, this is the cash and here is the actual account of expenses," he said dropping the whole cash in the private room of the overseer.

"Why you got it here?" The overseer was perturbed as he feared lest some official from the police, vigilance or his own department may raise objections to the presence of huge amount in his official residence. This could become suspicious raising fingers on the overseer himself.

"Lest you should say Ama Ganaie forgot honesty on the first sight of few cash bundles. Here is the list of actual expenses. Rest is your job to deal with," he placed his account book in front of the overseer.

Ama Ganaie played a powerful card to win the overseer's confidence. The overseer did not read the accounts but had a glimpse of last column, depicting total expenditure. He took the amount from the heap and handed it over to Ama Ganai.

"First clear your accounts with the metal supplier and the labour mates, "the overseer advised.

Without waiting for his share from the rest of the booty, Ama Ganaie got up and straightway reached the metal supplier's place to clear his accounts. By evening all labour claims had been cleared. Ama Ganaie received appreciation for his good work and a pat on the back for his honesty.

Couple of days passed and the overseer cleared all accounts with his officers and the office staff. Then he sent a word to Ama Ganaie that he is visiting his place. Ama Ganaie waited at home and got a sumptuous lunch prepared for the overseer and couple of people who accompanied him. Rice, chicken, couple of mutton dishes, *chutney* prepared out of walnuts, radish and green chillies mixed with curd proved delicious.

"Ama Kaka, you have restored our honour in the area by executing good work. Also you have increased your faith with the officers by exemplary honesty. You will be rewarded for it in the long run. Take this share of yours," the overseer said while handing over few bundles of currency notes.

Ama Ganaie took the money in his hand and stared at the notes.

"What happened . . . . is it not sufficient . . . . you feel it is lesser amount?" Overseer enquired as his jowly face moved.

"Bob Jee, no. In fact, I have never seen so much of cash at a time. This is really large enough to handle for me. I am thankful to you. It is all because of you. You have helped me; God will surely help you and your family. I can pray only," Ama Ganaie was a bit emotional.

"I have one more suggestion for you. You now get a permanent contractor's enlistment card. That will help you in tendering for bigger works," the overseer responded. "You get property certificate and bank certificate, rest I will see. You will get a contractor's card."

The overseer left the place and Ama Ganaie showed the money to his wife whose eyes remained wide open on seeing so much money at a time. And when she heard it belonged to her husband she prayed for the overseer. Then she touched the fluffy packing on the note bundles to ascertain whether all she heard was true. Pinching her left arm she assured herself that she was not in a dream. Ama smiled and winked. Both decided to dump the money in the wooden trunk with the advice that a new padlock should be brought to make it more secure.

In a week's time Ama Ganaie got a certificate from the revenue officials by paying a sum. The certificate was issued in case of his immovable property which was his agricultural land and a bank certificate where he opened an account for the first time. In another fortnight his enlistment card was ready and he was now able to submit tenders for the construction works. His construction business flourished by leaps and bounds. Money flow increased and so increased his influence in the department. The senior most officers on their visit to the area made it a point to have a sumptuous lunch with local mutton delicacies commonly known as *wazwan.* Ama Ganaie made it a point to serve the *wazwan* in some nearby scenic spot like a forest area or in the vicinity of the spring.

Wazwan previously used to be a ten meal course of various mutton dishes. The local names given to these various varieties include *rista, tabak maaz, rogan josh, korma, kabab and goshtaba.* Rista is a round shaped meatball prepared out of minced meat. Kabab is around eight inch long meat stick prepared out of minced meat but sizzled over embers. Tabakmaaz is prepared out of sheep ribs and soaked in hot ghee. Goshtaba is again a meat ball but bigger in size. Minced meat is mixed with lots of fat, turned into orange size balls and finally prepared in curd. Piping hot Goshtaba is a delight to enjoy. For these preparations, special community of chefs locally known as Wazas take the responsibility.

With passage of time Ama Ganaie's mud brick house made way for the burnt brick three story house. Reinforced concrete slab was laid. Thatched roof made way for the corrugated galvanized iron (CGI) sheet roof. Inner walls were plastered and synthetic paint applied on the walls. The drawing room had new sofa although hardly anybody sat in it. Needless to mention cement, steel and CGI sheets came from the works allotted to Ama where saving of such materials was enforced. He showed such 'austerity' during the execution of government works and he used the spared material in construction of his own house. And official help came at every spot. The house took around four years to get completed. In addition to it, additional land holdings were purchased by Ama Ganaie where labourers from upper belt worked. Since work opportunities in the upper regions were scarce, the labourers from mountainous regions provided cheap labour compared to one from the plain areas.

With every passing year wealth of Ama Ganaie multiplied along with intimacy with senior officers. This proportionately increased the arrogance. Although officers counted him a galoot but Ama projected himself a clever person and at times sapient. Ama Ganaie stopped caring for the lower rung officials who were now complaining against him. With Ama being able to befriend senior officers, nobody heeded to the complaints of lower rung officials. What followed was some irritation over one or the other thing as Ama indulged in flippancy. He berated these officials and quibbled of and on.

Ama Ganaie continued to construct big structures and road stretches but the irritating behaviour gave birth to animosity with lower rung officials. As time passed, due to continuous complaints, the officers also had some effect. Or at least they pretended to show off lest their subordinates turned hostile.

Ama Ganaie did not leave the habit of offering Namaz all five times a day. Morning, evening and night prayers would be offered by him in his home or local mosque, but he being on work, offered afternoon prayers somewhere near the office of the works department. And if, he did not find time to reach the mosque, he offered Namaz in the premises of the works office wherein some green park area had been carved out. Few flower beds had been created and couple of trees offered cover from the scorching sun. The area had timber lattice work erected along the periphery. The timber work had green colour painted over its surface. Small wicket gate restricted entry of cattle and canines into the area. Along one side black topped road led to the main office building while as on the other side a small stream flowed. This stream had unpolluted water and those offering prayers used it for ablutions. One road worker had been assigned the job to look after this green space and he used stream water for upkeep of the space.

One afternoon, during the Namaz, Ama remembered his latest encounter with the officer. The officer had not released his payment for some time and Ama entered his office in the same manner as in past. He did not require any permission or sending a name slip for seeking entry. As he entered the office he said Salaam, to which, the officer responded with his head movement only. He was seated behind a wooden table with a glass sheet over it. Dressed in dark blue suit, white shirt and inclined strapped matching necktie, the officer continued scanning a couple of files placed in front of him. Before Ama Ganaie would raise the issue of his payment, the officer looked at him with squinted eyes and tightened forehead which exhibited some anger.

Chide in silence!

He pressed the call bell, the peon appeared and the officer handed him some papers informing that Ama Ganaie's bills be shown to him at the site of work. This was a clear message to Ama that all was not well and his influence had got a dent. May be the officer wanted to see his wings clipped. Ama realized the gravity of the situation, rose from the chair and politely saying Salaam again, came out of the office chambers. But gall of defeat pierced deep into his mind.

On a sunny afternoon, Ama Ganaie was offering Zuhar Namaz. While he sat for *Atayat*, he was lost in some thoughts.

"*Yi Dee Dala* . . . . This bloody engineer," he shouted abruptly and next moment got busy with the unfinished Namaz.

Other colleagues walking past heard the abuses and they stopped fearing Ama Ganaie had some mental problem.

"Ama Kak, why you abused Dee Sahib during Namaz?" asked one of the persons.

"This bloody fool . . . . he is not releasing my payments . . . . it weighed heavily on my mind . . . . And I could not resist even during Namaz."

All laughed.

Ama Ganaie continued to earn money and enemies in equal proportions. But none, particularly from the lower rung officialdom, dared to touch him or question him in the process. He developed strong relations not only with the officers of works departments but with those holding important posts in the district administration; police, revenue, banks and others. He invested his earned money in building empire for him. Land, buildings, vehicles and the like attracted his fresh investment. Many people worked with him. Although most of them complained about his behaviour and non-payment of wages on time but they still continued to work in his estate and the works being executed by him. He would occasionally arrange a feast with local Wazwan dishes. All senior officers would be his guests which had an impact on psychology of his workers who did not dare raise voice. Ama remained callused towards lower rung officials and even to his own workers.

Building fortune with earned money was fine but Ama had a big void in his life. He had no children. Consulting senior doctors during that period was out of question as none in the area thought bearing no child could be a medical problem. Nobody had any knowledge about Xand Y chromosomes. Hardly anyone knew about faulty egg fertilization. The only thing known in the area about childless couples was that they are cursed by the divine power and stands as a punishment for their misdeeds which could be erased or corrected by the divine help only. Some saint should extend help. Some Moulvi may provide a tumulut. Some offerings at a shrine may bestow with a gift. Fixing days in Makhdoom Sahib Shrine was another advice. This shrine is revered one and is situated in the midst of capital city atop a hillock. A flight of chiselled stone steps takes the pilgrims to the hill top.

"Visit the shrine early morning on seven Thursdays. But right from the first step you both have to walk barefoot." This proposal was put forward by another well wisher. Ama did everything but to no avail.

Final advice came from his father-in-law.

"You both should visit the shrine at Baba Rishi near picturesque Gulmarg. The hearth in the shrine is the holy place and one who paints it with special clay does get favours from the saint. Many have benefitted. Visit on Thursdays is auspicious. Allah and the saint will listen to you also."

Not much time was wasted and in few days time coming Thursday was fixed. Ama and his wife had bath and put on fresh dress. Half a dozen close relatives embarked into the second hand vehicle of Ama Ganaie. Home preparation of Wazwan was loaded in the back (dickey) portion. Two big and fat sheep were tied at top of the car with the carrier. The car rolled early in the morning and by noon all reached the shrine. People from far off places had gathered in the shrine premises. After some time, having ablution, the duo entered the hearth area and mopped and painted it as advised by the elders and the priest present there. They offered some money to the priest present there who prayed for them. Coming out of the hearth area they donated the sheep to the shrine. Offered Namaz and then sat in one corner to have the feast. They spread a sheet, took out utensils and had a good meal with wazwan and rice. Some poor fellows sat nearby and they were also offered some mutton and rice. By evening the group returned home.

About a year passed and Ama's wife conceived. Nobody had the inkling as to what made the duo gifted after so much of time post marriage. Those who advised a particular doctor thought their prescription worked. Some talked about a particular Pir, others of an offering. But Ama's father-in-law was sure about the gift has come from the shrine of Baba Rishi.

In the process Ama had four children; two sons and two daughters. The first son was born when Ama lived in the mud brick house and the new house was still under construction. And the local midwife helped his wife in the delivery. This was a routine in the area that local midwives acted as nurses and helped in the delivery. But by the time his wife was pregnant second time he took her to the district hospital. He wanted his baby be born in a more hygienic environment. He often complained that we in villages live like our own cattle. In the process he had started building his burnt brick house and then purchased a second hand white ambassador car.

The colour of the car was intentionally chosen to be white as most of the officers and the politicians used white ambassador official cars. His car had a weak battery and needed a push every morning for start up. The local people passing by would gladly help the driver to start the car daily.

'Ama Kakani Jama naaw, daka di di paka naaw'(Push on Ama's frozen boat). Small children walking nearby had developed their own rhythm to ridicule the daily practice of pushing the weak battery car. They feared or respected Ama Ganaie so would shout till Ama appeared. After that complete silence was observed.

When his third child, a girl, was to be born he took his wife to the private nursing home in capital city, Srinagar. There was only one nursing home in the whole valley and admission in it spoke of affluence. Ama called it the 'nursa home' and so did call all his neighbours who invariably thought it to be some place in the city almost forbidden for poor people. It became talk of the town then that Ama Ganaie has admitted his wife in the 'nursa home' for delivery. Some envied his affluence others had sarcastic remarks 'when one has enough money he needs ways to spend it.' So happened when his fourth child again a girl was born. On these three occasions Ama arranged a feast for the people. In one feast locals and the officers of works department participated. On other two occasion officers of district administration, police, banks and some politicians also participated. Politician was the new entrant in the list of guests.

With passing time Ama had become a known person in the valley in whose house lots of money was available. Money came from works, agriculture and other business establishments including his rented accommodations to various offices as not much government accommodation was available in the area.

'Money makes mare go' is an old adage. So happened in Ama's house. The government introduced schemes which encouraged use of modern machines in the field of agriculture. Old type plough made way for tractors. Use of long handled brooms for painting fruit trees with pesticides became obsolete and introduction of mechanical sprayers was encouraged. These items were offered on cost subsidies by the government. Ama took full advantage of such schemes as government officials themselves came to his house to explain and offered help to receive cash doles in return as gifts. Transition from an ordinary farmer to a modern one with machines at his disposal was swift.

Now old ambassador car had been replaced with new SUVs. He was the only person who had an excavator in the area. He used machine controlled sprayer in his orchards. He owned a couple of loaders. He had added a Hamam to live comfortably during chilling winter months. Hamam is a local version of heating arrangements where a room is kept hollow beneath stone slabs. An oven is kept in the middle of one of the walls where fire wood is burnt. The heat and smoke pass beneath to find outlet through two pipe openings. The stone slabs heat up the room and make it cosy during winter months. Ama had no dearth of firewood needed as rejection wood from his fruit and non fruit bearing trees was available in abundance.

Time keeps changing like a revolving wheel. And with influx of money it changes the life faster. Ama's wife also had the effect of cash bundles she continued to see for some time now. Earlier, she was a simple village woman who worked herself hard in the small agricultural field and wore traditional dress. She had some silver ornaments which she had received from her mother on her wedding. Her mother had also received these when she was married. These items in fact had a family history attached. Ama's wife used these on special occasions. Otherwise, she used jewellery of ordinary metals bought from local village shops. Glass bangles purchased from the itinerary vendors and chintz cloth dresses were her usual dress. But as days passed, her glass bangles and silver ornaments made way for costly gold items. Mogul-e-Azam gold set was one such item. Better design gold ornaments came from registered goldsmiths in the towns and the capital city. She usually remained attired in costly dresses and embellished in designer jewellery particularly when she travelled to some far off place on select occasions. Though she did not change to modern English dresses like jeans and tops but her traditional dresses cost her much more. She was now supervising household work being done by servants and hardly participated herself.

Ama now had wealth, recognition, property, family, acquaintance and what not. He even had importance as the local political leaders always visited him and kept him in good humour because he helped them financially by providing election funds and use his influence over the voters in favour of the candidate of his choice. His trucks would also be used by the election candidates to take out rallies for campaigning. Youth would jump into the trucks carrying banners and shouting slogans in favour of the particular candidate.

"*Mir sahib aage badho hum tumhare saath hai* (Mir Sahib, move forward. We are with you).

The Rebellion

Rebellion had been born many years before when a Kashmiri nationalist leader was hanged in Tihar jail and buried in the jail premises. This was perceived as a revenge killing by the Indian establishment against the murder of a diplomat. The hanged leader had become Maqbool (popular) among the Kashmiri youth. In order to thwart a situation, that his grave could become a rallying point for his followers, his remains even were not handed over to the relatives.

The situation continued till 1989. The ruling class had turned the election results, two years before, the way they wanted it to be. Declaring the results in favour of the candidate of their own choice was order of the day. Protests by the candidate, declared defeated, were usually confined to the extent of a press conference and, subsequently, every one forgot it. The loud bangs of upholding the democracy was laughed at by one and all as nobody believed the rhetoric. Democracy had been used as a whore and abused at will during previous elections.

However, after rigged elections of 1987 the volcano was simmering. Though nobody had any inkling as to what was in store but some candidates having allegiance to a conglomerate of religious groups had become popular. People listened to them more than the ruling class. Protests, on one pretext or the other continued. A complete strike observed on the death anniversary, to protest against withholding the remains of the nationalist leader, showed popularity of the cause and demand for complete freedom. Police and paramilitary personnel were deployed on all important installations.

Senior police officers increased the number of their static guard. Even then one evening some armed youth attacked the house of a senior police officer. Till then police had dealt with stone pelting crowds. Arms and ammunition in the hands of local youth was a new phenomenon. The static guard was at an advantageous position. Fire was returned which continued for some time till the group leader of the attackers received fatal bullet injury. His accomplices managed to retreat. Though locals did not believe the police theory about this incident but, subsequently, many blasts occurred. A bus was blown up in city centre. Telegraph office attacked. Paramilitary pickets fired upon and the cross fire continued late in the night. Then news of bomb blasts and firings reached from different places.

This was new to everyone in Kashmir. Local newspapers published banner headlines about incidents of firing, blasts, and warnings through bills pasted on mosque walls. Political workers, through paid advertisements, got published their press releases repenting their association with political parties. Some even came to mosques to apologize for their follies. They atoned for their past misdeeds, exploitation and political lineage. In the first instance these things happened in the capital city Srinagar only. But, subsequently, the incidents spread to other parts of Kashmir. A shoot out in the city centre and alleged molestation bid by the Para military forces ignited the fire. First protests were organized. But later in a short period of time big processions took shape in nook and corner of the valley.

When armed struggle spread, number of deaths also increased. But processions increased manifold. In case of a death in some locality people swarmed in for the four days till Fatiha was offered in a big congregation. The people participating in the processions had a favourite slogan;

"*Ai shahido Alsalam*" (Martyrs, peace be upon you)

The people's participation was overwhelmed. Those who could not walk down the long distances, they prepared foods, packed it in small pouches and threw it towards the vehicles passing by. This was done to express solidarity and show the acknowledgement of the new scenario.

Ama Ganaie was not able to walk long distances or pretended to be old enough to traverse far off. His sons participated in these processions. But, he himself wanted to be counted and become part of the new scenario. He would donate fully and asked his labourers prepare some food, pack in pouches and himself supervised its delivery when vehicles carrying people passed near his house. Word spread that Ama Ganaie is donating and participating fully in the Tehrik (movement). So his status as a big donor did not get any dent.

Ama's wife and his two daughters watched the passage of processions from the attic of their house. Their big three storey house had attic which they called tower. Attic usually is called *Kaeni* in Kashmir but with the introduction of burnt brick big houses and reinforced cement concrete (RCC) slabs the word changed to tower. Nobody being sure how it could be the tower but none objected to its use also. And so tower became watch tower for such ladies who had tall structures to live in.

*   *   *

It was middle of winter when one evening, Ama Ganaie's door was beaten. He asked his servant to look out. His son also came out to open the door. Around half dozen gun wielding youth appeared. They had concealed their faces with *Naqab*. They wanted to spend the night there.

Why Ama Ganaie's house?

One, the house had a Hamam and second, the affluent and the influential person could be helpful if forces personnel appeared from somewhere. The toilet system inside the house would help them remain inside and conceal them from the prying eyes of the forces.

An ideal hide out!

For Ama Ganaie and his family, it was a privilege to give shelter and food to the Mujahidin. If the news broke in the morning it would enhance his status as being close and acquainted to the Mujahidin. If the news did not break itself it would be done intentionally. The 'Tehrik dost' was every body's desire. The group of Mujahidin entered to a warm welcome. With affluence, Ama Ganaie had bought LPG stove, pressure cooker and other kitchen utensils which showed off his better monetary condition. Now it was not difficult for his wife to get the eatables prepared. No hearth was now needed. Ama's wife herself supervised the preparation by the servant.

The group of Mujahidin consisted of half a dozen youngsters. Four of them had grown longer beard while two sported stubble. Religious people among Muslims sport a good beard. All of them were in late twenties may be one in early thirties. Dressed in Kameez Shalwar, they wore heavy and long jackets over it. They had pulled the trousers above their ankles. Sports shoes enabled them to move faster if they had to run away for safety of life. Pouches of ammunition were tied to their belts and concealed under the long jackets. Even the Kalashnikov rifles could be covered under the jackets. But they preferred to brandish their guns. Soon after their entry into the house they asked to be guided to the washroom for ablution. Ama's servant was happy to show the bath room and then he laid some rugs in the drawing room for offering Namaz. One of the members whom they referred to as Ameer, the leader, led the prayers. After prayers they returned to the Hamam took out small sized Qur'an from their pockets and recited few pages silently.

Ama's children also participated in service to the Mujahidin. They wanted to be part of the brigade to keep these people happy 'as they belonged to the nation'. The little girls were asked to go and sleep by their mother but they remained awake to see the arrangements to their own satisfaction. They repeatedly half opened the door, had a glimpse of Mujahidin, hugged each other, giggled and expressed happiness that the 'nation's important property' was present in their home. Ama saw the little girls peeping through the half open door. He called out to his younger daughter.

"Delicion, it is getting late. Go and sleep."

The little girl had red cheeks, so Ama compared her to a variety of apples called Delicious. But Ama, the semi-literate person, pronounced it as 'Delicion'. He used to call his younger daughter "my delicion" with love. The little girl usually pranced and shouted "I am Totha's delicion . . . . I am Totha's delicion." Despite Ama's advice the two girls remained in the corridor.

They repeatedly talked to each other and pictured the next morning scene in their school when they would talk to their classmates about presence of Mujahidin in their home.

They felt elevated compared to other school friends when they described the men and the machines they carried and rested these against the walls in their Hamam.

The group of Mujahidin stayed for the night, had a sumptuous meal with chicken and mutton and a cup of *kehwa* before sleep. The Kalashnikovs stood against the Hamam walls.

Show of strength!

The supper was a delight for all except Ama Ganaie who recognized one among the group being from a neighbouring village. The reason which made Ama uneasy was that he remembered the incident when he had exchange of hot words with this fellow about a year back during execution of a work. The boy was a works supervisor then and had now joined militant ranks. Years of hard work, and acquaintance with senior officers, had made semiliterate Ama Ganaie a bit more clever and taught him nitty gritty of certain situations. He had understood how to meet the situations when powerful and powerless are to be tackled.

Euphemism in front of the powerful!

The gun exhibited power.

Ama felt this boy had in fact tried to take a revenge. He may have intentionally brought the group to his home suspecting that Ama will object to their entry and stay. The incident will incite the group against Ama Ganaie making him a target of the militants.

He was not wrong!

But his good luck had saved him from such a problem. He sensed the trouble and did not create an iota of suspicion among the group that he was not happy with their stay. Instead, he asked them about their comfort. While the group members thanked him for the hospitality neither the identified member nor Ama Ganaie expressed any reservations about the whole episode as if nothing had happened in the past or there was any baggage about the past incident. Ama intentionally engaged this particular member in long drawn talks and enquired about the hardships faced during travel across LOC on the hilly rugged terrain and the training course in arms. The Mujahidin kept explaining and Ama listened with patience and attention.

Mujahid the narrator, the raconteur!

The overall condition and the enthusiasm of the people across LOC was main subject of discussion. The response towards the armed struggle was thoroughly analyzed. The number of youngsters undergoing training in the camps there became point of discussion. Till late in the night all remained awake with Rehman, the servant, occasionally going out to check whether everything was safe.

In the morning the group members had salt tea and breakfast. They wore *Naqabs* again and left the place brandishing their weapons.

*　　*　　*

Religious leaders have been very popular in Kashmir and they have been able to turn the tide in their favour time and again. They have, as such, been closer to political establishment also because politicians took their support whenever they needed it. One such religious leader belonged to the family of preachers, who, over centuries had established a clout among the masses. His forefathers had been responsible to introduce education among the Muslim population during the times of disgraceful subjugation of Kashmiris. While other preachers had followers this family had disciples. And the tradition continued.

During the inception of militancy, one morning some youth were reported to have come for a meeting with the religious leader and subsequently fired upon him. With his death needle of suspicion started trembling. It pointed to militants on one moment while next moment it moved in the direction of forces personnel. On one hand, local governor was blamed for the killing, as some incidents of mass killings had taken place when forces personnel fired upon huge crowds who demanded Azadi, while the governor, on his part, blamed the militants whom he termed enemies of peace.

Whosoever was responsible for the killing, the dastardly act was condemned and the disciples of the slain leader came out on the streets to protest. Hundreds of thousands followed the procession which received the dead body of the religious leader from the hospital. The procession proceeded towards the grand mosque where the preacher used to address the faithful on every Friday. It was a routine of decades that he delivered religious sermon weekly on the auspicious day. In between the soldiers manning a security bunker fired upon the crowd. People received bullets, in all parts of bodies. Head, chest, abdomen, legs and fell like trees chopped or sawn at stem. Hard core followers of the preacher braved the bullets but did not allow the coffin to fall off the shoulders. If the front group succumbed others were ready to offer their shoulders. Guns emptied bullets but could not take away the passion of the people mourning and protesting in the procession. Scores of people were down on the ground. Some dead, some injured. Some pretended to be dead to save themselves from the wrath of trigger happy soldiers. While the pallbearers walked past the bunker hundreds were down on the black topped road turned wet with human blood which spilled like an overflowing stream. Those who ran to save themselves left their footwear there.

After sometime, segregation of the bodies started.

Dead to be transported to the police control room and injured, but still surviving, to the hospital. Vehicles, both hospital and private, made a beeline to the spot to help in lifting the bodies and the injured. Those living nearby thronged to help. But soldiers fearing the crowds may go out of control did not allow them to reach nearer. Cocking their guns upon the swelling crowds they restricted the movement towards the spot.

Blood dripping down the injuries and in semi conscious state, some writhed in pain, while others bearing acute pain still pretended dead fearing the soldiers might shoot if they made any movement. The soldiers, segregating the dead and the injured, searched their pockets and took away any valuables like purses, watchs and currency notes.

Curfew was imposed to thwart any mass protest.

*   *   *

This year the winter went almost dry with few showers here and there. There was scant snow fall in the plains and meagre in the hills. The power supply has always been a problem in the valley but this year it proved bit more troublesome. Although power supply was a bit better in the city but villages had more of dearth. Evenings, as such, happened to feel dreadful.

The ghost town!

The news about corpses scattered here and there made the environment more frightening.

No one knew why somebody's corpse was hanging down the tree.

None had an inkling why bullet ridden body was on the roadside.

None had any clue why the head and torso of some person was at different places.

The self concocted stories made rounds. About one, the label of Mukhbir (the army informer), about another political worker, and someone else the Mujahid's *dakh loor or soiyath* (Militant's helper).

Fear engulfed the whole valley and it increased with every passing hour after sun set. In the evening the doors were closed before dinner. Lights went off in all rooms except the one where the food was served. Passing of vehicles broke the silence but increased heart beats.

What if army convoy passes and stops near our house. What if Mujahidin came and asked for night stay.

What if this . . . . what if that . . . .

Some fifteen days had passed when Ama Ganaie served food to a group of militants and they stayed back in his Hamam during the night. With guns dangling their shoulders they looked very powerful and none could say no to them even if one wanted to. Ama Ganaie was thinking about this incident time and again.

"I am not able to reconcile with that incident," Ama squinted his eyes and roamed in his room from one corner to other. "How could I? Ama you were forced to serve food to that boy who insulted and humiliated you in front of dozens of people. Ama you had to sit in front of him like a faithful servant. Like a weak dog," he cupped his face in his hands, and then pressed his temples with his palms to give his head some relief. He took a cigarette from his pocket lighted it and had few deep puffs, releasing smoke through his nostrils in between.

He was not bothered about the late night food preparation but the idea of one person's presence in the group pinched him a lot. The very thought of his presence in the group struck thorns . . . . no nails . . . . no spikes . . . . rather wedges into his heart.

"No Ama no, you can't accept his authority and sit like a coward. I have to take a decision . . . . a strong decision!"

Soliloquy continued!

He felt someone was hitting him with a hammer on his head and his medulla will break any time. This man had spoken to him harshly a year back. And the pictures of that incident rolled like a film.

"What authority you have . . . . you are just a works supervisor . . . . Your chief stands up when I visit his office . . . . who the hell are you to object to my work . . . . what you know about specifications . . . . how can you yell at me . . . ." Ama Ganaie had responded harshly to the man.

But now this man, having joined militant ranks, became master of the area. Despite having so much of influence in the area, Ama Ganaie had to serve him without expressing a word of dissent or protest.

How could one tolerate this . . . . and Ama Ganaie the influential person . . . . no way!

Ama Ganaie and his family had their evening meals. The women folk, Ama's wife and daughters, got up to other room to sleep. He signalled his two sons to remain seated as he had something important to talk about.

"The situation in Kashmir has turned bad. Gun men are ruling the roost. Gun has become very powerful. No one dares to say *no*. Since we are well off we can be first targets. We shall have to shell out whole property . . . . may be in instalments . . . . may be in one go . . . ."

"Why you say so *totha*. Who can grab our property?" elder son Nazir asked.

"Partly the persons we served last time. Partly government of India,"

"Hmmm . . . . but why?"

"I was asking the Pandit post master what will happen to the Kisan Vikas Patra and other deposits with the banks if Kashmir gets independence or becomes part of Pakistan . . . . his reply was it will all go to government of India accounts . . . ."

"How can that be? The Pandit is an Indian agent and he wants the Tehreek to fail. He is spreading concords. Such Pandits are killed by Mujahidin and then some people say Mujahidin are wrong, "his elder son responded.

Then his sons watched him with despair. His sons were in their teens with a difference of around two years in age. They had grown taller and their skin was fair like most Kashmiris have. Economic stability in their home was visible from the dresses they wore. They usually liked modern dresses of high class brands. Availibility of vehicles in the home had made it possible for them to learn driving in their young age. The youngsters looked stout bodied.

"And you know among the group we last served was the son of Rahim Dar of neighbouring village. They don't have sufficient food as their harvested crops don't last for full year but now with gun in hand he has become the master of this nation . . . ."

Ama Ganaie was sarcastic and used derogatory language. Indulging in ribaldry, he tried to spook his sons. He wanted to abuse the person more but somehow stopped short of it. Presence of his own sons forced him to be morally on high ground and don't indulge in more filth speak.

"Then what you want us to do?"

"One of you shall have to cross Line of Control (LOC) and become Pak trained Mujahid. That is the only security." Ama Ganaie was clear and forthright.

During past some time Mujahid was the buzz word and everyone who had a gun hanging down his shoulder was a hero. Even when some Mujahid died in the encounter with the army his funeral procession would be a thing to watch. All people, men and women, young and old joined the procession from all parts of nearby localities and offered Salaam and Fatiha to the slain Mujahid. The youth were specially lured by the turn of events towards the gun. Emotions ran high.

This was a special occasion when Ama Ganaie asked his sons to travel across LOC and get trained in firearms. The main aim of this whole exercise of exfiltration and infiltration was to liberate Kashmir from Indian rule but Ama Ganaie analyzed other aspects. The presence of the armed youngster disturbed his peace of mind time and again. He wanted protection in his home so that his neighbours don't force him into submission. Both his sons were young and incidentally lured by the gun.

"Whom do you want to cross over?"

"Farooq . . . ." he named his younger son.

After this nobody talked. They got up and went to sleep.

*   *   *

Fearing violent reaction from the gun wielding Mujahid and a type of social boycott by the population for their anti Tahreek steps, all pro India politicians had left valley to seek temporary residences in Jammu and Delhi. If some daring ones remained in the valley they had, at least, two tier security blanket.

Two more days passed. Nobody talked about the plan in the house. Ama Ganaie had himself chalked out a programme with some pro Tehreek political worker who used to book groups to be taken to Line Of Control and handed over to some Gujjar guide who had complete knowledge about mountainous terrain and secret routes and who could safely make them cross LOC. LOC is an artificial line which divides two parts of the state of Jammu and Kashmir. One part, around two thirds in area, is controlled by India and the other one third is controlled by Pakistan. Both have a claim over the entire state and have fought full-fledged wars over the issue.

Gun culture stood introduced in the state particularly the Muslim dominated areas. And volunteers among the pro militancy political parties had sprung up who arranged the travel and guidance for the enthusiastic youth to cross line of control between two parts of Kashmir. With these arrangements it was very easy for the youth to cross over and get trained in fire arms. Only the youth had to make up their mind rest of the service was at hand.

In the wee hours Farooq lifted his ruck sack filled with warm clothes, wind cheater, woollen cap, and a galosh that could be helpful in ascending the mountain peaks in between on way to LOC. The long shoes had Duck Back mark on back side. He wore pants and shirt with sports shoes. All his family members bade him farewell as he left home. Mother and his young sisters went upstairs to watch him move on the road outside from their watch tower.

"He looks a real Mujahid," Shazi nudged her sister.

"*Khoday ani nus wari wate. Chashmi bad nish bachawinas* (May God, he returns safe and sound. Allah saves him from whammy and evil eye." Their mother prayed with head towards the sky.

"*Amen*" Both sisters responded.

*　　*　　*

With number of attacks by the armed Mujahidin increasing, the encounters rose in number. A grenade attack on an army vehicle, a rocket launch on military establishment, a gun fire on the patrol party became the order of the day. Ambush by the Mujahidin to attack the convoys resulted in loss to forces personnel. While these attacks infuriated the uniformed men, the death of attacking militants or the people caught in cross fire or revenge fire also increased. This increased the number of mourners participating in the funerals. The political leaders advocating freedom thronged such spots. All Fatiha congregations turned into rallies and the freedom loving elements got a readymade audience to address the nation.

"Be united and the glittering sun of independence is to rise soon. The martyr's blood won't go waste. Mujahidin are the sacred property of the nation, we need to protect them. Every household has to be their safe abode. They are offering their precious lives for our better tomorrow. Government may try to place a wedge among various groups of the nation to safe guard its own interests, but we have to exhibit that we are one and in unison. Beware . . . . and India shall have to go . . . . leave this territory despite its huge military power."

The oratory by the leadership happened to be similar at all places as if it was a written statement distributed among the concerned.

Rhapsody was at its peak!

The funeral congregations were held either in some bigger area near the house of the martyred Mujahidin or some open space near the graveyards. The participation of both men and women was witnessed. A temporary partition segregated the groups of male and female participants. At certain places women speakers organized Fatiha congregation separately. New breed of educated women who had allegiance to freedom loving groups spoke at the occasion. Emotionally charged participants vowed to take the struggle to its logical end.

The enthusiasm of new breed of youngsters encouraged the number of recruiting organizations to multiply. And so increased the number of new outfits.

The increase in armed attacks increased the number of deaths and injuries to forces personnel. This led to rethinking about Kashmir policy. Introduction of army into the fray was mooted and so came into force some of the laws. With dreaded law Armed Forces Special Powers Act (AFSPA) coming into force the lower rung armed forces personnel got enormous powers. Power makes people arrogant and absolute power breeds absolute arrogance. Number of dead bodies also increased. The deaths did not remain confined to armed persons only but included those killed in the cross fire and the revenge taken at places by the army after getting attacked.

Attacks

Deaths

Destruction of property

Funerals

Congregations

Revenge

And introduction of Martyrs graveyards took place.

In almost all localities separate spots were identified to bury the Mujahidin killed in action and the civilians in retaliatory action by the forces personnel particularly when their own men fell to bullets. Fluttering green flags on the periphery and tin boards identified these graveyards and similar spots from far off distances. The individual graves lined with marble and granite tombstones appeared through contributions by the locals.

Shaheed . . . .

The advice by the speakers that every home belongs to the Mujahidin was taken sportingly by the common people; but not by the army. They received reports that some over ground freedom loving elements visit the congregations after every death of a Mujahid. And the armed trained militants who returned from across happen to hide in the localities. Who gave this information?

Army established its own networks. They filtered their informers to receive pointed information. It was done either through some willing locals who liked to work for money. Some others who were tortured on suspicion of being sympathizers and could not bear the brunt of third degree physical torture. They then spoke out whatever they knew about. How could they bear?

Tied through wrists and ankles to the ceiling beam in the shape of an aeroplane.

A roller inching over the naked body.

An iron rod twisted in the rectum.

Electric shocks to the private parts.

Pumping of water into anus under tremendous pressure.

Then in addition some of the trained persons arrested in some places along with arms or letter heads of various organizations were pivotal in providing the vital information.

The information about locals giving shelter to armed militants who attacked the army infuriated the uniformed men. They looked with suspicion to everybody. They presumed every youth to be a militant or at least a sympathizer and every home a hideout concealing firearms. Pheran, the long Kashmiri robe, became the source of suspicion of highest order because it was very easy to conceal a Kalashnikov underneath it and fire at the army when they came within the striking distance.

To counter attacks by Pheran clad boys, army devised a novel reaction. All people wearing Pheran must have their arms stretched out of the Pheran. 'Hands Up' became the catch phrase.

Over the years people had installed amplifiers in the mosques which were used for Azan, a call to the faithful to offer prayers or delivering religious sermon by the Molvis particularly on Fridays. However, these amplifiers were subjected to alternative use by the forces. Search operations became order of the day.

Mosque loud speakers were used to order people of Dandipora to come out in the open and assemble in the play ground near the village. Why was Dandipora chosen for the searches? Couple of days back, on the hillock, militants had targeted a patrol party and injured a couple of army men. The news came that they were injured but who knows they might have died later. The assailants ran towards Dandipora village. Army suspected they melted in the local population to deceive the army. On hearing the announcement people came out of their homes and ran towards the play ground. Before actual identification started, couple of lower rung soldiers ordered some youth to do menial job. One cleaned the soldier's shoes. Few were asked to do physical exercise like jumping up and down. A middle aged man lost in some thoughts had his left hand first finger dipped in his nostril. He was clearing boogers from his nose. His behaviour irritated the soldier and as a punishment he was ordered to get engaged in frog jumps. Few more were made to do a circus act . . . . pirouette. Then, after some time exercise to identify the 'suspected attackers' began. People, particularly youth, walked past the Gypsy. God knows who sat in the Gypsy with his head covered with a black cloth and eyes only open. Time ran. Minutes, half hours, hours and full day was consumed. Morning, afternoon and evening went by. In all twelve persons were in army custody but nobody had the slightest information about each other.

Dandipora rejoiced when people, assembled in the play ground, were released by evening. The locality plunged into darkness due to always absent electricity. Kerosene lamps gave some feeble light. People, hungry for the whole day, had dinner and as was a daily routine slept early. However, twelve homes whose men had not returned from the search operation commonly called a crackdown could neither eat nor sleep. Who could search for them?

Their very young children.

The illiterate womenfolk.

Or the frightened siblings.

And when some time later gun shots ricocheted, all inmates of Dandipora hid themselves into quilts, put off their kerosene lanterns, bolted their doors and windows. The relatives of missing persons even went into frightened slumber praying silently.

The ghost town became more horrifying.

In the morning Numbardar, the village head was summoned by the army. He was accompanied by the village Chowkidar. They identified the twelve bodies with their heads and torsos strewn in the dry Nallah between the village boundary and the hill slopes.

"They attacked the army patrol with weapons and our commandos killed them with *khukris* .... you know these Gurkha soldiers don't waste Indian bullets. *Gala kat dete hain* (they slit throats)" the army officer had explained to the village representatives.

Decapitation!

These representatives had no guts to describe the lurid details regarding the sanguinary episode. News, however, spread to the village about one dozen people lying headless in the ravine. Strict orders from the army officer were conveyed that no mourning should take place.

No screams

No beating of chests

No hollering

No slogans . . . .

Kashmiris say' *Khoon chu baraw diwan'* (Spelt blood can't be concealed. It speaks out). News did not remain confined to the village only. It reached somehow to the district administration and the local police station, though late. The Station House Officer accompanied by some of his sepoys reached the spot. Around ten hours had passed when villagers and the relatives came to know about the identity of the headless bodies. Forbidden not to weep, they just watched helplessly. When local police appeared on the scene after around ten hours to do *panchnama* of the dead bodies, first cry came from the mouth of the woman whose husband was one among the dead. Deep emotional sighs wheezed out of the trachea.

Then screams followed.

Word spread in the village about the arrival of the local police. Then hordes of people appeared from nowhere. All lanes and by lanes converged at the dry ravine.

Even the weakest can't be silenced for long. The frightened can't be suppressed into subjugation. The powerful have to face revolt and resilience. The pusillanimous gave vent to their feelings. Screaming villagers shouted, tore their shirts, bared their chests and stood in front of the soldiers.

"Shoot us, come on fire!"

"You killed our brethren, now kill us also."

"Shoot here, shoot here!"

The soldiers beat a retreat. Few fired shots in air.

"We want freedom!"

Ricocheting gun fire was met with reverberating Azadi slogan.

*   *   *

With number of organizations increasing, number of press notes multiplied. Demand of protest strikes increased. The local newspapers published the press notes either threatening Indian army to leave or paying glowing tributes to the slain militants, Mujahidin in local parlance. And with attacks increasing, army resorted to establishment of new camps in new localities. Government buildings, schools, deserted houses and even orchards or open fields were occupied to set up camps. Barbed wire fencing around the new camps, restricted movements with speed breakers, concertina wire barricades, drop gates, watch towers on raised platforms filled the new landscape. Anybody visiting any locality would have the first impression of his entry into a war zone. Weak hearted feared and restricted their ventures outside. Errands diminished.

Over the years Ama Ganaie had established a big orchard near his house. He purchased more land from adjoining neighbours and extended his original piece of land with this new annexed land. Orchards need continuous vigil against theft, and damages to fruit trees. So Ama constructed a small hut in which he kept ground floor for the watch and ward labourers and on first floor two rooms were nicely furnished. These furnished rooms were used occasionally when Ama and his family had guests from city who wanted to enjoy early spring blossom which is greatly liked by the people. Visiting the orchard having blossoming trees and having mid day meal on the green top surface would be a picnic that too free from hustle and bustle of city or any other tourist spot. The ground floor was furnished with grass and a thick sheet laid over it. The first floor was nicely furnished with an attached bathroom where doors of the bath room opened in both rooms. Few chairs and cots also found their place as some furniture. Ama Ganiae also shifted his cow shed from the premises of his house into one corner of the orchard. The reason behind this being that he felt cow dung smelt filthy and officers visiting his place would feel uncomfortable. Secondly, the chowkidar in the orchard would feed and look after the cow and bring fresh milk to Ama Ganaie's house in the morning. The cow would also feed on the grass and some fruit available in the orchard itself.

Life moved on smoothly till one day a senior officer namely Brig. Ajay Ranawat came in a caravan of twenty vehicles of the army and decided to establish additional camp in the vicinity. Ama Ganaie's orchard proved to be an ideal place. The hut could be used by the officers and fenced orchard by the security personnel. Ama Ganaie did not want to let the orchard go to army but who had the guts to say no. Army was much more powerful than the groups of militants and could not be threatened by information that Ama's son Farooq was also a trained militant, though he had not returned yet to the valley. The security personnel arrived one day with full baggage, ammunition, big mouthed guns, dozens of big and small vehicles, tents, and hundreds of personnel. The whole area of the orchard was sanitized first. Existing residential accommodation was reserved for the major and couple of more officers. Some pre-fabricated boards were used to erect few more billets as residential huts for middle level officers. Futon and sleeping bags provided the urgently required furnishings and beddings. Fenced area was strengthened by concertina wires. Watch towers were erected at corners and sand and earth filled bags erected at many places. Search lights of big size were fixed on watch towers to keep vigil and thwart any possible attack by the militants. The inner area in the orchard was paved with pebbles to make passages in a criss cross manner to pave way for movement within the camp. Near the main gate some area was reserved for parking of vehicles.

When after few days the army men actually transferred to this new camp the entry into it was completely blocked. Passing trucks, loaded with stone ballast or nallah boulders were stopped to drop some quantity of their material near the gate.

Local taxes extra!

The parking area was paved with stone ballast in a few days and now no wheel tracks were visible there. Bricks unloaded from passing trucks were used to enclose certain area for planting ferns and flower saplings. Triangle headed arrow marks of iron or steel pointed towards various spots like officers mess, general mess, volley ball court, office and the like.

The back side of the orchard had a downward slope and at the foot of the slope ran small stream. This water was used by some villagers living downstream for irrigation as well as drinking purpose. The army men used the declivity for erecting country type dry latrines for the use of lower rung soldiers. Trenches were dug out and timber posts erected. Thick polythene was used to cover these blocks on three sides and the front side had a removable polythene cover which could be lifted for allowing entry. This was a source of health hazard for those who used the stream water but nobody dared to protest.

In fact the orchard was distributed into three parts. One adjoining Ama's house was left vacant, middle portion in which the hut stood was occupied by the army and the other part again left vacant. Ama Ganaie did not object to the occupation. He was clever enough to understand that nobody will listen to his objections and he understood this could prove an additional security for himself and his family. He even used wile to influence the commander of the camp.

Sweet tongue, rather words coated with sugar!

He now had arranged two tier security system, one through his son who joined militant ranks and God had sent in another through army. He knew nobody could raise finger on him for giving land to the army because army had occupied such spots at many places and, as such, he could not be singled out.

Hunt with the hounds and run with the rabbit!

The villagers lived in the area in congested localities and some had constructed houses a bit far away from the village itself. They had left the congested area of the village and used their open spaces either in the orchards or paddy fields. However, these houses were scattered and the inmates looked frightened in the night hours. Anybody could come and attack and nobody would be able to help. Communication was very difficult because telephone lines would remain mostly disturbed and all did not have the facility available. Secondly, all central government departments had shifted their offices to Jammu as they feared reprisal and may be attacks by the militants. Even some telephone exchanges had been blasted with grenades.

Nexus

"Yes, in the first instance these six people . . . . *behenchod.* Sister Fuckers" Major Salvan moved his pen swiftly on the paper, "I have ticked the names. But people must see them outside . . . . understand,"

"Sir, "JCO, standing across the table, took the paper from him. He then thumped in 'Savdan' and left the office room of the major.

After the army established its camp in Ama Ganaie's orchard, the major in charge, one day, thought of establishing rapport with local population. He sent a word to at least half a dozen people to meet him in the camp. When they assembled, they realized it was a trick played by the major. All the six invitees belonged to the militancy in a direct way. Their sons were either active militants or were still across. It was intentionally done and they were made to wait on a bench for around one hour near the gate. It was done with the purpose of exposing them to the general public who travelled in the buses and had to alight from the bus and walk the distance. It would be the sweat wills of the JCO in charge that he may or not ask the ladies to disembark and walk the distance. Sometimes his mood would allow the comfort to the females to remain seated.

Half dozen people of the area directly linked to active militancy waited for the call from inside . . . .

All waited helpless!

And when the call came, they were taken to the frisking room and then guided to major's office for a chat. Some water and some tea was served. And then followed the sermon to which these men could respond in affirmative only.

"See, India is not so weak that we will leave Kashmir for the fear of few hundred guns. And Indian army is so powerful . . . . these *behenchod* Pakistanis are not able to face directly so they want your sons to indulge in guerrilla warfare . . . . can they face . . . . so better ask your sons to surrender . . . . otherwise who is where and which area . . . . few bullets will finish them off . . . ." he continued his advice.

After this there was silence.

No warning . . . . or a sermon . . . . for some time and then the major asked the sentry to guide them to the gate.

These six men could not talk much among themselves till they reached Ama's home. Curious to know what could be the purpose of this meeting they indulged in discussions as they entered the courtyard.

"Gulam Ahmad, what is your assessment of today's meeting?" asked one among the group.

"He is frightened of recurring Mujahidin attacks. Be at ease. Will Mujahidin surrender . . . . no way!" Ama was confident. "Come inside and have a cup of tea."

"Thanks. Family members must be anxious as to why were we called to attend the camp." All said almost simultaneously.

They then quietly dispersed and left for their places.

When Ama Ganaie entered his home, anxious family members asked him about the meeting. And Ama replied sarcastically,

"*Wanaan hasa shanil. Timan weni tan yiman athas manz bandook chu* (He is boasting of his power. Why shouldn't he tell those who have guns in hand)?

Ama Ganaie did not understand the intelligence of the major. He, for some time, thought that the major was actually afraid of militant attacks lest he may lose his life and, as such, resorted to threatening him and his other colleagues in order to affect surrender by the active militants. May be this surrender by half a dozen militants would pave way for others to follow. Then Kashmir would be free from militancy and old time peaceful environment would return. The major actually had different plans in his mind. The militant organizations had for past some time been warning common people to desist from keeping liaison with army, fearing that information about their movements may be passed on by someone. So the major killed a couple of birds with one stone. One, he exposed the relatives of active militants to the general public lest someone among the militants would have to think over the strategy afresh. Second, he established a direct contact with the relatives of the militants . . . . rather with the militants themselves. The major wanted a close liaison with Ama Ganaie which didn't come to Ama's mind immediately. This thing, Ama understood few days later when time and again his phone rang and the major was on line enquiring welfare and if he needed anything. Even to the extent if Ama could 'provide a fresh glass of pure milk because army supply used to be powder milk only'.

Days passed and the proximity increased. The new breed of people with power had surfaced; militants on one side and the army on other. Civil administration was almost defunct. Actually gun only ruled and, whosoever carried it, was the master of trades. Works departments were worst hit by the new dispensations. Some persons exposed their links with the militant organizations to have a clear control in the offices. Some even managed to get the officers and engineers abducted and then enforced their release from militant captivity against some negotiated price. Others interfered in the tendering process to achieve whatever they wanted. Ama used the double advantage. His son was a 'Pak trained' Mujahid and he had established very good relations with the other source of power, the army major.

*　　*　　*

Kashmiris say '*Jab Allah deta hai to chappar phad ked deta hai*' (*When God bestowes He does in plenty*). A windfall happens.

This came true for Ama Ganaie.

The people attached to the works division, he mostly worked with, became his slaves and his diktat ran. The officers, officials, workers and the contractors all remained subdued in front of him. Anything, among the works he felt was profitable, went to him. And any diversion of funds, he liked to have, became easy for him.

In the month of July incessant rains continued for many days. The hills had heavy rainfall and the nallahs flowing down brought gushing streams overflowing the banks. The discharge was enough to breach weak spots first and then washed away a portion of an important bridge connecting the two districts. The population of hundreds of thousands was rendered connectivity less. None cared for the general public but the army movement became cumbersome as they had to detour via some other route. And in case of war like situation the army found it unsafe. The road opening patrol parties found it very difficult to maintain the route incident free. The emergency was there.

In the wee hours when few people had finished their Namaz in the mosques and others were still asleep, army had encircled a large area in the vicinity of the bridge. People listened to the orders on the mosque amplifiers to assemble near the bridge.

New use of Mosque amplifiers!

Hundreds in number without proper breakfast!

The scene near the bridge was like a congregation around a shrine where devotees throng with reverence and faith. Men of all ages descended the place without even an iota of protest as they had now gained the experience that even a stare on the face of an army man would invite trouble and result in severe beating. In order to save themselves getting sloshed they silently arranged themselves in groups, some excavating the stones and boulders from the river bed, few removing the lichen, others pouring these into baskets and few more helping load these baskets on the shoulders and rest transporting them to the actual bridge site. The people had complied orders to get baskets, shovels and the manual excavators of various kinds from their homes.

Some of the army men dressed in full combat and holding sticks in their hands mingled with the groups of people lest someone needed a 'lesson' to be taught if he played some trick or rested a while escaping the gaze of these soldiers. Some soldiers, arrogant and mad with absolute power tried to stultify the naive villagers. Large contingent of soldiers in full combat dresses remained spread around the area to thwart any attacks by the armed militants who may like to keep the connectivity snapped. The damage to the bridge was extensive which needed technical expertise and time to rebuild. So the temporary approach was to be connected with the stone filling in the yawning gap developed due to collapse of bridge pier and part of the slab. This damaged portion needed filling.

As time passed women folk received the news about long drawn activity the men folk were engaged in. They realized that these men won't be allowed to leave sooner and needed some food items. Through whispers women decided to reach the venue in groups with food items, bread, rice, bagels and the like to feed their relatives. Though the soldiers, guarding the area on the outer circle, first rejected the idea of allowing these women into the area, but fearing a protest which could result in a backlash they were later instructed by Major Salvan to allow the entry. The men doing forcible labour job on the bridge site were then allowed to have few morsels of food by rotation. After food they engaged themselves again in the labour work. One middle aged man was holding a big boulder over his shoulder when he farted. Two soldiers, standing nearby, laughed loud. They did it intentionally to catch the attention of group of three young women who were returning after serving food to their relatives. As they looked towards the laughing soldiers, one of them winked his eye to convey his obscene intention. Couple of them indulged in ribaldry.

"They care for their relatives, who will care for us?" The soldier passed the lewd and suggestive remark as these young women passed by. Other one tried to shrink and obstruct the passage. When the women tried to pass by he indulged in spanking.

Ama Ganaie managed hundreds of wire crate from the stocks he had saved when he executed works previously. And then, under the watchful eyes of the army major and his subordinates, people brought stones and boulders from the river bed and filled the crates at the damaged spot. In between filling with smaller stones was done. The breach was bigger so it took around a week to be restored. The difference between day one and other days was that people had not to be called in from their houses. And from day two, the junior engineer of the area supervised the work while assistant engineer also paid couple of visits.

Payment of bills was not source of any fuss or arguments because the execution of "emergent natured" work was supervised by the engineering staff themselves and the DEE Sahib was invited by Ama, supported by a telephone call by the major, to the residence of Ama Ganaie. All had a sumptuous meal and cheques were handed over to Ama Ganaie at the venue itself.

Trouvaille had taken place!

Kashmir is known worldwide for its natural beauty. Though due to conflict, life became miserable and hardly anybody ventured out to take a sojourn towards the beautiful landscape of vast meadows, gushing nallahs, snow capped mountains but the beauty of verdant remained intact. In addition Kashmiris weave world famous hand woven carpets second only to Iran. These carpets are woven on specially developed manual looms. These looms consist of wooden poles tied with iron locking system and kept vertical in a room. The threads of silk or other manufacturing material pass over it vertically. Then other threads pass vertically and transversally with a couple of workers sitting around and enforcing knots between these threads. The spectrum of the carpets depends upon the instruction sheets 'Kaleen Taleem' the carpet lessons in local parlance. This *taleem* is written in some sort of code words which needs some training for the workers and can't be understood by one and all. It resembles the music notes according to which musicians pull strings on their musical instruments to come out with interesting and enjoyable musical numbers.

The workers with the help of these notes are able to produce world famous carpets lined with pictures of birds, shrines, flowers and the like which are so soothing to eyes and only rich can afford these due to very heavy price tags.

The government had banned cutting down of walnut trees because it is used as raw material for the local walnut industry crafting furniture which is a beauty to watch. After a week's time Ama Ganaie's load carrier was loaded with a beautiful walnut sofa set and a world famous Kashmiri carpet to be dispatched to Jammu and then onwards through a transport agency to major's home address.

*   *   *

The diversified views of the parties involved in the possible resolution of the vexed issue had thrown up various organizations on either side of the fence. The armed groups supporting them took sides according to their outlook. This, not only threw contradictions open among the groups having different aspirations but also subjected the groups to enmity for want of supremacy. The so called green brigade who aspired to fight for implementation of UN resolutions which promised referendum for inclusion in Pakistan or India was at loggerheads with the groups supporting complete freedom. The aspirants of complete freedom were on the forefront when armed struggle began. They, in fact, started the armed struggle as their stated policy and strived for nationalist Independent Kashmir state. The manifesto was drafted and ratified by their leader decades back. He was subsequently hanged and buried in the jail premises. While there was difference of outlook so possible skirmishes was inevitable but such happenings among the groups of green brigade did not augur well. The acts were internecine. The issue was highlighted with kidnapping of two foreign engineers working at a hydro power project. The other group used its force and got the duo released.

The faggot lost its constituents one by one!

Leaders of various groups involved themselves with oratory, press notes and calls for unity. The calls for unity were so much in abundance that it was amply clear all is not well. The nation was either acephalous or had more leaders than followers. The saner elements tried to forge unity among various groups under the umbrella organization. The number of frequent and individual strike calls by the militant groups diminished and Umbrella took charge of proposed strike calls and continued with a joint political front.

*　　*　　*

The national days of India like Independence Day, Republic day etc remained an all-official function only; hardly any civilian attended the functions. Some parades by the contingents of police and central police forces would be the highlight and the district administrator took salute in functions which being very low key affair. There were two problems facing it. One the non participation of locals, complete strike by the transport and the business establishments and second the separate parades by the militant organizations who celebrated Independence Day of Pakistan a day earlier than India. The security establishment faced added problems during these days because the venue of green brigade arranging a flag march with hundreds of armed militants would be a secret and tackling such big groups was a problem.

This year's Pakistan day was celebrated with fanfare.

Morning sun had just got above the mountain tops and the far off snow peaks shone like diamonds when around one hundred militants dressed in full combat fatigue, brandishing Kalashnikovs and pouches tied to their bodies appeared from different directions and assembled in the open field. The commander looked a brave and confident man with stout body from his appearance. With an imposing height of around 5ft 10inches he had broad shoulders and was dressed in a sky blue Kameez Shalwar. The sports shoes made him elegant. He sported black beard as long as one fist on his fair skinned face. His body guards flanking him were dressed in Pathan suits with their trousers pulled up above their ankles. They also sported beards some longer others stubble. The Kalashnikovs earlier dangling their shoulders were now cocked in ready to fire position held in hands with muzzles pointed forward. From the nearby villages some youngsters had got inkling about such a parade and they arrived in time to watch. Striplings rejoiced as they watched from one edge of the area.

The Commander took salute as the contingent marched in front of him. Some raised slogans 'Allah-o-Akbar' which were reciprocated by others. Those watching on the periphery responded with enthusiasm. Before the march would be over around two dozen army men appeared and spread in different directions to encircle the open field. However, the militant commander sangfroid and unfazed by the sudden development continued his speech.

"We are all on the path of Jihad. Even if we lose our lives our Allah and beloved Prophet (SAW) shall be happy with us. We shall get rewarded on the day of resurrection. As Muslims we can't be cowed down by any force on the earth, howsoever, powerful it be,"

Suddenly, his speech was disturbed by the hand held mega phone.

"You are under siege. Better lay down arms to avoid any loss of life,"

"First look around. There is another circle around your men,"

As the army officer looked around he was astonished to see another group of Kashmiri militants brandishing Kalashnikovs giving cover to the contingent in the inner circle.

Militant commander's gumption!

The recalcitrant militant commander sauntered towards the raised platform around the open field. He was flanked by four militants. Others stood in their positions as the commander pointed to them with his raised hand.

"So decide . . . ." he continued as he reached near the army officer holding the mega phone.

"Agreed . . . . you leave this side we will go that side . . . . no use spilling blood . . . ." The army officer reconciled with the new development and signalled with his stretched arms.

Pakistan day, as such, had passed off peacefully in the sense that armed militants arranged flag marches at least at three places but no untoward incident happened. And on India's Independence Day whole of Kashmir came to a standstill. By evening on 14th August itself the Kashmir Bandh call came into effect with Umbrella Organization declaring 15th August as black day and asking people to observe complete shutdown. It was impressed upon the local population to observe black out in the evening. Before sun set the locals put off lights in their homes and the area looked like ghost town with no movement of people or vehicles. The area was engulfed by complete darkness.

No traffic

Shadows Beyond the Ghost Town

No business establishment open
No movement
Complete dark
Ghost Town!

* * *

Love at first sight

Due to proximity with the army major, Ama Ganaie had an advantage that he, his family and his workers could go nearer the camp walls from his side to look after the fruit trees. On Independence Day of India and Pakistan whole population of Kashmir used to spend at least three to four days in their homes fearing some kind of attacks and counter attacks. Ama Ganaie's elder son Nazir had also returned from Srinagar where he did engineering and stayed in the hostel. He was around twenty one years of age. Engineering was the second favourite subject for Kashmiris after medical. Intelligent students took up engineering while extra intelligent took up medical science. Ama Ganaie had added love for engineering. The overseer had helped him around twenty five years back and now he felt that his own son would also help. Secondly, he wanted him to look after his business after him so he felt engineering the best suited subject for him. Nazir also did not say no.

Nazir, back from Srinagar for few days, entered his orchard wearing jeans and a T-shirt. Six feet tall, sharp Kashmir features, fair complexion and robust body, Nazir could easily be mistaken for a model or an actor. He roamed in the orchard where labourers were working. And so walked, here and there, his two younger sisters Ruby and Shazi.

The two girls had average height and body structure. Fair skinned, bubbly faced Ruby, the elder one, had a dimple on lower side of her right cheek which made her more attractive when she talked. The younger girl Shazi had sharp features. Shazi, the red cheeked 'delicion' of her father. Both wore *Kameez shalwar* and low heeled sandals.

Although village girls had been now taking to school for studies but recent incidents of violence had frightened them and the parents were always apprehensive about their safety. However, Ama Ganaie and his sons did not object to their studies and Ruby and Shazi, the young girls continued studying in the local English medium school.

The part of the orchard, under army occupation, had a barbed wire fencing separating it with the rest of the land. The army area was partly blinded by jute coverings hanging down the erect angle iron posts and barbed wire lines. In between empty glass bottles were hung in groups of twos and threes. The bottles were hung as a precautionary measure lest someone tried to jump over it. If so, the bottles would strike each other and act as alarm. At intervals wooden or iron posts were erected with timber planks spread above to form watch towers. These watch towers overlooked the orchard portions on either side. However, these were unmanned along the fenced area where Ama Ganaie's big house stood.

The orchard had big and spread out apple trees. Half a dozen men in two groups were engaged in sprinkling pesticides over the trees. 4 ft by 2 ft sized aluminium tub was used to contain pesticides mixed with adequate quantity of water. A machine run sprinkler had its inlet venturimeter dipped into the tub. The outlet was a one meter long brass stick instrument with an oval shaped head having lots of small sized holes which released the liquid under pressure to reach farther and shower the branches all over.

As the two girls reached near the fence separating the army occupied area they heard a female voice coming from the area,

"What are you people doing with these plants?"

They peeped through to see who was calling and found a lady officer in full army fatigue. They came nearer.

'Arti' . . . . Read her name plate on the left breast. The officer had two stars on the shoulders.

"Mam . . . . these trees need regular maintenance and insecticide is sprinkled to guard the fruit against any disease. So these people are attending," elder girl Ruby said pointing towards few labourers who were at work.

At some distance their brother Nazir got attentive as to what was being asked about.

"So you live in that house?"

"Yes . . . . your neighbours," Ruby said with a smile.

"Are you also in army?" the younger girl looked inquisitive and asked with surprise.

"Yes . . . . *main bhi fauji hoon* . . . . and there are many girls in the army now,"

"*Darti nahin camp main?*"(Are you not afraid?)

"*Are dar kis baat ka . . . . mujh se hi Log darte hain . . . . army wale bhi* (Why should I fear . . . . People are scared of me including army men)

The two girls smiled.

Lt. Arti looked a confident and educated girl while speaking. She had around 5ft 6 inches height, too good for Indian girls. Her face was round and wheatish with darker tinge not as fair as the two Kashmiri girls. Her body structure was thinner which gave her height impression of additional inches. Her hair was braided in such a way that all could be concealed under the bottle green army cap which was tilted towards right side of her face.

"I will come to your house one day,"

"Most welcome!"

"Write your name and phone number," she handed over a piece of paper and ball pen.

Ruby recorded and handed over the paper back to Arti.

"Here is my name . . . ." Arti pointed to her name plate and placed the ball pen in a space on her left shoulder.

Lt. Arti, in the course of conversation with the girls, raised her eyes towards Nazir who was moving here and there. Before leaving, the girls felt the necessity of telling Arti about their brother. Since they had seen Arti looking at Nazir time and again they felt she might get suspicious about him and his presence near the army camp which in many cases in the valley had turned fatal.

"He is our brother, Nazir Ahmad . . . . He is doing engineering in NIT Srinagar."

"Ok . . . . will meet you soon . . . . Bye"

Arti said while leaving the spot. The two girls waved their hands towards Arti till both lost sight of each other.

By afternoon bicycle borne hawker appeared in the village to sell his Urdu newspapers. While people in the village purchased at least one paper each, Ama Ganaie used to buy almost all newspapers published from Srinagar. In the days of Hartal these newspapers gave him leisure moments to know the present status of the movement. After Zuher Namaz, he sat in his room and scanned through the newspapers. The photographs of celebrations of 14th August, the Pakistan Independence day, had taken space in all major news papers. While Ama watched the photograph, he felt his blood pressure rising. Uneasy, Ama Ganaie felt embers all over his body. Ama, with one of the newspapers in his hand got up from his place went near the switch board and increased the speed of the ceiling fan running in the room.

But a whoosh of air from the ceiling fan did not give any respite to Ama. With squinting eyes, he again stared at the photograph. With every concentration dots per inch in the photograph increased to give him detailed sight of the boy. He unbuttoned his Khan Suit shirt near his throat as the trachea felt a bit suffocated. Then he poured some water into the glass tumbler and *gulp gulp* drank it. He tried to calm himself with more sips of water and diverted his attention towards other items of news. But somehow the image of the boy repeatedly pinched him deep. Intentional insouciance was of no help. The postage stamp sized face looked like a monster which rose from nowhere and readied to swallow Ama Ganaie in one suck.

The loquacious Ama felt his power of speech is lost.

His eyes had itching in the corners. He recognized the same boy in the front row of one of the parades who worked in works department and who had taken food in his house after which Ama decided to send Farooq for arms training.

*　　*　　*

Early in the morning Rashid heard a knock at his door and rushed to open it. He was surprised to see his cousin Farooq at the door. After return from across the border he straightway went to his cousin Rashid's house so as to keep himself safe from army. He had deliberately chosen wee hours to reach there, lest information about his arrival goes out. Farooq, the militant son of Ama Ganaie was back. He was in his early twenties. Rashid hugged him tight and in hush hush tones led him to his room upstairs. Rashid made him change his dirty soiled clothes which smelt sweat. Then he had a thorough bath and shaped his beard.

Coming out of the bath room he looked a different person. He was now dressed in blue jeans and a denim shirt. His black trimmed and arranged beard gave him elegance. Sharp features and raised nose over fair skinned face made him attractive. He then spend almost full day with Rashid.

"Now sip tea, have omelettes and tell me story of your departure and arrival," Rashid showed his curiosity.

"Right from home up to the LOC there was no problem faced as we travelled in a taxi. Army did not get suspicious," Farooq said sipping tea.

"And beyond that?"

"It is as good as sacrificing one's life. Dangers of many kinds are looming large. A slip down the slope means the end. Mere suspicion by the army results in a shower of bullets,"

"Oh my God!"

"It is a miracle that boys are returning safe. Weak hearted can't move. They either die in the middle or get caught by the army,"

"And the passes?"

"Most treacherous. We were led by a tribal through mountain passes during night hours when soldiers became delinquent. The pedestrian walk along the slopes of mountains some with thistle, some verdant some naked rocks took us to the other side of the border. Steep slopes are like cannibals and the hawks keep flying above, waiting eagerly if someone goes groggy and falls,"

"The attitude of the people across LOC?"

"They welcome with open arms and big hearts. Call us Mujahidin," Farooq continued.

"What about training?"

"I don't know who organizes it. But experts are there who teach the basics. It is sort of short term course,"

"Why not full training?" Rashid was inquisitive.

"On two counts there seems some hegemony of a particular party. I won't elaborate lest it becomes a source of feud among parties,"

"Your choice. I won't force,"

"Some groups tried to exhibit their strong manpower and dominate others. Even which group should return and which should delay was a bone of contention resulting in frequent verbal clashes,"

"The tribal guides?"

"The tribal guides sometimes play double cross and took money from both which resulted in many deaths to the trained Mujahidin," Farooq sighed and his eyes became moist.

"Farooq . . . ." Rashid did not complete the sentence. He wanted to know the reason.

"Dead bodies were spread at many places. The eyes were gouged out by hawks. I saw some bangles protruding out of the chest pocket of a young boy who lay dead over a big stone. He must have bought it for his sister but could not deliver. I remembered Ruby wearing such bangles when I saw them in his pocket," Farooq had a deep breath and couple of tears rolled down his cheeks.

"Have one more cup. Should I inform uncle about your arrival?" Rashid changed the topic.

"Inform him about my arrival only. Don't talk about the hardships I faced. And don't tell Mom anything in particular."

"Sure . . . . nothing."

*   *   *

Ama Ganaie had taken his meals when he felt sleepy. August heat was at its peak. He and his wife were alone in the house with little girls in the school and the servant doing some work in kitchen garden. Ama decided to take siesta and soon fell asleep. Not much time had gone by when Rashid, his nephew appeared in the house. He met his aunt who was awake. His sudden appearance at this hour surprised her and she asked the reason.

"Nothing *Chachi*, I was just passing from this place returning from the orchard near the bridge so thought to enquire your howabouts."

"Ok . . . . if so sit and have lunch."

She loudly called her servant to fetch lunch for Rashid.

Before servant would listen, Rashid stopped his aunt.

"I swear, I have already taken lunch,"

"Then have some tea,"

By their conversation Ama Ganaie's sleep got disturbed and he woke up.

"*Ho Rash Lala tche kar sa aakh* (Dear Rashid when you came?)" Ama asked while sitting against the wall cushion.

"*Ada sa kariw thohi petra bapathur katha batha be anouw chaie* (Let you uncle and nephew talk I will get you some tea)"

Rashid was a young man in his late twenties. Tall fair skinned boy dressed in maroon colored Khan Suit sported stubble over his face. During militancy period more and more youngsters had sported beards, some longer some stubble. This had twin effect; one, they wanted to show off being more religious and second they were identified as closer to militancy which increased their influence among the general public. He was feeling more of heat as he had walked some distance in the scorching sun. Sweat beads slipped down his face and neck which he continuously wiped with a white towel surface handkerchief. Rashid poured water from the jug kept nearby and sipped. Ama realizing that Rashid was tired due to excessive heat signalled towards his wife to increase the speed of the ceiling fan.

Ama's wife got up, turned the fan regulator clockwise and left the room.

"Chacha I have come to inform you, Farooq has returned. He is this time in our home. He came there secretly. Nobody knows. I thought you may like to meet him. I did not tell anything about it to Chachi." Rashid informed his uncle taking long and deep swigs of water in between.

"You did the right thing. But it won't be proper for me to come now . . . . someone may get suspicious . . . . I will come in the evening," wide smile and deep thoughts, causing wrinkles on his forehead, appeared on his face alternately.

"As you deem proper . . . ."

Servant entered with a tray containing few cups and kettle. Chachi followed him. Ama and Rashid changed the topic abruptly lest someone got suspicious.

Having taken some tea and biscuits Rashid left for his home and there was some understanding expressed between the duo. The day passed off and in the evening Ama expressed his desire to offer Maghrib Namaz in the main mosque within the village area. Although this was unusual during the turmoil times to go far off in the evenings, his wife did not suspect anything. With a promise to return soon, Ama Ganaie left his place. Instead of visiting the mosque he wandered in the lanes for some time till it was dark and entered his brother's house in such a way that nobody detects his arrival. His nephew Rashid and militant son Farooq were watching his arrival from the third storey window. Rashid took him directly to the room where he hugged his son. For some time they remained like that till both were satisfied.

Sometime even silence says more!

After a long conversation through their silence they both parted and sat along the wall in the room.

"How are Mom, Nazir Bhaya, Ruby and Shazi?"

"Everyone is OK . . . . Nazir stays in the hostel at the college and visits here after a fortnight. Ruby and Shazi attend the school . . . ."

"Hmmmm . . . . I heard schools are not running . . . ."

"Government schools are running for just few days in a month . . . . but private schools are better off . . . . the overall situation in Kashmir is not OK . . . . army has set up a camp in our orchard . . . . though they are nice but the major knows about your travel to PAK. He talked about you couple of times."

"How can I meet Mom and sisters?"

"I advise you to take precautions while roaming. This major is friendly with me but if you are armed how he can ignore . . . ."

"Hummmmm . . . . I stayed for so much time just to meet you . . . . I know precautions have to be taken . . . ."

"You know that Rahim Dar's son . . . . PWD employee . . . . he has joined Holy Warriors . . . . I saw his photograph in the newspaper on 15th August,"

"So what? Our Tanzeem Justice Force is the biggest of all,"

"Just to inform you . . . ." Ama Ganaie tried to downplay what he feared most.

Before leaving Ama Ganaie hugged his son, kissed on his forehead and prayed a lot for his welfare. He was accompanied by Rashid for some distance till they both decided to depart towards their own destinations. Till Ama reached his home only two vehicles passed on the road. The head lights of these passing vehicles helped Ama Ganaie walk easily on the pot holed road surface.

The army had issued strict instructions that no civilian vehicle shall pass on this road after 8PM. So, hardly any passenger vehicle travelled during late hours on this road. Moreover, the conductor of the vehicle had to lift the drop gate himself, get the number noted by the sentry and then vehicle would pass and the drop gate downed by the conductor again.

* * *

Few more days passed and one evening Lt. Arti spoke on phone with Ruby. Here and there, Arti directly came to the point of interest.

"When should I attend your home?"

"Your convenience . . . . I am always ready to welcome you," Ruby replied.

"What about tomorrow morning?"

"Simply no problem. Tomorrow is Sunday so all are home,"

"All means?"

"Me, Shazi, Nazir Bhaya, Dad"

"Otherwise where does your Dad go?"

"He is a PWD contractor . . . ."

"But his workers must be doing his job,"

"But he has to attend the office for clearing his papers, bills etc . . . . He has additional responsibility . . . . he is head of the Contractor's Association also,"

"So tomorrow morning . . . ."

"Yes . . . . but please have breakfast in our home,"

"Ok agreed."

The phone dropped and all in Ruby's home enquired whom she was talking to in Urdu. Mom, the illiterate woman called it *Paerim*.

"We are expecting a guest in the morning. Arti mam, the lady army officer,"

"*Ada yi tan so tey korie chi* (Let her come. She is like a daughter)" Mother expressed her motherly love.

Dinner was served in the usual way with rice, mutton and vegetables being the menu. Ruby laid the *dastarkhwan*; Shazi brought copper plates and other utensils. Mom put rice in plates and bowls. Water was poured into copper tumblers. All the family members sat around the *dastarkhwan* and had their dinner. The servant used a separate *dastarkhwan*. In Kashmiri style, food was taken with hands.

Most of Kashmiri population takes food prepared from rice purchased from Public Distribution System (PDS) shops. PDS is a distribution system where rice brought from Punjab or UP is sold through government controlled system and issued to consumers against ration cards. But the affluent class and those who produce rice from their fields use the local rice. Koshur (Kashmiri) is synonymous with local produce and Punjabi with non local produce. Since Ama Ganaie had lot of rice producing fields so his family used *Koshur tumul* (local rice) for their food.

While the family was about to retire to their bed rooms a knock on the door was heard. All had a moment of anxiety as to who could come so late. Late night knocks had become most dreadful in Kashmir. Knock by army could mean arrest or a shoot out by the army even on mere suspicion. Knock by the militants could result in annihilation in the name of Mukhbir, the informer. Even some killings had taken place on the supposed information about someone being sympathizer of one or the other armed group. The servant was asked to peep through as to who knocked. He, before opening the main door which opened under the canopy outside, enquired who the person was. The reply from outside had a pleasant surprise not only for him but whole family.

"*Rehmana darwaz khol be chus Farooq* (Rehman, open the door I am Farooq)" he heard the voice in a whisper.

Rehman without any delay opened the door and held Farooq in a tight hug.

"*Farooq Saeba Log ya Rehman balayi* (May God give you my life)".

As the inmates heard name of Farooq they rushed towards the door. Farooq's brother Nazir, his sisters and mother. Ama Ganaie followed them quietly.

"Close the door first then talk," Ama Ganaie had an advice for all.

All assembled within the lobby area where from first floor stairs took off. The ground floor rooms also opened in the lobby. For some time they remained standing and hurdled in the lobby area hugging and kissing each other.

"Brother, come inside and have dinner," Ruby invited him.

"I have already taken dinner. I just came to meet you. I can't stay for long. I have to leave,"

"*Hata kya chukh tse wanan. Raatus roz. mey kati aawu tasla* (What are you saying. Stay for the night. I am not satisfied yet)" Mother said.

Farooq turned his eyes towards Nazir and Ama Ganaie in a bid to convey that they convince mother to let him leave. Nazir and Ama Ganaie understood the meaning of silent conversation and Nazir intervened.

"He can't stay for long, may be army has got the information of his visit. Let him leave or stay as per his convenience,"

"Yes, you are right," said Ama Ganaie.

His sisters also nodded in affirmative so did Rehman, the servant. Farooq took his mother towards one corner of the lobby, hugged her tight again. So did his sisters one by one. Nazir signalled Rehman who opened the door and raising his right arm walked slowly outside to check whether everything was in order and nobody was in the courtyard. Farooq followed, gun hanging down his right shoulder. Wearing a sports shoe, he took short but fast steps to cross over towards the brick fencing wall, jumped over it and melted in the darkness.

His parents and siblings watched. All prayed for his safety and success.

"*Rehmana subhas wathi zi suli pahan. Tahri dula kadi zi* (Rehman, get up early in the morning and prepare Tehar)," Ama and his wife addressed Rehman almost simultaneously.

"*Theekh haz* (All right)" Rehman replied with enthusiasm.

Divine intervention is sought by people at every step when they feel they are somehow weak and vulnerable. To ward off evil spirits Kashmiris believe in donating some food. They have over centuries resorted to preparation of yellow boiled rice mixed with turmeric powder. This is known as *Tehar* which is then distributed among the passersby.

Farooq's safety was of prime concern.

Would *Tehar* provide some succour?

Rehman closed the main door and all went to their bed rooms to sleep at ease. Mother and sisters were extremely happy that they could see Farooq after a gap of around one and half year. And that too hale and hearty!

As they all lay in their beds there was a sense of pleasure and anxiety in store for them. On one hand they were happy to see Farooq in his spirits but what could be in store for him was a worrying factor. They all took turns in the beds and sleep seemed gone far away from their eyes. Though they did not express to each other but fear of future loomed large in their hearts and minds. Catch and kill by the armed forces was in vogue. Killing on mere suspicion had taken place. Frequent search operations commonly called the crackdown by the army were a routine.

Night stretched too long for the Ganaie family. And when it ended all felt as if they had been awake for the whole night.

It passed off any how!

When Ama and his wife finished their morning prayers Rehman was ready with *Tehar*. Before children were awake Rehman lifted *Tehar* in a big copper container and distributed outside the gate.

Tehar, the protector!

*   *   *

As dawn came and they prepared for the breakfast, couple of army men flanked Arti when she entered the courtyard of Ama Ganaie. Arti was a welcome guest led by Ruby and Shazi into the drawing room. Their mother came out to greet her. She hugged and kissed Arti and prayed for her. Arti could understand no words as mother spoke in Kashmiri. The only thing she could understand was the language of love and affection. The ladies sat in the drawing room. Soon a series of items appeared in the tray held by Rehman, the servant. Chicken, boiled eggs, butter and omelettes covered with additional plates lest they get colder. Two kettles, one filled with sugar tea and other with salt tea, followed. Rehman placed the items in front of Ruby and served some tea and snacks to the army men seated and keeping guard on the veranda.

"Where are the male members? Call them also," Arti asked smilingly.

Shazi got up and in few minutes time Ama Ganaie and Nazir entered. Arti stood up to greet them with folded hands. Her eyes remained glued to Nazir for few moments.

"Uncle, please be seated. I have seen you with major Sahib. He seem to be your friend."

"Yes *beta* . . . . this is Nazir. He is doing engineering in NIT,"

"Yes, Ruby told me. And I am Arti Ranawat from a place in between Punjab and Himachal. My father retired some time back while serving in the valley itself. Brig. Ajay Ranawat,"

Ruby started serving breakfast to Arti and placed a plate filled with a couple of chicken pieces in front of her.

"I will have it if all of you share it with me,"

"We shall take later. You are our guest,"

"If you treat me as a guest then I won't come here again,"

"No, you are always welcome," Ama Ganaie intervened.

Now everyone sat and Arti herself served the breakfast.

"*Khaye na, sab army wale zaalim nahin hote* (All army guys are not tyrants)," she again smiled.

But more so her smile was directed at Nazir, which, none except him detected.

"How do you people contact Nazir Ahmad when needed in between Sundays?" Arti asked.

"A telephonic message is kept in the office which reaches my hostel room . . . . 225 B," Nazir informed himself." I usually come after a fortnight,"

The information was conveyed intentionally in such a manner so that it is easy to remember and nobody suspected. The breakfast session continued for about one hour and then Arti left thanking all and informing Ruby and her sister that she would invite them for a lunch in coming days to the camp and that they can't say no.

Before Arti left, ladies hugged her and she had a parting smile towards Nazir.

Smile is the first language of love!

Two pairs of eyes dropped!

Her Adonis was there!

*　　*　　*

"Master Jee seems to be in a hurry. He does not recognize people even from his neighbouring village," Rahim shouted loud upon seeing Abdullah who was looking somewhere else and did not have any attention towards Rahim Dar.

"Ohh . . . . Dar Sahib . . . . Asalam-u-Alikum . . . . sorry in fact I am in a hurry and the bus has left. Now I was thinking what to do and how to reach the school in time," Abdullah was apologetic.

"We better hire a taxi. I, also, have some important work to attend. I need to reach in time." Rahim's suggestion came.

Abdullah nodded in affirmative and Rahim Dar called out to a taxi driver. The driver came running. May be due to some respect or fear of him, he being father of a top militant in the area. While the trio indulged in some low tone talks for a while, the driver then ran faster and drove his taxi towards them. Rahim and Abdullah sat in the back seat while another passenger sat on the front seat on the left side of the driver. On the advice of back seat passengers the driver sped faster.

"We have examination time so we need to reach earlier," said Abdullah.

"It is you teacher community's duty to impart proper education. Students must be morally and educationally perfect. Then only can they move forward and participate in Jihad also"

"Although the situation is not as good yet we are doing our best. Repeated Hartal calls are ruining the career of students,"

"I have conveyed my resentment against these strikes through Zulqarnain," Rahim Dar referred to his son.

"I know Zulqanain personally. He is a real Mujahid. He is my taught and whenever we meet he expresses his respect. In fact some bad elements have intruded the pious ranks. They are giving the Tehreek a bad name,"

"True . . . . but with a flood all kinds of debris also is washed away . . . . but you know Zulqarnain was telling me some days back we will finish off these elements who have no conviction towards Jihad,"

Before Abdullah could say anything his attention was diverted towards the driver who slowed down his vehicle.

"What is the matter, brother?" He asked the driver.

"Army convoy,"

"What the hell, you move forward,"

"Sir, they will beat up. We have to stop till it passes. We experience this daily,"

"Hey major we also have to attend the duty. We are getting late," Abdullah rolled the window glass down and shouted towards the soldier blocking the traffic from link road. The soldier turned his head and had a belligerent look towards Abdullah.

"What duty you do?" the soldier asked while reaching near the vehicle.

"I am a teacher,"

"You teachers give bad sermons to the students in your schools that is why they have picked guns and ruined this whole state," the soldier blamed the whole teacher community while opening the vehicle door. "*Behenchod* . . . . Guru Salla. "He slapped Abdullah.

Abdullah lost control and pushed the soldier. Coming down from the vehicle he indulged in a fight. One more soldier standing nearby rushed towards them.

"Stop stop," he shouted.

With a firm push and a hit on head with the gun butt, Abdullah fell down. Blood was profusely oozing out of his head injury.

"Shoot him . . . . shoot him . . . . he tried to snatch my rifle," the first one shouted asking his companion to shoot Abdullah.

"Please don't shoot. It was a misunderstanding," Rahim Dar implored while rushing and came in between the soldiers and Abdullah.

While the soldier pointed his gun Rahim Dar lost courage, lest he should become the target, moved aside still imploring not to shoot. However, good luck prevailed when a small army convoy was seen passing from the other side. In one vehicle Lt. Arti was seated. She asked his driver to stop when the soldiers signalled and attracted her attention. She came down to enquire.

"Mam, this man tried to snatch my rifle,"

"Hey soldier why are you telling lies to your officer," Abdullah shouted in broken voice.

Lt. Arti turned towards the driver and Rahim Dar to enquire further.

"There was a misunderstanding. He had to attend examination duty,"

"Now first take him to a hospital. Get him treated first. He is bleeding."

Rahim and the driver helped Abdullah to sit in the vehicle.

* * *

The Venal

The army had not taken the celebration of Pakistan day lightly. The parade conducted by the militant groups infuriated the army and they wanted to convey their message as to whose writ ran and who actually ruled. They gave some breathing time in between to convey as if they had taken the issue lightly and, subsequently, forgotten. But that was not to be. The villages near the parade sites became the prime targets. Early morning raids led to encircling the vast areas and proclamation of orders through mosque amplifiers. The people were ordered to assemble in the local play ground, school grounds or any of the open spaces where ever available. What then followed was herding of the people particularly males like cattle. While male members ran towards the spots ordered by the army the sepoys roamed the lanes and by lanes of the localities to ascertain that no persons remained in the houses. In between they hurled choicest abuse on the frightened villagers.

"*Behenchod bhag jaldi Azadi tumhare intizar main hai* (Run fast, Independence is waiting for you)"

"*Pakistani saale . . . . kapde bhi wohi pehne hain,* (You Pakistani bastard. He is dressed like them)" some referred to the Pathan suit.

"*Ye dadhi wala HW ka aatankwadi lagta hai* (This bearded looks a HW militant)"

About an hour passed when almost whole of male population was driven like cattle to the open space. None dared to protest against the belligerent soldiers spread over the locality. All took the humble pie in front of the gun wielding and abusing army men. Hundreds of men assembled in the play ground created a mess as lot of noise was emanating from the crowd. The play ground was encircled by army men and at places heavy machine guns had been fixed. Dozens of army vehicles surrounded the area. As some officer's vehicles were seen from the far off distance approaching the venue, the JCO immediately ordered for a complete silence.

"Be silent, Colonel Sahib is approaching," he shouted.

Pin drop silence!

The flag car approached nearer, though still outside the encircled area and the people engaged themselves in side-talks in low tone.

Kashmiris have a peculiar kind of sense of humour. Even when they are in distress they crack jokes. Subjugated for centuries by tyrants they would satisfy their hurt sentiments by calling the rulers by nick names. While seated subdued, like frightened pigeons, someone in the group tried to be a *Turbaz*. Turbaz is one who exaggerates things to make the situation funny.

"*Khodayas aesi wu mangan pan ni kothi gotch maqbara watnawun . . . . az ani naw* (You always prayed to God that we should reach the grave yard when we are physically fit . . . . now you have reached)," a middle aged man said in humour pointing towards the graveyard nearby.

People sitting nearby had a laugh. The petulant Junior Commissioned Officer (JCO) looked askance at the villagers.

He moved his eyes towards them in anger and then filth came out of his mouth. He was not amused by the hearty laugh by the villagers who, in his thinking ought to remain subdued.

"*Bahenchod haste ho* (You sister fuckers. How dare you laugh.)," the snarky officer indulged in bawdry.

He signalled with his right hand first finger and picked a couple of persons from the group who, he thought, initiated the laugh. One of them was a young man with beard. The bearded man was around thirty plus wearing Kameez Shalwar. Sharp featured man had long pointed nose and was of good height which made him lanky in structure. The JCO commanded them to come nearer.

Chatakh

One on right

One on left.

The JCO displayed his full quota of anger on the bearded man slapping on his face right and left.

"*Hans raha Saale . . . . Dadhi wala aatankwadi* (The bearded terrorist . . . . you have courage to laugh)" The JCO indulged in ribaldry and filth came out of the mouth of other soldier, standing nearby. He got encouraged and used his gun butt to 'teach the Kashmiris a lesson'.

The duo's good luck favoured them as the flag car came towards the venue. The JCO's attention got diverted. He then moved swiftly towards the approaching officer's car.

A ground thumping salute!

The colonel was flanked by a couple of middle rung officers. He had a casual look towards the assembled crowd and whispered few words to his colleagues who nodded in affirmative. He then left towards a tent in one corner of the ground where few chairs were arranged. In few minutes operation started.

Few lower rung army men spread and picked some of the youngsters at random by pointing towards them. Youth, particularly with beards, became the first target. Not less than twenty boys were ordered to board the waiting vehicles which left immediately.

All panicked.

Then people were distributed in four groups of around a hundred each and asked to walk past the olive green Gypsies standing in a row. They were made to look towards the windscreen.

One

Two

Three

Four

The people walked past, looked into the windscreen. Occasionally horn of the vehicles blew which sounded like a death warrant. People whose passage made the horn blow were bundled in the bunker vehicles parked nearby. These vehicles are sarcastically called a *tabut* (coffin) vehicle. Such vehicles were middle sized with a driver's cabin. Behind it the body of the vehicle consists of thick bullet proof iron sheets having very small glazed openings through which one can peep only. The back side had hinged openings resembling two shutter doors with a locking system both inside and outside.

Rumour doing rounds in the valley was that whosoever is made to board the *tabut* vehicle hardly returns safe. The esoteric instructions were intended for the officer's close aides.

So panic at its peak!

The process continued for hours together till it was evening. Many rounds were conducted and the spotters, seated inside the vehicles, indentified the suspected militants or their sympathizers. The spotted were bundled in vehicles. In the evening the colonel fulminated and delivered a warning speech to the frightened crowd who now included mostly middle aged or elderly persons.

"You have to think over yourself. Live in peace with the army or perish like flies . . . . choice is yours," he thundered and left the scene. The lucky ones were let off as the army lifted the siege.

The army men on duty jumped into their vehicles which were covered with camouflage nets. Behind the driver's cabin in the big vehicles couple of men took positions with their light machine guns (LMGs). In smaller vehicles the men stood with their faces covered with black cloth.

As the tired and exhausted people were getting ready to leave the spot, the army trucks leaving the spot raised a dust storm on the earthen track connecting to the metalled road.

*   *   *

It was very early in the morning. Sun had risen above the mountain ranges and very few vehicles plied on the road outside. Ama Ganaie and his family were preparing for the breakfast. It was usual for the family to sit on the elevated portion of the kitchen area. Standing kitchen consisted of a reinforced concrete slab laid about thirty inches higher from the floor. Marble sheets had been spread over it. A kitchen sink was fixed in between. Few cabinets of ply board above it made space for extra utensils and kitchen ware. The cement concrete floor had been laid and ceramic tiles fixed on them which made it easier to mop after finishing the food preparation. On the lower level portion of the kitchen area foods would be prepared if the servant did not like to keep standing or felt tired due to some reason.

Before the breakfast Ama Ganaie's servant Rehman used to bake homemade bread. The youngsters enjoyed omelettes. Ama Ganaie had been served only one cup of salt tea yet when the wicket gate opened. His seating arrangement was such that he could have direct sight of the gate through a small window on the corner of the kitchen wall. Kashmiris prefer to sit in their kitchens with their family members and, as such, their kitchens have larger space. They construct houses in such an alignment that their vision from the kitchen to the main gate is not hindered. He could recognize at least a couple of men who entered the courtyard. In all six people entered. All were dressed in Pathan suites and some were wearing Karakul caps while others donned skull caps. He asked Rehman to open the door of his drawing room and let the people in.

The main door of the drawing room opened on the veranda which had a flight of few steps. The drawing room popularly called *Bhaithak* was a big hall. Just near the entry was placed a sofa and a central table. This would be usually used by those wearing pants who found it difficult to sit cross legged. On the opposite wall was fixed 5ft by 4 ft size and around 9inch deep almirah. The almirah had many partitions in which were placed different objects like calligraphic Quranic verses, brass vases and a few family photographs. Incidentally, photograph of Farooq had been lifted from the place soon after he left for arms training. Rehman made the visitors sit in one corner of the big drawing room and left towards kitchen to call his employer in. Few minutes later Ama Ganaie entered saying Salaam. All the guests stood up to shake hands with Ama. Formal introduction was done by the two people whom Ama Ganaie knew personally. Rahim Dar was one of them.

"Is everything alright. How come you came so early?" Ama asked.

Before anyone could speak, Rehman entered with a kettle and tray containing cups and local bread.

"We just had tea, why you took the trouble," Rahim Dar said.

"You are my guests. Tea is must," Ama replied.

Rehman placed cups in front of all and understood the signal of Ama Ganaie to leave. He left, closing the door which opened in the lobby area.

"Is everything all right?" Ama enquired.

"Nothing is OK. Army has now retaliated fiercely. The boys had celebrated Pakistan day and conducted some parades at different places. Army conducted crackdown and arrested many boys from different locations," Rahim Dar said in one breath.

"In our locality thirty boys were picked, ten were let off by evening. All have been tortured and are nursing injuries," the other visitor said.

"My elder son you know is with Holy Warriors. They could not catch him but his younger brother was picked up. They say until Mujahid surrenders we won't release the brother," Rahim Dar completed.

Ama Ganaie supported his left jaw with his hand and elbow resting on his knee. Nobody cared about the tea which was getting colder.

"All of us have same story. My son, his son, this man's brother . . . ."

"My son in law had come after three months but was arrested. They listened to no argument. I pleaded his innocence but they said he has left his place after attacking the army convoy and is hiding here," another person completed his story.

"I know you can help. You have good relations with Major Salvan. Even if they are not kept all here in his camp, he can use his influence in other camps," Rahim Dar pleaded.

Ama Ganaie did not reply but the image of the militant who, in a way, was the driving force behind his decision to make his son Farooq take a plunge into militancy came up on his mind screen. Now his father was seeking Ama's help to get younger son released.

What a pity!

Irony of sorts!

"Do they think I am in a way working for the army?" the idea struck Ama Ganaie like a thunder.

"But you know my own son has become a Mujahid," Ama tried to analyze their mind.

"Who does not know . . . . but since army camp is located in your orchard . . . . you may use your influence. See Mujahid is a Mujahid. Let them catch him. That is a battle between gun and gun. But what have innocents to do with it . . . . these people don't understand that," Rahim Dar promptly tried to clarify doubts.

"They understand all but are pressurizing us," another visitor tried to present the whole episode simpler.

"They can't become friends. They know how to extract their own work. But since you are pestering hard, I will try," Ama Ganaie stood up and left the room.

Around ten minutes passed and Ama Ganaie was dressed neatly in the Kameez Shalwar, long waist coat and a *karakul* cap. He again entered the drawing room where his visitors were seated.

All stood up and left through the door opening on the veranda. Rehman brought Ama Ganaie's black leather chapels polished bright.

Ama Ganaie and his visitors moved towards the army camp around 300meters from his gate. Few vehicles were lined up around 150 meters from the main gate of the camp. Around twenty persons both men and women waited some 50 meters from the gate. Ama Ganaie was recognized by the sentry who frisked him and allowed him in.

Frisking was a two edged sword. It was a deliberate attempt by Ama Ganaie to show that army does not believe him blindly. On the other hand army did not believe any Kashmiri, howsoever, close to them. Others accompanying Ama were asked to wait far from the gate where other people waited. In few minutes time Ama was in the room of the major. He was as usual served water and a cup of tea till major came to meet him.

"So Gulam Ahmad how you came so early in the morning?" the major asked.

It took just few minutes for Ama Ganaie to narrate the whole story because the major did not take much time to understand.

"I don't think you should intervene in the matter. Army top brass has taken the issue very seriously. We can tolerate anything but no Pakistan,"

"So . . . . what to do?"

"Be silent. Your own son is a trained militant and we know he has returned and is active. So you need to be more cautious,"

"If the parents of those arrested are ready to pay handsome amount then . . . . ?" Ama Ganaie used sesame.

"None will accept. Indian army is not like that,"

"But if few militants or their sympathizers are released do you think Kashmir will secede and be free and independent," Ama Ganaie struck the right cord.

"True . . . . But army officers won't accept,"

"No harm in trying,"

"Ok . . . . but it has to be very secret,"

The serpent traverses curved paths till it reaches the hole. Then suddenly its path becomes straight.

"You know me fully . . . . I have that sense," Ama threw lasso.

"That is why I sometimes deal with you. Meanwhile, I tell you ask your son to be very cautious. He is on the hit list of both army and HW,"

"Why HW?"

"HW wants its supremacy. They will annihilate all others and rule themselves. Finally we won't allow even them to rule,"

Ama Ganaie shivered from top to bottom. He took another glass of water. Shaking hands with the major and exhibiting a fake smile, he left.

As Ama Ganaie came out of the gate, his morning visitors became restive at the waiting spot and rushed to seek some information. Ama did not say anything but kept on walking towards his home. He avoided them to enter inside the drawing room but engaged them in the courtyard itself.

"*Myon hi mainiw bata khet nirew* (Better listen to me, have lunch)," he extended half hearted invitation.

"It is too early for lunch yet. Shall we hope for better?"

"I talked to the major. He did not respond nicely as he was in a hurry. He has some important work to do, may be some meeting. I just conveyed and assured him some money even. Rest is in the hands of God. Don't disclose to anyone,"

"Be assured,"

The visitors took leave of Ama Ganaie and left the spot.

*   *   *

Couple of days passed when a new development took place. The JCO, who had beaten up a bearded man during the crackdown in front of many villagers, had pain in his right hand. The pain was first attributed to some muscle cramp but it continued to increase. The doctors advised one or the other medicine. Some advised exercise. He did everything but the pain persisted. The cream was rubbed. Saline water used to wash the area. Heat therapy and so on was tried but of no avail. Somehow the news was disclosed to the person who supplied vegetables to the army camp. He used his horse driven cart every morning and unloaded a good quantum of fresh vegetables for the army mess. The tomatoes, brinjal, turnip, potatoes and some leafy vegetables were supplied by him. As he came to know about the pain in the arm of the JCO he hit upon an idea. Whether it was a prank or had good intention, nobody knew.

"I will tell you the secret of this pain," he took the JCO into confidence.

"What?"

"But first promise you won't disclose it to anyone,"

"I swear I won't tell anybody,"

Pain is pain and it hurts all. It can't be segregated into class, race, religion or status. It can't even be quantified. It makes everybody scream.

"You know you slapped a bearded man few days back during the crackdown?"

"Yes . . . . so?"

"He is a religious man. People know him as a saint. His way of life is inscrutable and his expressions esoteric. You humiliated him and this pain is the punishment,"

"Are you sure?"

"Very much"

"Then what should I do?"

"It would be better if you go to his house and plead him to forgive you but that will create suspicion among the Mujahidin and they can harm him,"

"Then?"

"Better call him here and nobody will suspect and everything will remain a secret, "he suggested.

The snarky JCO, disturbed by pain, nodded his head in agreement. It was a known fact in the area that this bearded person was a religious minded man and used to be called Moulvi Sahib. He had attended religious seminary for his education and used to lead the prayers in the local mosque. It was also believed that he had been benefited by a revered saint whose association helped him. Some believed it some brushed aside.

Subsequent to this, the JCO had some relief from the acute pain which teased him for few days. Whether it was some help from the bearded man or the doctor's prescription had its effect nobody knew. The Molvi's act enamoured the army officers. The bearded man became popular and even Major Salvan reposed faith in his spiritual supremacy. Major was so impressed by it that after few days someone in the camp stole his wallet which contained couple of thousand rupees. The wallet was found outside the camp barricade but money was not traced. Since the civilians were not allowed into the camp so it was ruled out that somebody from outside had done the mischief. The inmates could provide no solution. Major Salvan, acting on the advice of the JCO, sent a word to the Molvi Sahib and sought his help. The bearded man made all the suspects to assemble. He got some quantity of rice and in front of them recited something in very low voice and then blew air from his mouth over the rice. He offered a little quantity to each one of them.

"Turn backwards and eat this rice so that nobody watches you eating it. Whosoever has stolen the money shall spit blood after swallowing this rice, "he declared with confidence.

After observing the scene for few minutes, he instructed them to turn back and went to each one of them demanding the rice back. All but one failed to return because others had swallowed it. One suspect, fearing blood spit, did not consume it. And so he returned it to the bearded man.

"This man has stolen the money, "he declared.

And, in no time, he was subjected to some interrogation which made him cough whole money.

*   *   *

Army did not move nowadays in isolation. Minimum of three vehicles plied fearing attacks by the militants. Occasionally, IEDs were used to target vehicles through remote controls. Patrols were employed by the army in the wee hours and Road Opening Parties (ROP) cleared the routes first; then only army convoy was allowed to move. Routes without ROP were now out of bound for the convoys.

A convoy of four vehicles, a Gypsy and three one tonners, moved on the road. Following one tonner a Gypsy was part of the small convoy in which Lt. Arti sat on the front seat beside the driver. It was after noon and little hustle and bustle could be seen on the roads. Near the gates of National Institute of Technology (NIT) at Hazratbal, around fifteen students and other people were waiting for the bus to take them to the city, when this small convoy came to a screeching halt. Army men jumped out of the vehicles to give cover, fearing some attack or possible arrest among the gathering. The people in the gathering, particularly the young students, got panicky. Everyone feared the army presence. Arti dressed in complete army fatigue alighted and asked her Jawans to remain calm with a raised arm. She proceeded towards the security post at the gate.

"*Duty par koun hain*? (Who is on duty)" she asked.

"Sir . . . . , *main hoon*," a middle aged peon wearing khaki dress came forward. Out of fear he stuttered.

"*Main sir nahin madam hoon. Naam bolo*, (I am not sir, I am madam. What is your name?)" Arti smiled.

"Gulam Rasool,"

Arti took the peon on one side and gave him a small white envelope and with the movement of her hands stressed upon something. The peon nodded his head in affirmative. Nobody knew what it was.

With Arti back in the Gypsy, the convoy proceeded forward.

*   *   *

Around evening when Nazir entered his hostel room Gulam Rasool, the gate keeper, himself handed over the letter to him.

"*Ye military afsar ne diya hai. Wo ladies thi. Bola sirf aap ke haath main hi dena. Military se to sab darte hain is liye main khud aaya. kisi ko dikhaya nahin.*(This was given to me by an army officer. She was a lady. She instructed me to handover to you personally. Everyone is afraid of army so I came myself)" Gulam Rasool completed in one breath.

"Ok, thanks," Nazir took out a fifty rupee note and handed over to the peon.

As the peon left the room, Nazir bolted the door and hurriedly opened the envelope. He was himself anxious and impatient to know what it contained.

"Meet me near SBI in cantonment area on 28th 3pm,"

Two line letter inside the envelope read. Blushed by the invitation, Nazir read it again and again. He had understood the romantic overtones of Arti when she talked to his sisters and on the day she attended his home and had breakfast with his family. Nazir read the letter again and again. He felt some sweet music struck his ears which grew louder and melodious with every passing moment.

Serenade!

It was a strange issue. An army officer taking interest in a Kashmiri boy. Army was known to have taken interest in catching or killing militants or their sympathizers and even at some places the local girls became the target of their sinister design.

Nazir concealed the letter in his cupboard. If anybody found it could have serious repercussions. Nobody would presume that Arti was romantic towards Nazir but all would suspect Nazir's credentials and may label him as the army informer. His father's closeness to the army major in the vicinity of his house could prove a point against him. It would even be difficult for his militant brother to explain.

The new development engulfed his thought process.

Letter

Arti

Dreams

Supposed meeting

What next

Results

Repercussions

Nazir, a faddist, was a person always interested in latest fashion. He read fashion magazines and watched films also. Though cinema halls had been closed with the onset of armed militancy but those interested got film prints either through CDs or some other form. Nowadays, elevated shoes with big toe were the craze. So Nazir had decided to purchase one. Money was never a problem for him. After class hours he had decided to move to Lal Chowk, the business hub in Srinagar where all sorts of designer wear would be available. Making rounds for some time in the market place he purchased an elevator, the shoe with thick sole. When he reached his hostel room and read Arti's letter many thoughts made rounds in his territory above neck. He wanted to check his new purchase and put the shoes on for a trial. Before he could decide what to do, he felt need to visit the toilet.

In such situations these things happen. Either one feels thirsty or passes more of urine.

The hostel block had a big space for the toilets. As he entered and wanted to use the urinal he felt as if the urinal pot has been lowered by couple of inches. He looked around to find out but no repair work had been done or at least he could not detect any.

"How come the urinal pots have been lowered and why?" Nazir kept thinking. Finally he unzipped and eased himself. He washed his hands at the sink and left for his room. The wash basin was also lowered. At ease, he read the letter again and again. In the meantime he heard some foot taps and expected his roommate to enter. He did not want to reveal the secret of the letter to anyone. So he rushed towards the cupboard to conceal the letter. He had to bend a bit more to open the suit case. The space where his suit case was kept had been lowered by a couple of inches. The door opened and his roommate entered.

'Ha . . . ha-ha . . . . ha-ha'

Nazir burst into laughter and could not control himself.

"What happened . . . . why are you laughing?" asked his roommate.

Tears came out of the corners of his eyes and he lay flat on the bed. Perplexed, his roommate stood in front of him.

It took him few minutes to control his laughter and then he sat at ease.

"I am laughing over my own follies. What a duffer I am!" he said wiping his eye corners with a handkerchief.

"You are . . . . who does not know. But this time explain your foolishness first,"

"With my new elevator on, I felt urinals have been lowered . . . . what a duffer,"

Then both roommates had a hearty laugh.

Two nights, a day and a half day passed off in troubling Nazir's mindset. Arti and a planned meeting sent mixed feelings in him.

* * *

Love of sorts

Army mostly avoided travel in the dark to ward off dangers of being targeted by the militants. New type of attacks through planting and detonating of IEDs became a source of headache for the forces. Many vehicles became targets of such IEDs blasting off the vehicles high above in the air and instant death to many uniformed men. So they usually returned to their camps before dusk unless required for some emergency duty. The members of the army unit, Arti was part of, returned from an operation. Back in the camp, they went for some bathing etc as the day long hard duty had made them tired. And the travel on metalled and squalid roads had put a layer of dirt and dust over their bodies. Before dinner Arti complained of pain, which she said, was increasing with every passing moment. The unit doctor examined. Major Salvan himself supervised.

But no relief!

After some time, the doctor on duty with some inputs from others proposed to shift Arti to the cantonment hospital in Srinagar. Arti was writhing in acute pain. She had put off her army uniform clothes and put on a rat skin colour track suit and rolled occasionally on her cot. She caught her belly and stomach area in both hands showing her body being in severe trouble which made her restless.

The unit doctor and some more men surrounded the cot. As the decision to shift her was announced a small bag was packed with additional clothes, towel, soap case, toothpaste and brush for her immediate use. The patient was shifted to a trolley lifted by four men and they footed the distance up to the main gate where ambulance was parked in the parking area. The driver was ready to move. The hand trolley, over which Arti rested, was shifted into the ambulance. She continued to writhe in pain which increased off and on making Arti restless. Couple of men remained in the ambulance as the driver inserted the key. The *klik klik* sound changed into *grrr* and the gear lever changed position under his hand. The tyres started rolling.

Soon the army guard standing in the front Gypsy engaged himself in blowing the whistle hung to the lanyard to alert the passersby leave the road open for faster movement of the vehicles particularly the ambulance.

"*Hey army ambulance chi tez dawan. Basan chu kati taam chu Mujihidaw hamla kormut. Army walie chi zakhmi basaan* (Army ambulance is running very fast. It seems Mujahidin have attacked and seriously injured soldiers.)"

"*Kya pat moodimeti ti ma aasan* (May be some are dead also)"

People walking or standing along the road concocted their own stories about the movement of the ambulance. They pictured the possible attack by the Mujahidin and inflicting some injuries, may be grave, to the army personnel who in their view were being shifted to the bigger hospital. After more than twenty minutes the caravan of the three vehicles reached the national highway which being a wider and smoother tar surfaced road allowed increase of speed by the drivers. The army personnel blew whistles, honked and even used the hoot fitted in the ambulance. Those driving on the highway made way for the entourage as the army vehicles drove in wrong side beaming head lights at places to overtake the civilian vehicles.

It took around an hour before Arti was shifted to Srinagar in an ambulance guarded by soldiers seated in a couple of vehicles.

In the cantonment hospital, Arti found her place in a separate room where two beds, couple of chairs and a small sized side Almirah found place as the furniture. The windows in the room had clean curtains and the floors lined with smooth ceramic tiles. The room had an attached washroom. Immediately after her arrival and admission into the hospital, she was administered dextrose through bottles hanging down the steel T-shaped shaft. A transparent pipe ran from the bottle to the arm of Arti where a needle remained inserted into her vein. This was wrapped under the criss crossed adhesive tape pieces. A white uniform clad nurse continuously monitored condition of Arti.

She spent the night in the hospital and couple of specialist doctors examined her periodically. Tests were conducted and under observation Arti showed signs of relief. Rest of the night passed off peacefully with Arti having sound sleep. In the morning again doctors attended on her at regular intervals. Some medicines and light food was advised. By afternoon Arti felt relaxed but doctors advised one more night under observation.

Around 2-30Pm Arti requested the nurse that she wanted to have a stroll around and she should take care of her attendance in the hospital. The nurse suspected nothing. Five minutes before 3pm Arti, dressed in casuals, was near the SBI spot. Nazir reached the venue in time.

The cantonment locality locally known as Batwara remained peaceful compared to other parts of the valley.

The reason being that due to heavy presence of army within the area, the militants avoided attacking such a place. The security system in the area was perfect and sneaking in with firearms was next to impossible. The drop gates at the entry points on both sides of the highway were in place and most of the civilian vehicles passing through had to undergo rigorous searches. The passengers were asked to disembark and walk down some distance. Even women passengers were at times asked to foot the distance. On the southern side of the locality the major river Jhelum flows. Across the river, army had set up its smaller units which provided security to the whole area against any possible attacks. Such system was set in place after couple of rocket attacks took place from across the river.

Within the locality, in civilian and army area, large number of army vehicles could be seen with gun totting soldiers roaming. Men, women and children traversed without any fear. School children, out of their schools, dressed in various coloured uniforms and heavy bags over their backs, walked towards their homes after disembarking from their school buses. Some of them looked somnolent out of their hard work and boring school books. Some soldiers, whose leave applications had been sanctioned, could be seen making purchases from the local shops as they bought Kashmir embroidered shawls and other local merchandise.

Arti and Nazir walked silently.

Politics

Militancy

Human Rights violations

Army civilian hostile relations

Foreign hand

Outside support

Muslim extremism

India

Pakistan

Kashmir

They discussed none.

For about thirty minutes the duo roamed in the lanes and by lanes of Batwara civilian area.

They had coffee, ice cream, some moments of smile, joy and inner satisfaction.

Of course no expression of romance!

But a promise to meet again.

Why?

None had the answer.

None pestered for a reply as to why they should meet.

None asked as to what was the attraction.

None deliberated what could be in store after such meetings.

None exhibited fear about such meetings.

Before they parted they exchanged smiles. Time and venue for next meeting was whispered and agreed upon.

Were they love birds?

God knows!

*   *   *

Begaar, the forced labour

Convoy duty became the most hated word among Kashmiris but none could agitate against it. As refusal to convoy duty amounted to rebellion and all rebellion are crushed with severe punishment . . . . even death. The army fearing planting of IEDs during night hours wanted to play safe. The militants would plant these under culverts or on road side shoulders and detonate when army convoys passed. Many gory incidents had already taken place and loss of life was reported. People living nearby had to face wrath whenever a mine blast took place. But as time passed and such attacks increased in number, army decided to advent a novel way of arresting such attacks. The locals were allotted the Convoy Duty. The male members of the locality, irrespective of health condition or age, were supposed to perform convoy duty in the best 'national interest'. Roosters were issued on the basis of information provided by various local informers. In a stretch of 2 kilometres at least two men were engaged every night to check planting of IEDs. The men would roam the road for full night with lanterns in hand. The lights emanating from lanterns gave signals to army that the men were on duty. However, when the clever devised a way of safety for themselves, army resorted to improvisation.

Hanzaw hatche zaal gadaw hetchi wota (The fishermen devised nets and the fish resorted to jumps)

Some youngsters kept the burning lantern on the road hanging at some post which would give the army men an impression about local men are on duty. But soon it was made known to the army that omnipresence was actually fake. Now the duty was changed from just roaming to actually reporting at the sentry posts at least twice a night to ascertain the attendance. This increased the to and fro distance for people on duty to around ten kilometres a night.

Exhausted by the very hard exercise the men on duty had no other option.

They suffered silently!

*   *   *

Although the construction work fetched Ama Ganaie all fortune, yet, he one day felt overloaded. Exercise to arrange men and material for the construction of road, culverts, buildings and other things was tiresome. Prolonged argument with the engineers about specifications became boring. So many problems regarding arrangement and availability of funds would creep in at times. Cumbersome travel from one place to other in these volatile situations created panic in him. Every time one would leave the house, the family members remained on tenterhooks whether he is safe. Barrage of questions at each frisking point was a source of discomfort. Walking with identity cards held high in hand was humiliating.

"There is every danger of a mine blast. Holy Warriors can attack . . . . these men at frisking points are arrogant . . . no safety for human life,"

Ama Ganaie, one day thought if on his way to the PWD office there is a mine blast and he himself becomes the target what should happen to his family. Or if some day the Holy Warriors militant, with whom he had a fight before, remembered the bad old days and fired upon him. If some day the sentry at frisking point did not acknowledge his I-card and start beating him in front of so many people.

Ama Ganaie thought over how to keep everything in his own command. He called his nephew Rashid and asked him to execute some work on his behalf.

"You have to arrange men and material only, I will look after the office work myself,"

Rashid nodded in affirmative.

Ama Ganaie then devised a whole new idea of earning money. Rather Major Salvan provided him the new avenue of minting money. He grabbed it with both hands like a vulture catching some small bird in its talons.

A very bad idea!

Rahim Dar, the Holy Warriors militant's father, and his accomplices had come to him with a human tragedy and Ama Ganaie struck a fruitful solution. He thought over and found a new way of earning money. The new source of income was easy.

He again went to the major and enquired from him if he had thought over the issue as around five days had passed. The people whose wards were arrested and kept in various army camps were daily visitors to the spots to find out any clues. Each time they were either turned away after a long wait or if someone would be allowed to meet the prisoners, he would feel more upset with their waning health condition. Men and women made a beeline in the early morning and waited outside the camps like beggars.

Ama Ganaie influenced the major with his sweat words. He emphasized that since too many people are visitors to his camp they actually want me to use my acquaintance to get their release. Though the major talked high of the army discipline but fell into the trap partly by greed and partly by consent. Soon he discussed the price tag.

Fifty thousand for purely innocent.

Seventy five for over ground worker.

One Lac for Kashmir trained militant.

Two hundred thousand for Pak trained militant.

Ama Ganaie liked the idea. He did not disclose the inner feelings to the major and left the camp with a promise that he 'will revert back after discussing the issue with the concerned parties.'

In few days time the beeline that used to be formed outside the army camp main gate shifted to Ama Ganaie's gate.

Compromise of interest!

Ama Ganaie did not convey the rate list to everyone. He assessed the financial background of the concerned parties and then raised the rates by one hundred percent. If someone pleaded for reduction his reply would be 'make the payment directly to the major'. All feared a backlash in case the major got infuriated over the secret deals getting leaked and may be the whole game is spoiled.

Ama Ganaie played another trick. He did not accept any deals if the involvement of a Pak trained militant was there. He would easily ignore it saying the major and his officers are adamant over the issue.

Not many days passed when some of the land deals were ratified in the area. The distress sales of land at three quarters or even half the prevalent prices were finalized. The parents wanted their sons back unharmed at any cost.

"If the life is saved, land can be purchased again." They would repeatedly say.

And the brokers took advantage of such emotional outbursts. One thing was common that those who had no involvement with the active militancy had to dispose of their land holdings or other property. The people who were even remotely connected to militancy pounced upon the comparatively affluent class to donate for the 'national cause'. The business men, landlords and the middle class employees became the target. The higher status officers could not be laid hands on because they had either migrated to cities or kept static guards in their official residences.

Money started pouring in. But Ama Ganaie intentionally made the process of release lengthy as well as cumbersome. He wanted to prove that the job is easier said than done so that he would not be identified as an agent of Indian army.

*   *   *

Major Salvan liked Ama Ganaie and day by day his love increased. He had become a good conduit for his nefarious designs of earning money. Moreover, Ama Ganaie used his business deals to transfer money to the major's family accounts in his home town. He even managed transfer of hard cash through his workers in fruit laden trucks. Currency notes were packed in small jute bags, concealed in fruit trucks and transported to the destination which the major identified.

In Kashmir it is said *Yeli Gohal aasi teli chi gada lagan* (when there is turbulence making the water muddy one can catch more fish). It came true. Ama roiled to catch more fish. One day Ama Ganaie was seated with the major enjoying some snacks and he posed a question,

"You owned one band saw machine previously. What happened to that?"

"The carriage of timber has become very difficult now so it is closed," Ama replied with squinted eye.

"Why can't you resume the work there?"

"And logs?"

"That I will manage . . . . But fifty fifty," Salvan winked.

In Kashmir the forest protection has been a very delicate issue for all times. Even the most honest forest officers have not been able to control the timber smuggling. Though a fool proof system is in place to safeguard the forest wealth but repeated attempts have been made by the professional smugglers to transport timber illegally. The forest department has developed check posts on all major and minor roads to check smuggling but the system has not worked efficiently. The small time smugglers brought timber on horse backs. Big fish devised their own ways. The forest guards and other officials have put in some effort commensurate with their ability. But onset of militancy forced the forest guards to vacate their check posts fearing for their lives. Secondly, they feared challenging the smugglers lest they should have some connections with militants and could prove costly. The new player who appeared in the timber smuggling arena was allegedly the army and other uniformed groups. With absolute powers in hand, no official had the guts to challenge the authority of uniformed men.

In another few days Ama Ganaie's band saw started running. Logs would be transported from the nearby forests through army trucks and unloaded in Ama Ganaie's dump yard about one km from the army camp. Ama Ganaie's men at work sawed the logs into smaller sizes to transport the same to the required destination.

Quality timber at very less rates!

*   *   *

Friendship

Ohe evening phone rang and Ruby picked up the receiver.

"*Ruby bol rahi hai* (Is Ruby speaking)?"

"Yes, Ruby on line,"

"Ruby, I am Arti, your neighbour,"

"*Are* Arti mam,"

"How are all in the family?"

"Fine, all is OK,"

"I could not talk to you for some time. I was very busy,"

"I know yours is a very tough job,"

"Any way you, auntie and Shazi will have breakfast with me tomorrow morning . . . . positive,"

"I don't think auntie will agree. She is not able to speak or understand any language other than mother tongue,"

"So what?"

"I will talk to her. Rest is her choice,"

Night passed off peacefully and in the morning two army men appeared at the gate. They knocked at the door and informed that they have been sent by Arti Mam.

"She has already talked to you," one of them told Ama Ganaie.

"But where is Mam?"

"In her room,"

"But some lady must accompany them. How can they come alone?"

"We are here,"

"No . . . ."

One of the army men left and after few minutes Arti appeared herself.

"*Beti naraz mat hona lekin ladkiyoon ka mamla hai* (Daughter, don't get annoyed. But this pertains to girls)" Ama Ganaie tried to convince Arti.

"Uncle I am not angry . . . . I understand . . . . that is why I came myself,"

"Thanks daughter,"

As Ama Ganaie and Arti engaged in talks, Ruby and her sister, attired in very beautiful dresses, came downstairs. The young girls looked graceful with their rosy cheeks. On seeing them Arti hugged them.

"Where is aunty?" Arti enquired.

"She won't come. She refused,"

"No, she has to come,"

"Don't compel her. She won't be comfortable," Ama Ganaie intervened.

"OK, as you wish," Arti smiled.

The three ladies left the spot and the army men flanked them with automatic weapons in hands. In between the two gates there were couple of army men on duty who thumped their feet to salute Arti. Similar welcome happened at the gate of the army camp. Arti straightway led them to her room which was in a barrack type structure constructed out of pre fabricated removable boards. Inside the room they were joined by two more lady officers who praised their dresses and the looks.

"*Kashmiri looks to duniya main mashoor hain* (Kashmiris are famous for their looks world over)" one of them said.

The breakfast was served on a table furnished with tidy bottle green sheets. The crockery was arranged in a systematic manner. Soup bowls were served first.

Despite affluence in Ama Ganaie's house, Chinese type vegetable or chicken soups had not found their way in the kitchen. But as Arti and her colleagues used the cutlery to enjoy the soup Ruby and Shazi followed them.

"We have not prepared any non vegetarian dishes fearing you may feel uncomfortable whether it is Halal or not," Arti explained.

"So nice of you to care for us," Ruby replied.

Neatly dressed two waiters entered after few minutes and removed the bowls from the table. Then breakfast dishes were arranged on the table.

Boiled eggs

Butter toasts

Pakoras

Muthi

Samosa

Omelettes

"Omelettes, toast and eggs . . . . we eat daily but from army side I like this one," Ruby picked some *pakoras* and a samosa.

"Muthi also," Shazi said while picking one.

The breakfast session lasted more than an hour. Then the girls thanked and hugged the lady officers and left. Arti accompanied them up to the gate and kept an eye on them till they were far from sight across the partly blind curve on the road.

Outside the gate more than twenty people, men and women, had assembled to meet their wards locked in the camp or otherwise seek information about them.

*   *   *

Ramadan, the holy month was in progress and the people kept fast during day time and indulged in additional religious duties like *Tarawih* which is performed during this month only. Towards the end of the holy month comes one night which falls on 26th of the month. The revered night is immensely graceful and equivalent to one thousand months. This night is spent in the worship to Allah and Muslims have firm belief that Allah forgives the sins during this night of great virtue. It is regarded as a profound duty by the Muslims to observe the night fully awake in worship. Mosques and other religious shrines witness large congregations during the night and Imams and Islamic scholars continue to give sermons about the grandeur of the revered night. However, the night prayers start around two hours later than on other days leaving a bigger gap between breaking the fast and the night prayers.

Major Salvan who had tried to develop his connection with the local population thought it better to arrange an Iftar party for the respected citizens in the area. He invited a big group of local persons of repute and some from the administration to participate in the party. The invitees came before dusk and the major had made elaborate arrangements. The vehicles were parked just outside the gate on the opposite side of the road and the soldiers themselves lifted the drop gates unlike on other occasions. Inside the area, separate spot was provided with furnishings for the faithful to offer Namaz. Separate temporary arrangement was there to perform ablution if needed. A big Shamiana was erected to have dinner. The local chef had prepared mutton dishes which were arranged systematically for a buffet. The arrangement of dates, water and fruit to be used to break the fast was in place. The major had roped in a local chef, the Waza, who prepared *wazwan* the local mutton dishes for the event.

The district's who's who and the local respected persons included the district commissioner, the police chief, the medical officer, half a dozen journalists, Ama Ganaie and others. As the sun set and time for Iftar arrived the people broke fast. Major Salvan had invited, among others, his senior officers for the event who included his commanding officer and the brigade commander. Before Iftar the guests were introduced to the senior army officers who shook hands with everyone present. The senior army officers, the district officers and Ama Ganaie sat close to the brigade commander. Major Salvan made it a point that Ama sat nearer to the senior army officers. Another important guest was the bearded Moulvi who remained an important person for the major in all civilian army functions. He gained importance after he was believed to have given remedy to the JCO's arm pain and helped the major reclaim his stolen money. With these acts he enamoured them. This man later led the prayers.

"*Khorus saeti khor, fekis saeti feuk, Safa kariw durast. Safa durst Namaz durst* (Stand serried. Feet with feet, shoulder with shoulder, perfect line makes the Namaz perfect)" the Molvi said while people assembled behind him to offer prayers.

Some non Muslim officers and the major's colleagues watched from a distance the people offer Namaz. After the Namaz they were led to dining area neatly carved out and secured. The brigade commander led the guests to the dining area.

"Where is Tabakh Maaz?" asked the brigade commander impatiently.

"Sir, here . . . . in this container, "Major Salvan pointed towards the said container.

"I love it the most,"

"Sir, *yeh love karne layaq cheez hai* (Sir, this is really the lovable thing)" Ama Ganaie intervened.

Sycophant!

All smiled.

Tabakh Maaz is a Kashmiri mutton dish prepared out of sheep ribs and made crisp in hot ghee.

The participants roamed from one container to other to pick dishes of their choice and had a good meal. Those who finished meal walked to the spot for sweet dish arranged neatly.

Few soldiers on duty near the venue talked to each other.

"Most Muslims grow beards," said one.

"It is essential that devout Muslim has a beard,"

"But some have long beards and some short,"

"And some keep their trousers above ankles,"

"There is a joke about the beard and the ankle high trousers,"

"Like?"

"The trousers shorten and the beard grows longer. And you know there are three types of beard. The people having longer beard have short trousers and such people are after God. Some have shorter beards and they are after the army and security forces attacking and killing or getting killed. Some have very short, skin touch beard, you can say stubble, and they are after girls."

All the three soldiers had a hearty laugh. But they soon fell in attention getting a call from some senior.

After the party, all shook hands with the senior army officers, the major and his close associates and left the spot.

Brutes

After observing fast for one lunar month, people waited eagerly around radio sets listening to the news about Eid moon. The Rouyati Hilal (moon sighting) committee in Pakistan was in the meeting to decide about the sight or otherwise of the moon. Kashmir itself has almost always found a hazy horizon and the moon, very thin on the first day, is hardly visible, so the people depend on the decision by the Pakistan Hilal committee. Some have emotional attachments with that country while others justify that geographically Pakistan is in the same axis so moon sighting in that country is more authentic with respect to Kashmir. The Moulana heading the committee in Pakistan explained the process before final announcement. He referred to the participants of different provincial committees and the ones who took part in his own meeting. The reference to reputed Moulanas gave credence to the comprised committee. Final decision from the committee came and the news was broadcast on Radio Pakistan about the sighting of the Eid moon. However, it was not the same in rest of India where people decided not to celebrate Eid the next day.

The Kashmir population through ages have been following Radio Pakistan particularly for news about Eid and Ramadan moon. And a good joke has been coined about it which goes like this;

'We follow decision of Pakistan about Eid moon because like India we have an unbreakable agreement with Pakistan also. With India we are bound by defence, foreign affairs and currency while with Pakistan we are bound by hockey, cricket and the decision about Ramadan and Eid moon.'

People have concocted another story about announcement regarding sighting of Eid moon. The head cleric in Kashmir records two statements about moon sighting for airing on the local radio and television. Whether Radio Pakistan announces 'yes' or 'no' about moon sighting similar statement is aired in Kashmir also.

As the news was broadcast about sighting of moon people, young and old, rejoiced. But Eid or other festivals are celebrated by the children with much fanfare. Within minutes children of the locality, some three miles from the Arwanpora village, came out on the streets and burst crackers. Crackers of different makes and colours made bangs with loud noise. The army camp nearby got an alert. The inmates, mostly non Muslims, did not comprehend as to what had happened. The only noise they knew was of blast of grenades and a possible attack by the armed militants. Since the crackers burst for quite some time, a contingent of army got into action in very short period of time. Within minutes a convoy of army men left the camp and drove towards the nearby village. As the army vehicles reached nearer, the villagers feared the worst. Hearing the vehicle noise the villagers, both men and women, swooped on the lanes and dragged their children to their homes. Some had batons in their hands and they cursed the little children, beat them up and forcibly took them inside.

Not much time passed when army was in the village. As the men alighted two boys still bursting crackers on the main road panicked. One of them instead of pointing the rocket towards the sky threw it on the ground. The cracker circled and stuck to the other boy's right foot. He shouted and screamed with pain and fell down on the road itself. Couple of army men had reached nearer and they caught the young boy by his hair and slapped him fiercely. Nobody attended the boy on the ground. He was writhing in pain and snot dripped down his nostrils. Instead the army men swooped on the village and broke open the doors and smashed window panes with the gun butts. They dragged the inmates irrespective of their gender beating up men, molesting women and slapping children.

"*Aatankwadi kidhar hain jo blast karte hai* (where are terrorists who blast grenades?)" they kept asking.

"Sir, little children played with crackers because of Eid," the villagers implored.

"In the garb of Eid these terrorists attack our camps and now are hiding in your village . . . . we know all," soldiers shouted at the gullible villagers who had no idea about presence of militants, Mujahidin in local parlance, in the village. "You veal eaters, sister fuckers, sons of hundred fathers . . . ."

The scene was of chaos, confusion and fear. Even the loquacious stuttered. Mewling was heard from some homes and little children squalled at other places.

The scene continued for around an hour and the beaten up villagers remained assembled near the main road. Some of the houses were ransacked with belongings strewed here and there. Even pipkins found their found place on the floors. It was done to show off that the soldiers had definite inputs about militant presence in the village and they wanted to remove their doubts. Hue and cry was raised from all corners of the village by the weeping men and screaming women. The people wanted to revolt against the soldier's inhuman treatment but could not gather courage. In between one of the junior ranked officers talked on his walkie talkie giving latest reports about the incident to his superiors.

After some time couple of more vehicles reached the village. In one of the Gypsys, Lt. Arti was seated who sighted some movement on the road and asked the driver to stop. With the help of the head lights beamed from the Gypsy, she realized some young boy was lying on the road. She alighted and came nearer signalling the troopers not to fire. As she reached nearer, she saw the boy writhing in pain and screaming. He had his foot burnt with the cracker which had struck him some time back. And in the mayhem, that subsequently occurred, nobody could attend to him and his pain. Arti arranged some water for him and then helped him board her vehicle. She then gave instructions to her juniors to finish off the operation and led the convoy back to the camp.

While she narrated about the whole incident to Major Salvan, an army doctor attended to the injured boy.

Night passed off peacefully but for the villagers who had received thrashing by the soldiers for the 'sins' their youngsters had committed by bursting crackers to celebrate the arrival of auspicious festival of Eid. It was an interesting story or irony of sorts that the people who had received thrashing some time back were now enquiring about the welfare of their neighbours.

"I was caught by four soldiers in the lane. They tried to beat me with gun butts but the narrow lane came to my rescue. Around ninety percent of their hits were received by the brick wall against which I was held," said one.

"*Hey gariban heund tchu khoda aasan* (God protects the poor and the downtrodden). Say Allah saved you. Otherwise one hit of the gun butt can crush your head," replied other.

"I have firm belief that Allah only helps the oppressed otherwise so much of beating can break ones bones,"

"You are right,"

"You know I was kicked, rolled, thrashed and all that for twenty minutes in my courtyard. My family members cried loud. You see my body . . . . not a scratch is there . . . . Allah is great," said another raising his shirt above his back.

"*Turbaz* . . . . You always rely on exaggeration. You must have ducked behind the women folk." Another companion joked.

All laughed.

Night passed off like that with each helping other by rubbing, hot water towel massage, some painkillers and the like.

But one young boy was without any solace from any side. That was Rizwan, the teacher's son whose guitar was broken by the invading soldiers. Nobody thought about his guitar or perceived how to mourn the broken instrument or 'massage' Rizwan's emotions.

Rizwan was playing on his guitar when soldiers barged into his house. He was playing some notes about Eid celebration song.

"You bastard. You first hurled grenades and now camouflage with your music instrument as if you know nothing," the soldier slapped and kicked him. The guitar fell from his hands as he caressed his belly to ward off pain from the kick. Then another soldier beat him up with the same instrument till it broke on his back and head. He received some scratches and wounds but the instrument was soon in pieces. Leaving him behind, the soldiers left his room and ransacked other rooms kicking everything that came in their way.

Rizwan regained his consciousness. His sisters offered him some water. He stared at the broken instrument. It was second time his guitar had been broken into pieces. The young boy was a music lover and liked his music instrument more than books. Out of his savings he had purchased one. Around four months back one evening when he was playing some tunes outer door of his house was beaten. His father opened the door.

"Who is indulging in music? Don't you know it is un-Islamic?" Gun wielding *Naqab Posh* thundered.

Before Rizwan's father could reply, the gun man pushed him aside and straightway rushed towards second storey. He kicked the half open door of the room from where music notes came. He cocked his gun at Rizwan.

"How dare you do un-Islamic things?"

Before Rizwan could gather his senses the gun man snatched his guitar and tossed it many times on the walls. The instrument was in pieces. His father reached the room humming with fast breath. With great difficulty breath wheezed out of his trachea.

"Master Ji, it is because of you I am leaving your son alive. You have taught in school and our commander has been your pupil. Commander Zulqarnain has taken serious view of un-Islamic activities. Teach your son the right virtues." He thundered while leaving the room.

Rizwan was shell shocked and felt as if everything was over. So remained his siblings and parents.

Quiet

Numb

Speechless.

*   *   *

Large gathering of people was present in the Eid Gah, a vast piece of vacant land. The space has a high brick wall around along the periphery and is mostly used by the locals of Arwanpora and the adjacent localities for offering Namaz on Eid. As such the space is used mostly on two days in a year. However, during turmoil such spaces have been used to offer the Nimazi-e-Jinaza, the funeral prayers, of the Mujahidin killed by forces. On such occasions, during earlier period of militancy, when Mujahidin ruled the roost large gatherings assembled to pay tributes. To accommodate bigger congregations larger space was needed for which Eid Gahs provided the ample space.

Today it was Eid and the people from adjoining localities had assembled in the Eid Gah to offer Namaz. The head Moulvi of the area gave religious sermon explaining the importance of month long fasting and the reverence attached to the Eid. One person with bigger vocal cords cried at his highest pitch 'Salaat . . . . Salaat . . . .' to invite the attention of those who roamed outside. He wanted them all to enter before the fixed time for Namaz. People dressed in fresh and clean clothes entered and sat on the required spots and listened to the sermon. One person representing the Umbrella Organization created rhapsody by his word power to arouse passion among the people so that support is garnered for the ongoing movement. Children looked happier with a hope that they will collect lots of gifts in cash. Although four days back the bursting of crackers in the nearby village had caused a furore and army punished the elders including women yet people now were in high spirits. In this backdrop bursting of crackers in the area was banned. Not only had army pronounced in advance but parents also advised the children to desist from such acts which could lead to similar situations. Some space had been carved out in the Eid Gah by erecting polythene vertically so that women could also offer prayers separately.

Few minutes before fixed time, the Moulvi stopped his sermon and prayed for the peace and tranquillity for the whole world particularly for his state. Then Namaz was offered and people waited for the Imam to pray again. At that moment attention got diverted towards the main gate of the Eid Gah wherefrom around twenty army men entered the area. The people panicked. Some got their heart beats faster others had pale faces. All looked towards each other. Out of fear some people, while trying to whisper, stuttered. Others might have run away and jumped over the boundary wall but they realized that the area had already been cordoned off by the army. The Imam, realizing the situation, asked the people to stay calm. Some order inside the hearts was restored by the hollow assurances by the Imam. Ama Ganaie was seated in the front row. He recognized the senior officers of the army. The colonel, the major and few more were among the group. As they reached nearer Ama Ganaie walked faster to greet the officers. He shook hands and asked if all was well.

"*Gulam Ahmad, colonel sahib Eid Mubarak karna chahte hain* (The colonel wants to say Eid greetings)" Major Salvan tried to clear the doubts.

Ama Ganaie turned towards the Imam and conveyed what he had been told by the major.

"*Gode karew haz dua . . . . tasulsul thawiw bar qarar* (First finish prayers. Don't disturb the continuum) a young boy among the people stood up and almost shouted.

"Be calm . . . . don't be emotional . . . . they can assail you some harm," advice came from nearby.

"Just four days before they injured the whole village now they want to rub salt over our wounds by hollow greetings," he continued in his native language but in low tone.

"OK . . . . OK . . . . that is right," the Imam responded. He took a middle path to avert any inconvenient situation which may arise from the arguments. Ama Ganaie also realized the situation and conveyed the major that they may have to wait for few minutes till religious duty is finished.

The Imam took few minutes to offer final prayers. The colonel flanked by Major Salvan approached the front elevated portion in the Eid Gah. People in the front row observed that the officers entered the area with their boots on. But none had guts to object.

"I offer my heartiest greetings to all people of Kashmir in general and this locality in particular. I pray to God that peace prevails in the area so that we don't have to resort to violence time and again and we all live in peace and harmony. I further request you all to abstain from giving shelter to foreign militants who in no case are your friends. I also request you to advise the local militants to surrender and live their life happily. I assure their safety and rehabilitation in case they drop guns . . . . if you have complaints or information please feel free to share with Major Salvan . . . . Once more Eid Mubarak."

The colonel left the spot shaking hands with those who were on the fringes of the Eid Gah.

The locals followed after the army soldiers left the spot.

*   *   *

The issue did not settle down with some compassionate officers like Arti but was blown over. The Umbrella Organization got a shot in the arm with such news of gross human rights violation. They highlighted the situation through press notes and gatherings. Newspapers wrote editorials about the incident. The news spread to all corners that besides thrashing of innocent villagers, the soldiers had indulged in molestation and theft of some valuable items like gold ornaments and costly crop saffron. The saffron cultivators are known to possess wealth as compared to other peasants in the valley. The saffron is cultivated in select area of the valley and the cultivators of this crop have better economic condition. The people in such areas have built palatial houses and have other amenities of life. The crop when dried fetches around one thousand rupees per ten grams of the crimson red three branched stigma taken out from the flower. And peasants keep the dried crop in earthen pots till a proper and good price is offered by the buyers. Earthen pots save it from getting destroyed due to moisture in the atmosphere. On the fateful night when soldiers attacked the village it was alleged that apart from severe human rights violations by the army men the saffron was stolen by them after breaking the earthen pots. The civil administration and the army were pulled up as the news got good overage in the local media. The enquiries were ordered both by civil administration and the army. The people became bold enough in front of the enquiry committees and candid statements about the whole episode were got recorded. One such daring act was done by a teacher namely Abdullah. Abdullah was a school teacher and, as such, was called as Master (teacher) Abdullah by the locals. He narrated the whole saga of late night torture to the people, molestation of few girls and the theft by the soldiers. He was burning with rage over the damage to his son Rizwan's guitar by the soldiers. He even was instrumental in instigating and encouraging others to speak out and not remain timid. Although Major Salvan and his subordinates impugned the statements recorded by villagers, describing these calumnies, Master Abdullah and his colleagues did not resile. The enquiry conducted did not see the light of the day except the usual promise from authorities that proper and tangible action shall be taken against the offenders.

*   *   *

People say student life, that too hostel era in a college, is the best part of one's life. The time is so happily spent that one hardly feels any boredom except during examination days. Since enjoyment is to the fullest it seems the time flies. Nazir was spending his time nicely in the college hostel. Many other students also occupied the hostel rooms. The city dwellers remained as day scholars but students from far off places were boarders. Since he studied in the national level college it housed many non local students also. The institution was infamous for occasional skirmishes between local and non local students which at times resulted in clashes. With the onset of militancy these skirmishes increased. During nights computerized placards appeared on the hostel blocks with names of hard core and first grade militant commanders.

'Syed Salahudin Hostel'

'Ashfaq Majeed Block'

This irritated the non local students who always were against the armed militancy. The irritation took shape of few quarrels.

But this night something special had happened. Next was the April Fool's day and the preceding night had cooked something very humorous. In the morning when hostellers visited the toilets the door would not open. Students waited first, then banged the doors for inmates to make hurry. With hands on pelvic portions they tried to control the pressures from inside.

"Don't know which fool has occupied the seat, "one irritated student said.

"What about the other?"

"That also is occupied . . . . I tried all,"

About a dozen students wanting to use toilets assembled to find out why the occupants are not coming out. Regular bang at the doors and detailed examination brought loud laughter. The persons who spent night in the toilet blocks had done a wonderful job. The bolts had pieces of strings attached to them. These had been passed though the small holes or crevices and pulled from outside till these fixed the union of male female combination of the bolts. Without being inside, the doors were bolted giving tough time to the people aspiring to use the toilets in the morning pressures.

While no quarrels over the 'night duty' results took place, April fool's day started off on a laughter note.

*   *   *

'Army is known for its discipline'. While it was a presumed fact in the area that people like Salvan minted money against release of arrestees the lower rung could not raise fingers against him or his superiors.

"He must be paying the share to his higher ups otherwise how could he survive their wrath. When money is involved discipline takes back seat." This is how people in Arwanpora area described Salvan's activities. They had little faith in the enquiries.

Major Salvan was reprimanded after enquiry report about the incident which involved supposed theft of saffron from the village during a raid and the alleged molestation by the soldiers. Master Abdullah remained a thorn in the eyes of the major. His outspoken narration and candidness had played havoc with the psyche of the major. He could not forget the humiliation he suffered when he was called to explain his position in the matter. Somehow he managed to thwart any departmental action against him or his subordinate staff.

As time passed, the raging fire against Master Abdullah continued to burn with more ferocity. Few more days gone by and a militant arrested from some place was gunned down in the vicinity of Abdullah's village. What followed was a search operation locally called crack down. The men folk were asked to assemble in the school ground. The identification parade continued for some time. Finally few young men were rounded up. Among others Master Abdullah's son Rizwan also was part of the group. For some time questioning continued. After that all assembled people were let off. However, most of the youngsters were taken along in the army vehicles with a promise that after thorough questioning they will be let off and no damage shall be assailed.

Rizwan was a young boy in his early twenties. Round faced and shorter in height he looked like a healthy baby whose photograph is usually painted on the tins containing baby food and seems to have enjoyed lots of milk. Wearing jeans and denim shirt the boy looked lovely. His main task was to play guitar which ironically was broken twice. Once, on the orders of Commander Zulqarnain by Holy Warriors militant for being un-Islamic and second time by soldiers for using it as a 'camouflage after hurling grenades'.

Rizwan was taken to a far off place in the area. Three vehicles made their journey towards the hillock where people used to work in stone quarries for extracting stone to be used in construction work. The extraction had made cave like intrusions in the rocks as hard stones came out and mild stones and unusable material remained behind to give the area shape of caves. The soldiers encircled the area and two men made blind folded Rizwan to walk before them. He was made to enter one of the caves.

Thadakh!

The grenade planted on his body went off with a sudden blast and ripped off his body. Flesh, cloth, bones flew in all directions and Rizwan had no shape of a young boy now.

The army vehicles left the scene after few minutes.

The army handout read out on the evening news on Radio and TV was both intriguing and shameful.

'According to army press note, one militant arrested during search operation was taken to identify his hideout. While fiddling with a grenade he was killed as the bomb went off. 'The news reader explained the position.

In his home Master Abdullah was target of all and sundry for his 'unnecessary fight' he had taken with the mighty army.

"A few *tolas* of saffron would not make any difference, "said one.

"Life is more important than this money and crop, "said another.

"We are helpless and can't fight the might of the soldiers,"

"Nobody asks them a question,"

His wife accused him of killing his own son.

Abdullah sobbed silently.

The people from the locality had assembled in large numbers. Rizwan's mother and sisters wailed at the height of their pitch. The ladies were joined by the women from the locality and relations. The yowl resounded. The sisters repeatedly screamed calling him by name and asking to have food, tea. Mother cried, out of the twinge, repeatedly asking where the 'groom' has gone. The other ladies helped them with swigs of water.

And when the body pieces shrouded in white cloth were lowered into the timber coffin to be carried to the burial ground large number of people followed it. The scene turned pathetic with mother showering a mixture of candies and almonds held in a steel plate and sisters threw rose petals as is done in case of grooms leaving for fetching their brides.

Even callused could not restrain their eyes getting moist.

*　　*　　*

As time progressed internal bickering among the militant groups and the political parties patronizing them surfaced which at times took ugly turn. One, the armed youth indulged in fights second, they went public with their press notes. The press notes were drafted by people adept in such jobs. Some noted scholars, journalists and educationists, under their ghost names, were engaged in witchcraft of writing eloquent and Theo-centric press notes and articles. As such the 'clean' linen was washed in public accusing each other of doing harm to the sacred movement. Best of vocabulary was used in the press releases. This came handy for the armed forces. While they arrested some people in raids and crackdowns they tried to be soft on some groups thereby giving credence what the groups accused of each other. The 'sell out' by one or the other group and '*grohi baladasti*', the organizational hegemony was the watch word. The major and Ama Ganaie enjoyed the new situation but Ama Ganaie feared also. Ama Ganaie was able to benefit from more arrests and more releases but feared at the same time because there were apprehensions of his own son becoming target of inter group rivalries. The major started getting inputs about the presence of the militant groups because some people were getting weary of their presence due to army harassment on one side and the inconvenience caused by their leanings which sometimes would tell upon the sympathizers of either group. Even on this count some killings also took place.

These killings started widening of gaps among various groups. Though political Umbrella tried either to downplay the incidents or forge unity, but the attempts proved superficial only as the yawning gap extended further. The major was able to raise his own army among the militant groups with one group helping him to annihilate the other. After some time formal groups under various names cropped up, first under cover then openly. They got full patronage of the major and his colleagues for any covert operation. First of all, at selected places, these groups developed their own infrastructure like camps in the vicinity of the army areas. These groups gave themselves many names but for all others they were renegades. One such camp came up in Ama Ganaie's neighbourhood. They even tried to set up the camp on the opposite side of Ama Ganaie's house but he was more powerful compared to them. He pleaded before the major that this should not happen and succeeded. With this development the renegade commander felt insulted but had to eat the humble pie. However, Ama Ganaie had given rise to many enemies.

The PWD employee who joined armed group Holly Warriors

The renegade commander.

The rival group of his son.

Some who thought he made money through release of arrested persons.

Some who hated him for interfering in PWD works.

Some who saw him looting forests through proxy.

And some who did not like his affluence even before militancy.

But as is said everything has a limit. One can't wield power always as power wielded every time does not matter because some don't take the things lightly. Ama Ganaie returned from his meeting with the PWD officers and then with the contractors whom he ruled. He had distributed the works that were tendered among his association members and collected some 'poll money'. He even kept a couple of works for himself also which were to be executed through his nephew Rashid. Normally contractors happen to be very vocal as they feel they are able to convey their point through larger vocal cords and thus extract maximum benefits. But Ama's power had suppressed them to such an extent that they uttered very few words as Ama Ganaie, the union president, spoke louder.

He rather 'ordered'.

He was tired as he spoke too much in the two meetings. In the evening Ama Ganaie returned to his home in his car. He wanted to have some salt tea and took his seat on the elevated portion of the kitchen where from he could have a complete look outside. As he looked outside, he became conscious of the fact that his other vehicle was not at the place.

"Where is the blue car?"

"Sir, Majid from the camp took it," his servant replied.

"Why?"

"He came with three gun men and asked for the key,"

"Where has he gone with the car?"

"He did not say. He said we have a mission,"

"Hmmmm"

Ama Ganaie felt disturbed not because his car was taken but he felt insulted for his authority was at stake. Some body, so small in stature, had challenged his power by taking the car without informing him or seeking his permission. He controlled his anger and sipped tea. Unmindful, he took a big swig of hot tea and almost burnt his tongue.

Evening came but the car was not returned. Night was there but no car. The family had dinner and the main gate was closed by the servant. After some time all went to sleep.

Night passed off peacefully for all in the vicinity but not for Ama Ganaie. But he did not express his inner volcanic eruptions.

Another day and then one more night passed. On the third day as sun was dipping down behind the mountain range, Ama Ganaie and the servant recognized the horn of the blue car. Servant rushed to the main gate and Ama Ganaie came out in the courtyard. Majid zoomed in with the car and parked it at the same place where from he had taken it the other day. He was accompanied by another person of his ilk.

"*Haji Saeb, Salam Alikum, asi ous mission tami kini ni maey gaedi* (Haji sahib, we had a mission to accomplish so I took your vehicle)" Majid said while handing over the key.

"Take it, have a bath there and sleep well. You must be tired and hungry so have a chicken," Ama Ganaie pointed to servant's room, stretched his right arm to handover two hundred rupee notes to Majid.

Overwhelmed by the response of Ama Ganaie, Majid thanked him and asked his companion to get a chicken.

For all, the night passed off peacefully including Ama Ganaie. But morning was very disturbed at least for those who drove or walked on the road. The renegades in the camp were very much angry. They beat up any body passing through the area.

Nobody knew why?

Nobody dared to ask why?

Nobody comprehended what had he done to invite such wrath.

More than an hour passed when local police came to the bridge site which Ama Ganaie had got repaired after a massive flood. Some people reached the spot along with the police party. Something hanging down the bridge railing, through a rope round the neck, was lowered down with the help of a long ladder.

A corpse!

Lying down on the ground, people recognized it.

Majid, the renegade.

After tiring for two days he was now in deep sleep.

And the police party as usual formed the *panchnama*.

*　　*　　*

The armed struggle was at its peak with both sides attacking and counter attacking each other. The number of casualties on both sides kept rising. And in the cross fire were caught the innocent unarmed common people. At times army thrashed them for being sympathetic and harbouring militants. At other times they had to experience the wrath of militants themselves for being informers to the military. And with the reports that some guest militants have sneaked in, and joined the armed rebellion, the common people became anxious. It was because reports suggested that their attacks are pin pointed and they don't leave the place without a long drawn fight. Long drawn fight, which resulted in complete destruction to the house, in which they would hide or take refuge. And finally the wrath of army who avenged their human loss was a disturbing factor.

In one of the upper reaches a local youth was thrashed by the army for not performing the convoy duty well. It had come to the notice of the army that he hung his lantern on one of the posts and went home for sleep. Hanging of the lantern was done to deceive the army as if convoy duty was on for whole night. He did not react angrily to his humiliation but lost his cool when his mother and sister were abused by the sepoys. They could not bear the torture to the youth and jumped in to save him. But the sepoys kicked and lifted the duo from over his body. Later it was revealed that the sepoys in fact molested the mother daughter duo and even pressed their breasts. He had not taken the incident lightly. Abuse apart, the molestation shook the youth.

"Anything even my death won't bother. But dignity of my mother and sister or for that matter any Kashmiri woman is dearest to me. I won't tolerate. I will make them pay the price." His simmering volcano kept him burning.

In order to inflict maximum damage to the party he secretly got in touch with the non local militants and procured some ready to blast IEDs.

He vowed revenge!

Not much time passed when he was on convoy duty again on his turn.

"We better sleep by turns. Nobody will come to know,"

He made his companion to sleep for some time. During that period he himself planted IEDs at two spots. And after a gap of couple of days the militants blasted off the IEDs. Two vehicles were damaged and many army men killed and wounded. What followed was mayhem. In retaliation, the army fired indiscriminately killing few peasants working on the agricultural fields. The whole area was cordoned off and searches conducted. During searches, apart from torture of youth, the soldiers resorted to very shameful weapon; the rape.

13 year old girl.

25 year unmarried one.

30 year married one.

42 year, a mother of two.

55 year, a grandmother even.

None was spared.

The sordid saga of extreme revenge was revealed to the world through media. Though first attempt was made to refute the allegations 'spread by militants and their sympathizers 'but then the administration caved in. Top officials rushed to the spot talking of enquiry and justice. The army unit was transferred from the place and some enquiry initiated. Captain Rajat was indicted in the preliminary investigation.

Media and political leaders of umbrella organization made a beeline to the area. The Umbrella organization group that visited the place comprised of around half a dozen people in different age groups. It varied from mid thirties to mid fifties. They had been authorized by the parent body to visit and assess the situation. All of them sported beards some black others a mixture of black and grey. Couple of them wore white Khan Suites with black short coats. Younger ones wore designer suites of some international brand. One was dressed in coat pant suit with a *karakul* cap. Two midsized SUV carried them to the spot.

TV crews, still cameras, note pads.

Local media persons, non local journalists, even some Delhi based correspondents working for foreign newspapers.

And two new vehicles carrying Umbrella politicians.

Politicians wearing designer suits of world famous brands.

Politicians talking of high moral ground on Azadi platform.

Politicians addressing the readymade and emotionally charged audience.

Before leaving the spot they wanted to meet the victims of brutal violence. They met and did not stop with their oratory.

Rebuked the army.

The government.

The indifferent world bodies.

The only thing that could stop them from speaking was when someone suggested that these victims should get some monetary support from the Umbrella organization.

"See we don't have any money in the *Baitul Maal.* But still we will do whatever is possible," said one.

"Whatever we have is from donations of the people," said another.

"We don't get any financial support from any country,"

The argument continued and someone from the crowd whispered to his colleague, "They must have enough money for their designer suits and big cars. *Baaki to chalta hai.*"

"Air travel also," another retorted.

"Costly hotels yaar,"

Fearing the crowd may get restive, they beat a retreat.

Romance

The morning was beautiful with snow capped mountains shining. Little of hustle and bustle in the area exposed the poor law and order situation. No tourists, no locals. Only few shops and a couple of road side *Dhabas* were open. The buildings wore a deserted look as if mourning some one's death. The CGI roofs had developed deep rust surface. The window frames and shutters had paper like peel offs. The birds flew in and out of the hotel rooms. In the market area, at least two hotels were occupied by the security forces who erected drop gate and iron spiked plates blocking the entry through the gate. Forced entry by any vehicle could rupture the tyres making the inmates safe against any attacks. Around the periphery barbed and concertina wires were fixed and empty bottles in twos and threes hung at short intervals in such a manner as if some desperate lovers committed suicide. This was done to thwart any suicide attack by armed militants. If someone tried to cross over the wires the empty bottles would strike each other making noise which would alert the inmates. Very few locals ventured near the security camps except if called for. Occasionally, army vehicles plied in groups of at least three at a time.

Going through the hazardous journey of frisking and searches Nazir reached the picturesque tourist spot. He had been searched at least at three spots, his I-card checked along with other passengers. A girl of good height but lean figure accompanied him. She wore a black robe called Abhaya and most part of her face except eyes was covered with a white scarf. When the duo reached the spot they decided to move towards the gushing nallah. The water flowing in the stream was pure and milk colour foam appeared when the water hit the big boulders. Trout fish in fewer numbers roamed in the stream.

Before militancy erupted, the nallah was full of beautiful and different colour trout fish living in the wild. Nobody would be allowed to use the fish tackle or some net by the officials of the department to control fish poaching. After gun battles between local militants and the soldiers took place, the officials of the department disappeared from the scene fearing for their lives. And the militants roaming the area used hand grenades to kill or suffocate the fish before being taken out and be part of a sumptuous feast in the nearby forest area. Subsequently, when army regained some control and militants took to secret destinations or hideouts, the security personnel dropped live electric wires into the water and killed the fish to enjoy on the tasty hydrophanes.

And if any fish still existed in the waters it was its own good luck.

Good luck for the girl wearing black robe accompanying Nazir. No one had recognized Arti. After she left the army camp wearing civvies with a valid out pass and permission to visit the market place, Nazir made her to wear the robe he had purchased himself.

A good camouflage!

But she was not too comfortable with it as she wore it first time in life. She always wondered how these women wearing Burka or the Abhaya could walk down at ease. She compared herself with these women. While she herself lived in an army camp and the subordinate army staff did not dare to stare at her but same men passed livid remarks on the Burka clad women passing by the camps.

As her comfort level gave in, she removed her scarf from the head and face and expressed her freedom. Then she started playing with the water flowing under her feet. She had taken her sandals off and placed them on one of the boulders nearby. Seated on another boulder she lifted water in her hands and showered it on Nazir. Nazir reciprocated.

Love birds of course!

Then there were photographic sessions.

Standing in the water.

With mountains in the background.

Forest trees rustling.

Memorable moments.

Playing with water.

"How you like my Kashmir, Arti?" Nazir asked in between.

"Don't ask me this question. I will weep bitterly,"

"Why?"

"Why, don't you think we all should weep?"

"Hmmmm"

"The glittering mountain peaks are sobbing. The beautiful hotel buildings are moaning. The forest trees are silent as if in a funeral. The gushing nallah is singing a dirge. The black topped road is in mourning. The ventilators on the buildings are dropping tears . . . . but I still love Kashmir as much as I love you. I know Kashmir will one day be the paradise again. Then you and I shall roam here without a camouflage. Without a black robe. Without a face cover. No fear of getting recognized. No fear of getting killed or arrested. No searches. No mine blasts. No cross fires . . . . no . . . ." Arti sobbed. Her voice choked.

She folded her Abhaya above knees. Bent down. Lifted lots of fresh water in her hands and washed her face. Tears rolling down her cheeks, she rinsed her face with water. Then she continued for long to enjoy the water splash on her face. Nazir took out a towel surface handkerchief and wiped Arti's face for a while. Smiled and planted a kiss on her cheek.

The love birds of course!

They spent some more time in the wilderness of the gushing nallah and the verdant adjoining the water course. After that Nazir and Arti walked side by side to the road edge and boarded a bus back to the destination.

Army rules are strict. Report back in time is very important.

*   *   *

All human beings grow up in their age. Little cute children become young. In their prime youth they become more attractive and smart. Various kinds of clothes on their bodies give them more grace. And if clothes are well designed and costly they add to the beauty of the person wearing them. And when mothers watch their children grow up they feel pleased. Their hearts rejoice. Their life is bestowed by the blessings of Almighty.

Ama Ganaie was one such person whose children were growing up. He was happy, so was his wife. Their sons were now in early twenties and daughters in teens. On alternate Mondays when her son Nazir left for NIT in the morning she would shower blessings. Accompany him up to the gate. Then she would run upstairs to the attic which she used as a watch tower for keeping an eye till he went behind the curved road. She followed similar procedure when her daughters left for school. Up to the gate and then to the watch tower till their bus left the spot.

Two more people had the same routine. One was Arti the army officer. On every alternate Monday she pretended to check the efficacy of the watch tower in the corner of the camp. Watch Nazir leave the spot. Only two people knew about this routine.

Nazir and Arti.

And daily one young man from the army camp, who would always be in civvies, watched Ruby and Shazi leave their home and board the bus for school.

Visits of Arti, Ruby and Shazi to each other's place became frequent as time passed. Arti managed her visit to have a glimpse of Nazir on every alternate Sunday when he visited home. Moreover, she called Ruby and Shazi to her camp on one pretext or the other. This was a boon for the young man in civvies. When he got an inkling that Ruby is to visit, he would stare at her from a distance.

Say nothing.

Just stare and praise her beauty.

The buxom girl was the only gift he yearned for.

He disclosed to none his purpose and his interest in Ruby. He feared reaction.

Ruby was in her 18th year. Bubbling with youth, donning rosy cheeks fluttering her frock, she always looked graceful.

He was not the only one who stared and praised her beauty.

One more youth had the same routine. He was a non Kashmiri but fair complexioned labourer who worked in the fields during day time. But before going for work he waited on the school route till Ruby passed by and entered the school premises. Nobody knew he always had a short gun under his garments. In the heart of hearts he always yearned to marry Ruby, say good bye to the gun non sense affair, and live happily with her in his home across the hated LOC.

Ignorant of what was going on through the lives of some youth, Ruby attended her school. One afternoon few army vehicles stood outside the school gate at a distance. As Ruby and her sister, after school hours, walked towards the bus stand few hundred meters away there was a volley of gun shots. All ran helter skelter. Those who were near the school gate returned. People ran which ever direction they felt safer, fearing bullet injuries. Ruby and her sister were walking near the army vehicles. Suddenly, a young man in civvies instructed them to sit down in the protection of army vehicles. Blushing with fear Ruby looked more beautiful to him.

"Don't panic, you are safe . . . . have some water," he stretched his arm with water bottle in hand.

Ruby and Shazi both took water.

"*Ama Ganaie ki beti ho na tum?* (Aren't you Ama Ganaie's daughters)" he asked.

Ruby was stunned. She looked at him to ascertain who he is.

"I know you. Don't panic,"

After few minutes, feeling safe, the two girls got up.

"Should I accompany you up to the bus stand?" he again asked.

Ruby did not reply and left the scene with her sister.

He kept watching till they disappeared.

Back in the vehicle his colleague asked, "*Kuch baat bani* (Any progress?),"

"Thank God, she did not suspect we did the aerial firing intentionally,"

"Why don't you tell her directly you love her?"

"She is Ama Ganaie's daughter who is so close to the major. If he complains about me, the major will shoot me,"

"Nothing will happen; maybe she is also interested,"

"I am still paying for the sins of others. They indulged in rape and I was put off duty,"

"Right . . . . but,"

"You know, those *behenchod* court martial people said you, as commander, have the responsibility . . . . what could a captain do to those soldiers whose friends had been killed,"

"Easy . . . . easy,"

"They could have killed even me . . . . Now this attachment to non sense military intelligence,"

"At least for some time you will be at ease,"

"*Yaar kya* ease? Only intelligence I could gather was about Ruby . . . ."

"Have patience and courage,"

"*Yaar*, I will die without Ruby."

Greed grows

With the onset of militancy the minority community of Kashmir popularly known as Kashmiri Pandits had left the valley. The issue of their departure remained controversial as always. Some blamed the then governor for encouraging the mass migration to give communal colour to the movement. The Pandit organizations put forth the newspapers in which warnings by some militant organizations had been published for Pandits to leave valley. Others blamed the Pandits for hobnobbing with the governor and leave Kashmiri Muslims at the risk of getting butchered by the ruthless army. The controversy apart, the Pandits left the valley leaving their properties like houses and land holdings unattended. Subsequently, they sought to sell their properties. New breed of property dealers popped up who gained profits out of these sales.

Ama Ganaie had an eye on the adjoining orchard estate belonging to a Pandit. When he heard about some property dealer trying to sell the orchard to different aspirants, he thought about an alternative plan. He called Rahim Dar to his home whose son was an active Holly Warriors militant, formerly a PWD employee. Ama Ganaie had helped Dar when he feared that the army major may be rude to him. Ama wanted something for that service.

Service for service.

Or mutual interest.

God Knows.

The duo discussed for a long time in the cosy environs of Ama Ganaie's drawing room. No threats from anywhere. The fathers of two active militants discussed the strategy. The army camp was in the vicinity. Nobody could venture in. While they sipped tea they discussed the plan threadbare. After a long discussion Rahim Dar left for his home and Ama Ganaie remained calm.

Night passed off peacefully. And in the morning the Muezzin called the faithful to pray.

Allah ho Akbar . . . . God is great

Alsalat u Khairu mina nawum . . . . Namaz is better than sleep.

The faithful heard the call and ignored the cosy environs of their beddings. Had ablution and left towards the mosques for morning prayers. As the faithful offered prayers and decided to leave the mosques, some educated persons assembled near the wall, where posters had been fixed.

"*Tanzeem ko pata chala hai ki kuch log mafroor panditoon ki zamin jaidad bechne/ khareedne ki koshish kar rahe hain. Yeh koshish tehreek se gadari ke mutradif hai. Aisi koshish main mulawis logon ko khabardar kiya jata hai ki baaz aayen. Warna wo khud zima dar honge.* (The organization has got the information that some people are trying to sell and purchase the Pandit property. This is treason against the holy movement. Such people are warned to desist from such activities otherwise they shall be themselves responsible for any consequences.)

Such posters appeared in almost all mosques in the area. The frightened land dealers left the task half way for fear of their lives.

Few more days passed. Ama Ganaie was dressed in a white Pathan suit and black short coat which he usually wore. A *karakul* cap was on his head. Rahim Dar was dressed in off white long round necked shirt which touched his knees. Under the long shirt he had matching colour trousers. He usually used skull cap which had lots of pores. Both liked to wear chapels as they were headed to plains of Jammu. Putting their small bags into the back portion of the private vehicle, owned by Ama Ganaie, they sat in the back seat. The driver turned the keys and rushed towards national highway which could take them to Jammu.

Having spent most of day time on the mountainous track travelling, they straightway went to the rented house of Pandit land owner. He had made arrangements for the petition writer who was present with the revenue and court papers which were to be submitted in the court for registration. After signing some pages as identified by the person they decided to spend the night in a local hotel. In the evening the duo roamed Jammu streets and market places. They made lot of purchases. Back in the hotel they talked for a long time. One thing they thought common to agree upon was that Jammu seems in celebration mood till late in the night while villages and towns in Kashmir turned ghost towns just after sunset.

Next day, the duo got their papers processed in the courts and then in revenue records. In a couple of days they returned to their homes.

Not a month passed when Ama Ganaie's labourers were erecting barbed wire fence around the adjacent land belonging to a Pandit. The land estate increased manifold with this annexation.

Rahim Dar himself increased his estate though not as big as Ama.

* * *

The brave heart

July and August months are mostly dangerous for the people who live nearer the rivers and other water bodies. Flash floods in the upper reaches cause instant floods and some of the rivers and Nallahs which originate from mountain areas witness speedy gush of water. In the mountainous regions heavy downpour brings lots of destruction due to river bank erosion. Debris in the form of boulders, muddy water and logs are driven away by the high velocity water. As the plain area is reached, the debris settles down and small sized pebbles and logs reach lower areas. It has been a practice that the people living in the lower regions take risk of their lives and try to catch hold of the drifting logs which can be used in the houses. Though this is a dangerous game but every time flash floods occur and people watch logs being driven away by the gushing water, they find their way into the rivers.

A wide river passes within the periphery of Arwanpora. Over the years flood water accumulates debris in the river bed at spots raising the level there and at places scours the river bed creating huge depressions. Around these depressions water depth increases and the protection bunds erected by the flood control department are eroded. This year again flash floods were witnessed and the people rushed to the river area to collect logs and other firewood drifted down by the high speed water from the forest region. The young and foolhardy villagers took a plunge into the river. After struggling for some time two of them ran the risk of going deeper into the river to catch a bigger log. But to their surprise and ill luck the water current pushed them more inside the river and they could, with great difficulty, catch hold of some solid object which helped them go to the safety of an island formed due to shoal accumulation in the middle of the river. Saving their lives they stood on the island at least one hundred fifty meters from the river banks. The water currents in the river made their lives vulnerable and attempts by them to return to the bank failed. With each passing minute hope of their safe return dwindled. News about the episode spread in the adjoining area and the people rushed to the banks. Men, women, children, boys and girls assembled on the river banks. Incessant rains, cloudburst, and lightening and speedy water currents made the chances of saving their lives bleak. The onlookers could do nothing. They either prayed or reprimanded them silently as to why they took such a big risk.

A log can't be costlier than the human life.

The news reached the district administration who asked the fire brigade department to come to their rescue. Some firemen came to the spot. They tied few ladders to reach the spot but crossing over 150 meters was not an easy task. Finally they surrendered and left the duo at the mercy of God. The relatives of these trapped persons had anxiety on their face. Women screamed, with each passing water current, which hit the island and made the lives more at risk. The fierce water currents almost touched their feet. The close relatives took to the age old practice of slaughtering some sheep in return for the life of human beings. After some time some army men came to the river bank to witness the situation which was out of control. The group included the captain also. Roaming here and there he had a glimpse of Ruby who was one among the onlookers. The captain made way to reach nearer so that he could see Ruby closely and vice versa.

Eye contact was made!

The captain's brain moved as fast as the flash flood water current. He decided to show his skills of a brave army officer and the heart of a soldier. He was not so much interested in saving the lives of trapped persons as he was enthusiastic to show off his bravery and impress Ruby. He sent couple of his colleagues to the camp and in no time a vehicle filled with requisite items reached the spot. He himself changed his clothes and wore the rafting kit. The swimming bags, life saving jackets, helmets and the like were now on three persons including the captain. The rafting boat was downed into the water and before plunging into it he had another look at Ruby.

Eye contact!

The trio sped the rafting boat fast towards the island against the water currents. The voyage was not easy. The boat would be drifted away by the current but they did not lose control and kept rowing against all odds. The boat would be swept away by hundreds of meters but the enthusiastic soldiers brought it back. To their good luck the rains stopped and it helped them reach the island with great difficulty. They used ropes to tie the rafting boat to one of the big boulders till they made the trapped persons sit in the boat. Loud cheers were heard from the assembled crowd for the feat.

A heart pumped blood at faster pace but this noise was not heard as it was lost in the din.

The soldiers had difficulty in returning to the bank safely but they managed the rescue of the trapped duo. The relatives hugged and kissed the duo as they reached the river bank safely. Some people among them shook hands with the soldiers and thanked them for the feat.

The eye contact again happened!

The locals helped the army men load the items back into the vehicle which left the spot amid cheers and acknowledgement of the brave effort.

*   *   *

Dubious democracy

Desperate with the ongoing criticism of human rights violations and non-functioning of democratic institutions, the government decided to hold elections at any cost. The mainstream political leaders who had gone into hiding in Jammu and Delhi were roped in to try their luck again. While they feared for their lives but promise of fool proof security gave them some confidence. The renegades who had been accused of severe human rights violations and wanton killings were also advised to plunge into the electoral fray. Their leaders received the advice that in case they fought elections possibly they may be elected and thus could be the masters in the new dispensation. Since people feared them they were of the opinion that due to the fear psychosis they may be voted to power.

On the other hand it was a challenge for the Umbrella politicians. They swung into action to defeat the purpose of elections calling it a futile exercise in absence of durable political solution to the problem. Since government of India had time and again presented the elections to the state assembly as a referendum in favour of accession to India the Umbrella organization wanted to exhibit that the elections are not an alternative to the demand for plebiscite. Three groups took the proposed elections as a challenge.

One, the government for which a small percentage of voter turnout was acceptable to show the world that new government has the people's mandate.

Two, the Umbrella elements for whom better participation would prove counterproductive and negation of their plebiscite demand.

Third, the army and other security agencies for whom better participation would prove that their writ runs.

All the three groups made up their mind to make their view point acceptable.

The politicians whose last few years had passed off without any tangible public contact were now desperate to revive the old ties. The political workers had either gone into hibernation due to militant fear or become passive to the electoral process. Some of them had even become militant sympathizers may be under threat to their life. But rejuvenating the political vacuum was of paramount importance for those who wanted to try their luck under ballot. One such politician was David.

David was now in his mid fifties. He was a fringe politician having spent more than twenty years in politics. Dressed in round necked brown colour coat and loose pants the short statured politician had no imposing personality. His structure was an average between watermelon and a pumpkin. Protruding cheeks gave an impression as if the extra flesh shall fall down any time. Flab appeared on almost all parts of his body. Sporting pencil thin moustaches he intentionally wore a local cap which is generally used by the peasants. This was done to influence the local peasant population who outnumbered others in the particular constituency. He had very less education may be around higher secondary but had started his political career as a student only. He had already plunged into electoral fray twice without any success. This was the reason that he got encouragement to try his luck in the new scenario.

David actually was named Dawood but due to his atheistic leanings people nick named him David. Popular among a select group of people and voters, who had resigned into oblivion, David tried his luck again and made an attempt to revive old and maintain fresh relations. Among the fresh relations he thought Ama Ganaie was the best bet. Ama had a couple of advantages. One his son was an active militant and second he had a lot of local acquaintances.

One day David reached Ama Ganaie's house under a blanket of security cover.

Many vehicles carried paramilitary forces to guard him.

A bullet proof car was there for his own use.

A jammer fitted vehicle to thwart any remote controlled blast.

Ama did not snub him. He, in fact, wanted to establish additional relations among the political class. But on the face he did not express anything. He just listened to David and his political sermon of better facilities to the masses.

"The militant activities have deprived people of basic facilities and even wanton killings and HR abuses have risen manifold. Nobody listens to the hapless people. Political and democratic rights will ensure their say is heard," David continued.

"Hmmmm," Ama Ganaie nodded his head.

"It is, as such, every body's duty to put in efforts. It will be a social service,"

Ama continued his *hoon haan* only.

"I have come to request you to help me in the election process. You can use your influence,"

Ama pushed the tray containing snacks towards David. David acknowledged the gesture.

Spending some time in the company of Ama Ganaie in his drawing room, David left with a positive attitude but mixed feelings as Ama did not reply directly whether he would support or not. But David's hope against hope remained alive. David, subsequently, entered the army camp to discuss some issues with Major Salvan. It was done intentionally to show off his close acquaintance with the army. This could be used on the polling day when army possibly would issue subtle directions to the electorate to cast vote or face the music.

The election process did not take off on any high note. Militant threats kept the whole exercise subdued. Some killings took place. Contesting candidates and their security vehicles came under fire. Suspected political workers got warnings. Candidates and their influential party leaders campaigned though in a low key affair. The Umbrella elements campaigned for election boycott. Both exercises continued simultaneously.

Few days before the Election Day, the local army units called meetings with the locality elders to impress upon them to make efforts so that the exercise succeeded. It was ensured that the close relatives of active militants participated. While participants were offered tea and snacks as a good will gesture but warnings were also issued that anybody violating their writ shall be dealt with severely. One such meeting was conducted by Major Salvan also. Ama Ganaie also participated. The major had sent invitation to about a dozen persons among them close relatives, fathers and brothers of active militants.

"Voting has to be done. This is an order and nobody can violate that, "the major was blunt.

"Sir, militant threats are there. They have declared anybody casting vote shall be killed," said one participant.

"If I don't see black indelible election ink on the fingers I will get those fingers chopped. To die is one thing but to live without hands in a deplorable condition is pathetic,"

Sir . . ."

"No *sir paer* . . . . nothing just casting votes . . . . my men will be on extra security that day . . . . *wo behenchod* militant . . . . I will pick their sisters to the camp if they don't behave . . . ," Salvan pontificated.

Though the abuse was not aimed at Ama Ganaie and Rahim Dar directly, but they felt humiliated because it went straight into their faces.

Their daughters were directly abused.

*   *   *

Some time before the voting day, Ama Ganaie's drawing room was buzzing with activity. Around twenty people from the area had assembled on the request of Ama. The servant served tea and snacks. The elderly and middle aged persons wore Pathan suits, some peculiar *tanidar* Kashmiri Pherans. They wore skull caps and a couple of them *karakul* caps. All the persons now attending the meeting had at some point of time been called by the major and instructed to get people into voting. Although they tried to express their helplessness in view of militant threats but the major listened none. He was categorical in his command. No obfuscation, nothing inscrutable. Every word was clear cut.

"You all know why we have assembled here today. I mean the two edged sword . . . . on one side Mujahidin and on the other the military . . . . You all have attended the meeting with the major . . . . ," Ama Ganaie initiated the discussion.

"Hmmm . . . . yes . . . . we all know," said one.

"I thought we better discuss and chalk out a strategy . . . . combined one . . . . ,"

"What is your suggestion?"

"What suggestion can I give? In such a situation mind turns palsy. A step here or there shall prove pernicious. Frankly speaking, my own son sent me a word that he won't tolerate anything against the Tehreek. And I know fully Rahim Dar must have got the similar message,"

"I swear it is similar . . . . nothing against the Tehreek,"

"Then, what to do?"

"We better wait. See Tehreek is first priority. But to save one's life is also important. If we feel army is adamant on voting and we have in any case to cast the vote . . . . we better vote for David,"

"Why David?"

"I believe he is better than others. Others, we have tested already . . . . ,"

"Right . . . . ,"

The meeting ended after some time and the participants dispersed. Ama was now running with the hare and hunting with the hounds.

A double cross!

Outside on the road, some vehicles plied with few people inside them. The loud speaker was fitted on the vehicle and through it, were played songs in favour of the contesting candidate. Security vehicles carrying alert uniformed men rolled past giving cover to these vehicles. The number plates of the vehicles had been concealed under a thick layer of mud. This was done to thwart identification by armed militants who may take action against the driver or the proprietor of the vehicle for participating in the election process. The political workers sitting in the vehicles covered their faces with black cloth lest they be identified. The vehicle was decorated with flags and buntings having election symbol painted or inscribed on them. These vehicles were allowed to pass by without stoppage or frisking of the passengers in them which otherwise was a routine for all other vehicles.

*   *   *

The elections to the local assembly were announced and every Tomatoes, Dolmos and Humus were persuaded to participate in the elections. The participation had many fold benefits for those who advocated it. Bigger inclusion would mean that the people had taken to electoral options with enthusiasm and fervour. The higher percentage would mean that the Umbrella elements had lost influence and sheen.

Killing many birds with one stone!

The renegade groups, originally trained to fight the armed forces, were now working under the directions of same force. When they got directions to plunge into electoral fray themselves they thought that they would be elected to the law making body without much fuss either through manipulations or fear in the minds of electorate. And this prompted them to remain prepared mentally that they would be propped up as the winners. Kashmiris have coined a sarcastic adage for such people who out of greed resort to all kinds of follies.

'*Lalchi photmut hotchi matchi koli* (The greedy drowns into a dry stream)'

That is how people of such attitude and outlook are described as. Their leaders plunged into electoral fray under some interesting party name.

"*Insaaf Party* (The Justice Party)"

The name itself made people laugh. Their justice used to be of unique nature. Justice would be done in a jiffy. It included chopping off the head, shooting someone on mere suspicion, abduction, framing selection list of proposed employees. They, however, took good advice from their mentors.

"Present some soft faces before the public who have acceptance among the common people," they were advised.

It was not a problem for them to make people their own 'friends' and 'well wishers' with the only difference that they would abduct a person from his home and till he accepted their command would remain in their custody. Among the group abducted and made to represent them in the coming polls was a person nick named as Johnny.

Johnny had public acceptance and had over the years received goodwill from the general public. His story from a common man to just short of celebrity status was interesting. Tall person having average body build, he had an attractive figure. He, in one of TV shows, played the character of a Gali ka Gunda (the local urchin). Wearing jeans and fast colour T-shirt he wore a handkerchief round his neck. Though he did not look like a Godfather of the local gang but he pretended to be same by his actions. His repeated adjectives in the show included 'Johnny is a bad man', 'Johnny is the Godfather 'and so on. Johnny, Bad Man and Godfather words stuck to his name like a postage stamp on a postal envelope. Some people, subsequently, did not understand the intricacies attached to the word godfather. Johnny continued to rule the hearts of the people. Johnny additionally was known to be passionate character about his friends and neighbours and attracted lots of goodwill.

So Johnny, one day, found himself among the people who wanted a soft face. He was surrounded by armed men in the room where the leader talked, advised, threatened and finally announced his decision.

"You have to fight elections on our party ticket,"
Quickest Justice System!

The renegade leader was usually addressed as boss by his group members. 'Yes Boss' stuck to them as a watch word. And the "Boss is always right "is known to all. He always pretended to be like a Bollywood film villain ready to spread terror, humiliate, thrash and even kill anybody. Being in early thirties he also had received arms training from a camp across the border. After joining the pro forces group, he would dress himself to look very fierce which included army uniform also to which his mentors did not object. Robust bodied boss gave the impression that he could kill anybody with his strong arms only and not needing any weapon for the purpose. Depriving people of vehicles particularly small sized cars was his pastime. Regular calls to affluent people in the area for donations were a sport for him. And with election round the corner the frequency of these calls had increased and people had to cough up 'election fund' which served as protection money for them.

Before Johnny could utter a single word to explain his position, the group commander left the place.

Heartbroken and dejected Johnny left the place. He had two options, rather a single one, before him. His only option was to die, which if bifurcated, would be to die with the pro election bullet or the anti election bullet.

Post this meeting which ended in a final threatening, advice came from friends and well wishers to seek help from various government agencies and even the Umbrella organization. The government agencies advised to listen to them and participate.

"We will provide fool proof security."

They wanted some acceptable faces in the fray. Who better than Johnny?

And anti election organizations turned out to be as confused as ever.

'Have faith in Allah'

'What can we say to such brutal organizations that are even after our lives? You know they in fact mellowed down the spirits of Azadi,'

Johnny finally ended up with taking unwilling plunge into electoral politics.

The guarded election rallies spread in all parts. So did the anti election campaign. The leaders among the Umbrella organization spread here and there to preach for non participation by the people. With their rhapsody they referred to the macabre events in which scores got killed. Their rhetoric was sardonic towards the forces and the pro election politicians. They implored to the public to be sentient to the feelings of those whose dear ones had been martyred. The new aspirants in politics were deadly against the anti election compaign. One day, when the top most leader of the Umbrella group was scheduled to visit and lead anti election campaign in Arwanpora area, the renegade leader decided to teach him a lesson.

"Today I will finish off the person. He will die today and the rest of problems shall be solved, "he declared to a group of four volunteers who were ready to annihilate him.

The group got ready and decided to wait for the leader's convoy to reach a destination which was around five kilometres from the village where from the leader was expected to start his anti election campaign. The group waited for hours together but the convoy of the leader did not pass through the point. Tired of their endless wait, they called off the programme thinking that either the leader had been sounded off by some sympathizer about the possible attack or due to certain preoccupations somewhere he decided to cancel the programme. They returned to the camp around evening where they got the shock of their life. The incident was revealed to them by their group leader.

"This *behenchod* Major Salvan seems to be an ISI agent. He only saved this *behenchod* Umbrella leader from dying today at our hands,"

"What are you saying?"

"*Aur kya* (what else). Salvan had deputed his men around twenty kilometres from the Arwanpora area. They picked up this *behenchod* Umbrella leader in their own vehicle giving an impression that he had been arrested. But the fact is that the army men took him in safe custody to this place,"

"Is it?"

"He roamed in the area for full day. Addressed anti election meetings in full protection of the army,"

"My God!"

"That is OK. Johnny is visiting this area for election campaign tomorrow. We have orders to arrange public meeting at all places in our area,"

"So . . . . ?"

"*Sab hum ko chutia banate hain. sirf order pass karte hain. Kaun sune ga hamari baat. Log thode pagal hain hamare aadmi ko vote den gey. Itna zulm jo hum ne kiya* (All make fool of we people. Who will listen to us. People are not insane that they will vote for our candidate. We have been tyrants),"

"Don't get emotional. Control yourself lest someone listens to what you been saying,"

"*Yaar yeh kute ki zindagi hai. Is se marna behter hai* (We are living a dog's life. It is better to die),"

"*Maare to jayen gey ek din . . . . bas kuch din sakoon se ji to len* (We shall get killed one day. May we live for few days happily),"

"*Chalo phir camp main thodi sharab pi kar sakoon dhoondhen* (Let us seek happiness in camp with some liquor)."

The whole group got up.

* * *

Few days before the elections, posters appeared on mosque walls. It contained dire warnings to those who were to contest elections and also to those who participated.

Life threats in abundance!

On the other hand army men roamed in villages and whosoever met conveyed their intention of taking strong action against those who did not vote. The population of common people was caught in between the two guns one held by army and other by militants. The people being in a fix could not decide what to do.

On the actual day of polling the army men had laid siege around the localities during night time. People who wanted to leave the place early to wander here and there so that they are free from the wrath of army men were stopped and ordered to go back to the village.

"Sir, *zameen par kaam karne Jana hai* (Sir, I am going to my fields to work)" the fleeing people tried to convince the soldiers.

"No problem. Cast your vote first then go," said one soldier.

"And listen we will check the indelible ink on your index finger that poll officials apply," instructed another.

Some had their brains working nightlong. They made some mixture of vegetable juice and painted their index fingers. Showed off the same to inquisitive soldiers and were able to skip the 'unholy' exercise of voting for the people they did not like.

As the polling actually started, army men roamed in the lanes and by lanes of the localities to thwart any attempt by the militants and their sympathizers to disturb polls. Among the soldiers one young man in civvies also roamed. He, in the name of gathering information about poll process, was looking for Ruby, his desired destination. He had presumed since her father Ama Ganaie was a close friend of the major and he may play some role in active participation in the ballot cast. Presumably, Ama Ganaie might ask his family members also to cast vote. He visited all polling booths in the village to have a glimpse or may be a chance to speak to her. Due to holiday, on account of polling, Ruby did not go to school. He, as such, had lost the opportunity of looking at her in the morning. He stared at all small groups of women to find out if Ruby included in any one. In a bid to search for his love he forgot to have lunch or even a visit to his office. Ballot time was over and in an hour or so ballot boxes and the staff were transported to their destinations. The localities sighed relief. The siege was over. Villagers were happy and relieved.

All rejoiced.

Government at successful polls.

Umbrella elements for very low percentage participation.

Security establishment for a comparatively peaceful day.

But this young man was in a bad mood!

*   *   *

For Arti and Nazir meetings on specified places and time became a usual phenomenon. They took utmost care so that they are not recognized by any one. And no one should come to know about their meetings. For an army officer to roam about freely with a local boy was against the discipline. It could land her in trouble and she could be charged with leaking vital information. While as for Nazir it was equally troublesome. He could be at the receiving end on both sides. He could be labelled as informer by the militants. Even he could be slapped with a case for providing information to militants. His brother, being an active militant, was a disadvantage to him.

But love sneaks deep and ignores all dangers!

Today the duo reached Dal lake area. Nazir, in his jeans and T shirt looked very smart. His fair complexioned face was shining. And when Arti descended from a bus wearing Abhaya and face cover nobody recognized her except Nazir who greeted her. Boulevard, the road along Dal lake banks witnessed little hustle and bustle. Occasionally, passenger buses and cars plied. The conductors on these buses attracted passers-by and waiting passengers as the buses slowed down.

Nishat, Shalimar, Harwan.

Though these calls were for passengers going to respective places but no tourists were waiting for these buses to take them to these tourist hubs which in present circumstances looked deserted. So were all such places. The tourism infrastructure was occupied by the uniformed men.

Arti and Nazir walked along the Dal banks. Every where one could see the sand bagged bunkers of army and other forces giving shabby look to the serene environs of the paradise on earth. These were like flecks and smudges over a beautiful body. The cancerous spots in a healthy body make it non functional till the whole body dies down if not given chemotherapy to arrest the spread of the disease. Even chemotherapy leaves the body disfigured. Hair loss and skin scars are the visible ones. The invisible can't be described.

Paradise burning!

Although Arti herself was part of the same establishment and she lived in the makeshift hut erected in an apple orchard but she hated the occupancy most. She would not express it to anyone but her heart sliced as she saw the beauty vandalized. They moved on and on till they reached a boat boarding spot. Half a dozen boats waited there for any passengers.

"*Wal haz dal chakra* (Come for Dal lake visit)", the boatman enquired.

Nazir looked into eyes of Arti to know her reaction. He intentionally did not speak to her lest the boatman understood she is a non local. It could cast doubts as to how a local boy is wandering with a non local girl. And further revelations could be harmful for Arti.

Arti blinked her eyes and signalled in affirmative. Nazir decided the rates with the boat man and both were enjoying the boat ride on Dal surface.

Dal looked calm. Very few boats rowed there. Occasionally a motor boat used by soldiers disturbed the waves and the decibels pierced the eardrums. Vast area of the lake looked still. None knew whether it was peace or a prelude to some typhoon.

Dal Lake resembled the love birds having a boat ride.

Calm or initiation of a typhoon.

Nobody knew.

The hills around the lake presented a scene of peace. But some patches of bruise were visible from a distance. The security bunkers erected over the slopes seemed scars of some incurable disease which made the environs unhealthy rather waiting for death.

The love birds held each other very tight to feel their warmth. Nazir had dropped his right arm around Arti who rested her left face on the chest of Nazir. She closed her eyes and the cool breeze across Dal waters sang in her ears.

*   *   *

For David it was a remarkable victory. For an ordinary political worker, who previously indulged in street talks or closed door meetings before militancy erupted, the horizon had become wider for him. He was now member of legislative assembly, the law makers' body. He now represented people and enjoyed lavish life style. Government accommodation, security setup for his protection, free air travel and other facilities. Now he would brush shoulders with ministers and call officers for review of development in his constituency. Media persons made a beeline to his place for interviews. Even occasionally, he would be asked to speak to the elite audience of academics and researchers on the political issues. He now did not need people like Ama Ganaie to support him. He had made a mark for himself.

The arrests by the security forces continued despite new dispensation being in office. People continued to be harassed, arrested, denied bail and bundled in security vehicles during nocturnal raids. Claims always continued to be that no innocents shall be touched but ground situation was different. With the people like David getting elected, Ama Ganaie and the people of his ilk lost grip over the issue. The harassed people now pinned their hopes on elected representatives for help in the matter. Early morning, such persons whose relatives had been arrested would reach the official residences for a *Mulakat*. Since David feared some militant attack in the weak security zone of his village, he preferred to stay in the capital cities where security had been beefed up. From far off places people boarded early morning buses, which usually stayed for the night there, to reach capital city as early as possible. They had to wait at the gates for long hours because David would not be available so early. He developed an elite lifestyle which included morning walks and a penchant for golf game. Previously in his village he would work in his fields and orchards that gave him some physical exercise but now the security system did not allow him to roam freely. And secondly, physical exercise had been curtailed drastically.

Though Ama Ganaie had congratulated David on phone for his electoral success and David acknowledged his support but Ama wanted to personally meet and shake hands with him. Ama had in fact realized that some changes have taken place and in the new scenario, the major had some restrictions which tied his hands in discharging his duties compared to previous. Though draconian laws continued to be in force but media and political government had imposed certain spanners in the wheel. Ama, as such, wanted to keep the political bosses in good humour.

One morning Ama left his place early in his car and reached David's official residence. However, he like others was not allowed to enter till word came from inside. And it was conveyed that Sahib meets people after 9-15am and as such nobody is allowed to enter the high security area. Ama felt humiliated and he remembered the major who allowed him enter any time though his was also a security sensitive area. While others waited outside but Ama would never be stopped by the sentry. Here sentry was different who did not know or recognize Ama Ganaie.

No friendship.

No personal acquaintance.

No neighbourhood.

No orchard occupied.

No secret deal or partnership for earning money.

Despite humiliation, Ama waited for about half an hour till all were allowed in. All visitors were asked to wait in the hall, an accommodation near the gates itself. Another fifteen minutes passed and David entered. He took his seat in a comfortable chair in front. He sat with his face towards the visitors. Ama expected a seat flanking David but that was not to be. David wished everybody individually and had a casual introduction to the problems faced by them. Ama was as common as everybody in the hall. People expressed their helplessness and explained their problems.

Some had community problems like bad roads or deficient water supply.

Some had a damaged transformer.

Some wanted employment.

Someone's son or sibling had been arrested.

"My son has been picked by the Tas Force (Special Operation Group of Police)," complained an elderly person.

Task Force was nicknamed as Tas (thrash) Force by the people for their brutal onslaught on the populace and people feared it the most.

"Why?" asked David.

"He is innocent. But I fear for his safety. Now one person was demanding one Lac rupees. I can't arrange so much money,"

"That time is over now. None can demand money. It is the people's government. And I represent people . . . . the *Gareeb Awam (Poor commoners)*,"

Ama Ganaie felt David taunted him. Possibly this was a reference to his minting money on arrests and other things in connivance with the army major. He did not say anything but silently got up from his seat and shaking hands with David left the spot.

"Time of payments for release of innocents is over. Anybody having such a problem should directly contact me. I will see to the issue," David thundered.

Those present in the hall whispered and expressed satisfaction. David smiled.

In the car, Ama quaffed two full tumblers of water to quench his thirst, rather extinguish his fire stoked by David's snub.

*　　*　　*

The watch tower

Captain, attached with the military intelligence (MI), had lost interest with this new job. He, in fact, was given such a job which was not to his liking. He felt he had been rendered useless with this development. Gathering information that would be useful to the army for operations against militants was the job of those trained specially for this. They would in turn use local contacts for gathering information. Captain, in fact was attached to this group as part of punishment, so without much responsibility. He wandered and now he found a good way out to spend his time. He fell in love for the local girl namely Ruby. He was so enthralled by her beauty that he took it as a full time job. Ruby had not responded to his expression of love for her. It, as such, seemed a one way and unilateral affair which could find no end result.

As time passed, he spent his morning in the watch tower to see her leave for school. In the evening he would again try to have a look. On holidays he would keep an eye if she roamed in her orchard. And he prayed always that Arti should call her to her camp for a breakfast or lunch or just for some time pass. This would be a very good chance for him to watch her move. During the week, at least a couple of times, he would wait for her near school gates to see her leave the school in the afternoon. Watching her movement from his vehicle window or the room opening in the camp would be a God's gift for him.

The gift of love.

The gift of blossoming sprouts.

The gift of emotional excellence.

The gift of utter satisfaction.

He occasionally indulged in serenade along the barbed wire fencing dividing the orchard expecting Ruby might show her face from the window of her house. Ruby herself felt that the captain was interested in her. But she did not know about him as to who he is. Though he was tall, well built and smart but being always in civvies created some doubts in her mind. Ruby cultivated some sort of affection for the captain as days passed by. She developed a soft corner for him. But to reciprocate was something which she feared of. She could not muster courage for a similar response. She knew nobody would endorse her proposal. It would only meet a negative response which in fact could be violent also. The man from army was on the other side of fence when personal relations came up. The civilian army relations were a taboo. The conditions were hostile. War between 'them' and 'us' was going on. We killed 'them' and they killed 'us'. There were many hurdles rather mountains to be crossed.

Hurdle of religion.

Hurdle of hostile environment.

Hurdle of enmity.

Hurdle of a complex situation.

Ruby thought about the issue many times but soon shunned it off her mind.

This is not possible.

No logical end is in sight.

No agreement on the issue is reachable.

She tried to erase the memory from her mind as soon as it came on the canvas.

The apple harvest was in full swing. Ama Ganaie had engaged about a dozen labourers to pluck fruit, collect and pack in timber or card board boxes. They used small ladders to rise to the top and gather apple in baskets which when lowered would be emptied by another person. The whole collection was done near an open hut where packing was done. There was lot of hustle and bustle in the orchard. Ruby wandered in the orchard. The captain always waiting for a chance meeting saw Ruby. The fence bifurcated the two parts one occupied by the army and other in use by the landlord. It was easy for the captain to reach nearer the fence and see Ruby from very little distance in between. The distance between the two was intentionally narrowed by them when they saw each other. The duo kept walking along the fence though on opposite sides.

"Ruby, apple harvest is on. I think this year there is good produce," he tried to test the mood.

"Yes," Ruby smiled.

"Where you send it after packing?"

"Different markets in India,"

"You get a good price?"

"Sure,'

"How much?"

"Don't know. Dad only knows,"

"No problem. I will ask Ama Ganaie. He knows me well,"

"Hmmmmm"

"I have to ask him one more thing,"

"What?"

"That is if you permit,"

"First I should know,"

"About you,"

"About me . . . . what?" Ruby smiled.

"If I have permission to talk to Ruby freely . . . . and,"

"But you are talking,"

"This is just an introduction. I want to talk freely and may be take you for a long drive,"

"Do you think he will agree?"

"First you have to agree,"

"If I don't . . . ."

"Then I will die before time,"

"Ohhhhhhhhhhhh," Ruby's broad smile made her dimple look elegant.

"Yes sure," the captain exasperated.

"Ruby Didi, Mummy is calling. Come fast." Before Ruby could reply, her sister Shazi cried loud to call her informing that mother was asking for her. The duo separated and the captain kept watching her. She occasionally moved around to smile at him.

As Ruby reached her house she found her mother at the main door. She took her inside to reprimand.

"I will break your legs,"

"Mom . . . ."

"Don't utter a single word."

Though Ruby tried to explain that it was just a chance meeting but mother did not accept her explanation. Her mother always used the attic as a watch tower to look at things in her own way.

Be it when her son left for arms training.

Be it when her daughters left for school.

Be it when her son left for NIT on alternate Mondays.

Be it her husband visiting army camp.

Be it her daughter taking a forbidden sojourn in the orchard!

In the first instance Ruby's mother and sister came to know about this development. May be some men working in the orchard just got suspicious. And possibly one among them shared the issue with Ama Ganaie's servant. By evening, Ama Ganaie had the information. He enquired about the development from his younger daughter and asked certain questions from his wife. The younger daughter did touch the firing incident near the school and the captain's help with water and duck behind the vehicle. He brushed aside his wife's apprehensions.

"May be that man tried to influence Ruby but when response was zero how can I blame her?"

"The conditions are very bad,"

"I know but we can't be over cautious," he tried to repose faith in his daughter. "We must not take any such step which may damage her reputation,"

"I think let us find some match for her,"

"She is so young . . . . just nineteen,"

"Nineteen is not young . . . . she is nubile."

"*Pranew wonmut Koor yeli jawan gatchi so chi aasan kalas peth nara tok* (The old and intelligent said a young girl is like a pot of embers on the head of parents.)

"It needs to be dropped down in such a way that we don't burn our hands and neither should the embers die down." Ama replied cooling off his wife's tempers.

The discussion on the issue continued till late in the night.

*   *   *

Conspiracy

David was the new face on the scene. With his political power he could dictate. For the army he became another conduit for furthering its agenda. He would now be seen in all army functions. Though Ama Ganaie had not lost his status as a respectable person in the area but now lime light had changed. The man in focus would be David. While the major kept his relations with Ama Ganaie in tact but David got preferential treatment when senior army officers were present.

David was least interested in people like Ama Ganaie but he wanted to strengthen his political base on his own. With many people visiting his place for different works, he consolidated his own position in the area. He clearly had an eye on next election. He would conduct tours and small meetings in government guest houses in his constituency to listen to the problems faced by the people. He wanted to be seen as a compassionate face.

David thought out a new plan. He gave his own list to the army and police officials. These lists contained names of the supporters of rival political parties who had played a role against him in the elections. Even some staunch opponents also figured who had not taken part in the election process because of their conviction. These people would be rounded up in nocturnal raids and kept in camps or police stations without any entry into the official records. This gave the security agencies a free hand to play with the law which otherwise also was at the mercy of uniformed men. The relatives of the arrested persons were compelled by the circumstances to approach David. David did not demand any money nor did he play a conduit to army officers to mint money.

"*Yeh David behenchod nayi musibat ban kar aa gaya. Hamen nahin pata tha aisa khel kheley ga hum ne rally ke doraan hi IED se hatwana tha* (David has nuisance value. Had I known earlier he would have died through IED blast during election rally)," Salvan thought.

Though Ama Ganaie was much better option in the eyes of officers who wanted money but they could not say no to David. When relatives of the arrested persons approached David, he gave them a patient hearing.

A weak groggy old man pleaded for release of his son.

A woman yowled for her disappeared husband.

A stuttering sister sought whereabouts of her brother.

Still David used to take around a week's time to approach the authorities for their release. This earned David fame in the area that he is the only person who cares for his electorate and does their work without spending even a penny.

Ama Ganaie was snubbed by David during his visit to the place. Now his means of earning good amount of money was at stake. He knew that the army officers hated David equally but being an important person they could not ignore him. David continued to be an eyesore for both Ama Ganaie and Major Salvan. Ama Ganaie knew if David succeeded in one way he could close his avenues of easy money in the works department also. He wanted to hatch a conspiracy.

But with whom?

With one's aspirations nature opens many windows to be fulfilled.

One evening after having dinner together, the major and Ama Ganaie discussed the fate of their common enemy . . . . David.

"See your own son is an active militant. And you have good rapport with the over ground workers of other Tanzeem also. You can formulate a plan," the major said.

"Major, will you tell me one thing. He is a pro India person. You also fight for India. Then why you hate him?" Ama asked. He in fact wanted to probe the major deep lest he is trying to extract information from him only which he could use somewhere against him.

"You are my friend and I don't conceal anything from you. We have helped each other nicely. I will tell you the truth. I have recently booked a penthouse in a posh area in the capital pinning hope that money flow will not stop till Ama Ganaie is there. But I never knew this *behenchod* David will damage our chances,"

"Right, he is like a snake who tries to bite us both,"

"I have always given you and your militant son protection. Otherwise I know when he visits home. I can catch him easily . . . . or even kill him,"

"Yes . . . . I know,"

"Even your daughter Ruby is in love with the captain in MI. But I reprimanded the captain. He won't move forward,"

Ama Ganaie did not say anything. He went in deep silence. The major, after waiting for few more minutes, understood Ama had been hurt deep with the reference about his daughter. Ama on the other hand took the point well. He analyzed what the major wanted to convey. He had no room to rejoice his friendship with the major.

He had no space to play in.

He recollected image of his son.

He felt his beloved daughter in his lap.

"So Gulam Ahmad . . . . think over the plan. Talk to the militants," the major said lifting himself up from the sofa in his private room.

Ama Ganaie also stood up. Both shook hands and Ama Ganaie left for his home.

Outside night had spread deep black cover. However, army camp was lit up with a special power line which they managed by threatening the electric engineer of the area. Ama Ganaie's house was given special connection from this line. Even when whole of area reeled under darkness the camp and Ama's house was lit up.

Despite his house being lit up with the electric energy, Ama's heart was in deep darkness. He felt his heart may sink any time, he may collapse on the road itself and he may not be able to walk up to his residence. But courageous man, as always, traversed the distance.

Ama in deep thoughts felt sleepy. He rested his head against the wall and soon snored. His militant son Farooq was trapped in the second storey of his nephew Rashid's house and the large contingent of army led by Major Salvan encircled the big house. The army had laid siege in three layers. Major announced on a hand held megaphone and instructed Farooq to let the inmates go out. As news spread that Farooq was trapped Ama's wife and his two daughters came out looking desperate as they feared for the safety of Farooq. The mother daughter trio walked the courtyard under the gaze of army men who were present everywhere ducking behind the solid structures to save themselves from the gun shots. As they walked Salvan again raised his voice through the hand held megaphone and asked Farooq and his three colleagues to surrender or be prepared for the inevitable death. In reply a gunshot was heard from within the house. Farooq was in no mood to surrender. Immediately bullets were fired from few more windows. In reply army guns roared and fired many shots towards the house. Windows tattered. Glass panes fell. The ensuing battle would be furious and may be gory. Ama watched the situation far from the house. His wife and daughters were seated on the edge of the road around 300metres from the house. As guns roared his wife ran towards the house fearing for Farooq's life but she was stopped by the soldiers and forced to go back. She returned to the spot running and implored Ama to approach the major to allow him to meet Farooq and persuade him to surrender. She did not want him to die.

Mothers don't want to see their sons lose life!

Ama walked but the soldiers, who till yesterday saw him being friendly with the major, did not allow him to move forward. When he persisted a soldier put the muzzle of his gun on his chest and threatened him to shoot. Ama returned. His eyes were moist as he saw his wife and daughters in a pitiable condition. Then continuous firing ricocheted. All of a sudden a loud bang was heard. Dust rose. CGI sheets flew in air. Noise of bricks and other material getting demolished was heard. Ama and his family felt that their hearts stopped beating or at least missed some beats. Soldiers shouted in celebration and all of a sudden the captain appeared from nowhere and pulled Ruby and forcibly made her to board a Gypsy. Ruby cried and implored Ama to save her but the vehicle sped fast. Ama, his wife and daughter rushed after the Gypsy but could not catch it. Their feet became heavier. The captain had abducted Ruby. As soldiers shouted that all militants are dead Ama's wife collapsed on the road side.

"Zoona, Zooni . . . ." Ama pulled and shook his wife to get her back into senses.

"*Kya sa dalil chi . . . . tchi ma sa chukh khwab wuchan . . . . woth seud shong bisturas manz* (What happened. Are you dreaming? Go to your bed." His wife heard his shouts and entered the room to awaken him from his bad dream.

"May God this turns out to be dream only." Ama got up slowly from his spot.

*   *   *

Nazir was now in his final year of engineering and his love affair with the lady army officer Arti continued. One thing was special about both of them that they did not disclose their secrets to anyone; Arti not to her colleagues, and Nazir not to his friends or family. Even the photographs taken jointly by them at various tourist spots were kept hidden. Nazir was now allowed by his father to use the small Maruti car and he would now take it to his hostel also. This facilitated his movement to and fro college and home. He used the car for furthering his love affair. Arti managed her out pass and met Nazir and they would roam about at various places.

Today they had planned a long drive and so Nazir filled the fuel tank full. Arti as usual left the camp in civvies and, subsequently, wore black robe and covered her face like local Muslim girls for fear of being identified. In a couple of hours they were driving fast on the road leading to picturesque Sonmarg. The road length of around 110Kms gave them a good benefit of long drive and road leading to Ladakh region being part of the national highway was comparatively in a better shape. So the drive became comfortable. In between they drove through few towns where hustle and bustle was comparatively better than the village portions. The village areas had clusters of houses in burnt brick with CGI sheet roof coverings. In higher reaches single story huts belonged to poorer peasants and shepherds. Some huts had mud sloped roofs, others had timber planks arranged in steep angles so that snow during winters dropped down easily without causing danger to the structure. The scene along fast flowing river was unique. Speedy water hitting the boulders caused splash. Some village girls with pitchers over their heads marched in groups towards the nallah to fetch water as they had no water supply in their villages. Some contained dirty clothes in plastic buckets to wash on the river banks. Though both liked the scene of young girls marching towards the river but none realized their pain of daily visit to the river irrespective of the weather conditions. Scorching sun or chilling winds, they were forced to take the stroll in the morning and even in evenings also. God knows whether someone like David had been voted to power in their localities also who would listen to their woes.

Nazir stopped his car at various places and took Arti to the river bed for taking photographs. She played with water and occasionally threw it on Nazir. Mesmerized by the beauty of Kashmir, Arti had in fact decided to finally settle in Kashmir. She always dreamt of marrying Nazir. Nazir himself was passionate about new development. He also pinned hopes that after completing his engineering degree he will get a job in the local Public Works department and persuade his parents who, he expected, will agree. Arti was a smart girl with comparatively blackish complexion. She time and again asked Nazir whether he will like to go along with her despite her dark complexion compared to Kashmiris fair complexion.

"*In Kashmir we say kheun gatchi trami din gatchi geshami* (When we have to feast do in big copper plate used here for *wazwan*. But shower love on black complexioned beauties)"

In reply Nazir would quote this Kashmiri popular sentence.

At places Nazir asked Arti to drive the vehicle who, as an army officer, was very much adept in driving. Before reaching Sonmarg they enjoyed wafers, soft drinks, tea and other snacks at the way side outlets erected during Amar Nath Yatra for the benefit of Yatris. Most of these outlets were closed after Yatra ended.

Amar Nath Yatra is performed by Hindus who attend the high altitude cave during months of June, July and August. Hundreds of thousands of pilgrims from the country visit and have *Darshan* of the huge icicle formed during winters. Two routes take the pilgrims to the high altitude cave. These routes pass through world famous tourist spots Pahalgam and Sonmarg.

Since they enjoyed the trip at leisure they reached Sonmarg around noon. Enchanting beauty of Sonmarg thrilled Arti who like a mountain goat ran from one green spot to other. Fear of recognition had gone out of her mind as she reached Sonmarg. Since the annual Yatra had finished about a month back the presence of people was very thin and hardly anybody was on the slopes. Even some of the security bunkers established additionally for Yatra security had been removed. Arti removed her black robe and head cover. She laid flat over the green surface and made Nazir to follow. Occasionally she rolled down the sloped track.

"I have come here earlier also once but that was in full army fatigue and on duty. Nobody allowed me to roll freely like this," Arti informed.

"Hmmmmmmmmmm . . . . so you like it?"

"Like? . . . . who does not like the heaven?"

"Right,"

"Thank God, now the conditions are getting better. Hope to revive old scenario,"

"Do you think conditions are getting better now?"

"Comparatively yes. May be the political set up improves things,"

"Politicians will improve . . . . hilarious . . . . these are the people who destroyed this place," Nazir expressed anger.

"As always,"

"Had they not rigged elections, youth would not feel deprived,"

"Anyway don't spoil your mood,"

Nazir smiled and caught Arti's hand to lift her. They walked along towards higher contours hand in hand. Arti pictured Nazir dressed magnificiantly seated in front of her family members including her father Brig. (R) Ajay Ranawat. Her mother, sister and brother were seated on other side.

"Son, I don't have any objection to your marriage. I know you both are educated and earning hands and I believe your decision must not be something emotional one only. But for my family you have to give us some space. The marriage shall have to take place as per Hindu customs and all rituals shall have to be followed."

"I understand Sir, I don't have any problems. And I assure you all Arti shall remain very happy with me." Nazir replied calmly.

"And how you live afterwards whether being religious or semi religious is your own choice. We won't interfere in that. I have lived army life and in army religion finds little place. There religion of patriotism only works."

A deep and pleasant smile spread over all faces and Arti grinned in excitement. Then all shifted to the big hall type room on the ground floor where the scene was very attractive. At a place small fire was raging and a Pandit was seated chanting religious verses in a low tone. He occasionally dropped ghee with the help of a long handled spoon which raised the fire. Fire of love continued to rage in Arti and Nazir's heart. More than fifty people were assembled who sipped tea or soft drinks and engaged themselves in low key discussions. Arti and Nazir were led to the spot. Then the Pandit raised his voice and continued chanting religious scriptures for some time. Afterwards Nazir and Arti were made to take seven rounds around the fire. Subsequently, both were showered gifts.

Gifts wrapped in glittering paper.

Gifts of love and affection.

Gifts of new relationship.

Very next moment Arti and Nazir were seated in front of a Moulvi. Arti looked gorgeous in her glittering trousseau. Ama Ganaie and his family members remained seated in the room.

"Arti alias Arshi daughter of Brig. Ajay Ranawat, you are entering into wedlock with Nazir Ahmad son of Gulam Ahmad Ganaie against a *meher* of one Lac rupees, do you accept?"

"Yes," Arti said hurriedly.

"Agreed" Moulvi again asked.

"Yes,"

"Agreed and accepted?"

"Yes"

"Congratulations." The Moulvi said and stood up to recite the verses which continued for about five minutes. Then news was disseminated down stairs and the women resumed their folk songs called *wanwun*. Celebration; celebration all over in the household followed.

"Honeymoon in Sonmarg," Arti whispered towards Nazir who blinked his eyes in smile. The talk was lost in the din.

Somewhere nearer a vehicle honked and Arti and Nazir were woken up from the day time dreams. Roaming till late in the afternoon the duo left for their destination.

*　　*　　*

Ama Ganaie, disturbed by the new development and hurt of his ego decided to discuss the matter with Rahim Dar. David had snubbed him and he was sure that his claim as the unchallenged boss of the area was waning. And David was one such person who would do it very fast. His income from arrested persons had almost halved. His timber saw mill was under scrutiny. Even the major had expressed his displeasure and freshly cultivated enmity towards David. He invited Rahim Dar to his home and one to one meeting was going on. Ama was clever enough not to disclose the deliberations with the major during his meeting with him. He exploited the secular credentials and David's atheistic ideology which was enough to infuriate Rahim Dar, a devout practicing Muslim. The relations between Islamic parties and presumably atheists had always remained hostile and the new development gave the scenario a bad shape.

"It is a shame for us both. Our two sons are active militants but this atheist has won elections," Ama Ganaie expressed his anger.

"But you helped him in elections,"

"I did not help, just put a word. If compelled, vote for him,"

"Does that not mean help?"

"It helped him. In fact he came to my home before elections and talked of repression and *zulum (tyranny)*. I thought he has changed his ideology. Even he offered prayers in my drawing room. How could I know? Rinse the crow with hundred soap cakes his black colour won't go that is what our elders said,"

"No problem I will convey the word. You also proceed,"

"Sure . . . . obnoxious . . . . the stink must vanish!" Ama said sarcastically.

Then Rahim Dar and Ama Ganaie had lunch.

*   *   *

In a day or two it was announced through the loud speaker fitted taxi, doing rounds in the area, that a public meeting is being held in the village. David, the MLA was to address a public gathering and distribute cheques among the poor who had been selected as the prospective beneficiaries under a central government sponsored scheme. Request was made to one and all for participation. This was a tactful act by David to further his political agenda and strengthen his base as much as possible. Ironically, the scheme under which these cheques were to be distributed to the needy was running for quite some time and David had no contribution in getting the scheme approved. But now David wanted to reap political benefits. The event would be recorded for transmission through local television.

By evening Major Salvan was in meeting with the leader of the renegade group working under his control and very much near the camp. The two had a closed door meeting in which no one else was allowed to participate. Major Salvan gave instructions and the group leader acknowledged to have understood the plan in full. After the meeting the group leader called his trusted few to his room and conveyed the instructions.

*   *   *

On the scheduled day arrangements had been made by the administration for distribution of cheques by the MLA.

The poor people in every society are taken for a ride, so in Kashmir.

'Comfort of the rich depends upon an abundant supply of the poor' is a thought provoking saying and comes true in all parts of the world.

The government has devised a scheme for the upliftment of the poor and around ten to fifteen thousand rupees are distributed among these down trodden to help them build their own houses. How could a sum of ten thousand rupees be sufficient for construction of a house to live in? Raise a CGI shed or a room without proper heating arrangement or ventilation. It is usually without window and door shutters so fully 'ventilated'. Who is so cunning to have devised such a formula where these poor people are humiliated by showing them on local TV receiving these small amount cheques is not known.

Doles from the benevolent government!

Either the officers try to influence the politicians at the cost of dignity of these poor people or the politicians extract sadistic pleasure in such events. The politicians on the dais pose as if they are the most benevolent on the earth and they donate these funds from their own accounts or the properties they received from their forefathers. The entrepreneurs receive subsidy amounting to millions without any information to the neighbours even. Their wealth grows through these subsidies and then they are able to donate good amounts to the political parties as election funds.

The same venue was to be turned into a political meeting. Full fledged dais, covered with a *shamiana*, was erected on one side of the school ground. A sofa set was placed over the dais for the VIP and few senior officers. Barricading was done with timber poles and iron pipes. To further strengthen the security grid concertina wires were spread in between the common people and the dais. Loud speakers were fitted so that VIP's voice could be heard in all directions. The incomers were frisked at entry points and metal detectors placed in place to thwart any sabotage.

David reached the venue around half an hour late. Some called it security strategy.

"No strategy *yaar* . . . . how can he prove he is a VIP unless he makes people wait for him," others had a sarcastic remark. All stood up to greet David who was led straight to the dais. He acknowledged the welcome by raising his right arm. Someone started to speak. Microphones blared.

Thadaaak

A loud noise, a blast occurred.

Fire raged

Dust spread

Human flesh flew

Mayhem

People ran

Chaos

The security personnel gathered courage after few moments. They arranged an ambulance and lifted David. Others were also boarded into any type of vehicle that was available. Word spread David died in the blast. Word also spread Holly Warriors has done it. No one confirmed but information went on like that. The crowd which had assembled to listen to David went restive and shouting slogans against HW, marched towards the orchard of HW militant hailing from the adjoining village. Incidentally, couple of renegades camping around Major Salvan's army camp were leading the hostile crowd. The crowd attacked the orchards of Rahim Dar whose son was an active militant commander belonging to HW. A crowd of around five hundred men ran amok. They pounced upon the trees and in a fit of rage uprooted, chopped, broke, sliced, cut and damaged whatever came their way in the orchard. Rahim Dar, living nearby in the village, somehow managed to send his wife, daughter and younger son to some relative's home. But before he was himself able to flee he was way laid by half a dozen people in the crowd. They beat up Rahim Dar to pulp who was screaming on the ground. Few bullet shots were heard and Rahim was in a pool of blood. The renegade group leader emerged out of the crowd smiling and returning his revolver back to the holster.

'La ilaha illal lah
Muhamdul Rasoolulaha'
Rahim Dar whispered and dropped his head on one side.

*   *   *

Major Salvan and the renegade group leader watched the evening TV news in major's room. The major had arranged top brands of whisky on his table to celebrate the event. He wanted to share the moment with the renegade leader. The renegade leader also felt elevated to share a drink with the senior army officer. Salvan knew such encouragement will come handy when needed in future. Anybody who was to be wiped out from the scene had to be cleverly done through these renegades as they were to be used as toilet paper. Use and throw was the best policy. And in such cases no direct blame could come on the 'highly disciplined army' itself.

Politicians across lines heaved a sigh of relief that David was saved and prayed for his early recovery. They denounced the dastardly attack that killed two people including a senior officer and injured half a dozen others. Attack by restive crowd and killing of Rahim Dar was declared fallout of the attack on David.

Salvan and group leader smiled.

Smiled on their success story.

Smiled on the naivety of the official spokesperson.

The renegade leader felt this was the best time to probe the major as he was happy and in a smiling mood.

"Sir, may I ask why you asked me to plant the bomb under the dais and why you wanted David to die?"

"That is a secret . . . . don't talk of it," Salvan had a big swig of whisky.

"And Rahim Dar's family fortune?"

"He was the father of that *behenchod* HW militant . . . . what is his name . . . . ,"

"Commander Zulqarnain,"

"Commander *behenchcod* . . . . it takes us decades to become commander in the army and these bastards become overnight. You also were one such commander,"

"Hmmmmm,"

"Yes that *behenchod* Zulqarnain . . . . it is his code name,"

"Sir,"

"He attacked our party some time back and killed my close friend. And you know he was on the forefront of celebrating *behenchod* Pakistan day. I got humiliated before my officers that evening when my commander referred to the event. I vowed that day I will not let him go scot free. He does not know I can pick his sister and get her to the camp," Salvan was talking rubbish.

"Hmmmm" renegade poured whisky for the major.

"Rahim Dar is no more . . . . and his major income generation is finished. Now let him get money from those *behenchod* Pakistanis,"

"But Sir, I am sure his party will help him in building lost property again,"

"Which party?"

"Islamic Party Sir, you don't know they are called *kikars*. They have spread their tentacles like *kikar* tree. Spreading fast and secretly. And like the *kikar* wood they are hard also,"

"What else about IP?"

"Sir, this party is cadre based. They started their schools to give education. They did the best work on that front. Had they not indulged in politics and taken part in elections they would rule the hearts . . . . but things have changed now,"

"Hmmm" Salvan sipped some more and put the tumbler on the peg table.

"And Sir, this is not the first time this party has witnessed such an onslaught . . . ."

"*matlab* (Means)?"

"Many years back the members of this party became target of the people here. They were attacked, beaten to pulp and their houses damaged. The apple and other fruit trees in their orchards were chopped indiscriminately like it was done in Rahim Dar's orchard today. People's ire against hanging of a Pakistan Prime Minister was used by the ruling party in Kashmir to settle scores,"

"What the hell! Anything you talk about in Kashmir, Pakistan is mentioned in between. Is this part of India or *behenchod* Pakistan," Salvan looked somnolent due to excess quantity.

The whisky round continued for some more time. Then Major Salvan got up, shook hands with the renegade leader, who then left the room.

Ama Ganaie could not sleep the whole night. He heard about the bomb blast in the public meeting soon after it happened. He was astonished as to how it took place and who masterminded it. He himself had not been able to contact his militant son and ask him to arrange such an attack as discussed with the major and Rahim Dar. Similar was the case with Rahim Dar who informed him about himself not being able to contact his son. Both could not share the proposed act with any colleague of their sons. In any case it was to be discussed in one to one meeting with the sons only.

'Then who carried this act and gave it the name of HW plan which culminated in destroying the apple orchard of Rahim Dar and subsequent killing of Rahim Dar himself,' he thought over but could not get a proper reply.

Ama Ganaie kept turning in his bed. Sleep was very far away from his eyes. His wife asked him time and again the reason for this worry and inconvenience. But Ama had no reply. He could not tell her as to how had a plan been hijacked by someone. He could not tell her even the hijacked plan failed in getting desired results. He could not tell her why Rahim Dar lost his orchard and his life.

Could it be himself now?

Will he lose his property and life in a jiffy to similar attack?

Will his family have to run without foot wear or head scarves?

Will someone molest or abduct his daughter while she will run for her safety?

Be it a militant, a renegade . . . . or even the captain?

The questions frightened him He was shaken from top to toe by the very idea. He felt sweat dripping all over his body.

Ama consumed his full night taking puffs from his *hookah*. Early morning he felt giddy due to sleeplessness.

Honour killing

The pilgrims thronged the area in large numbers to seek blessings on the birthday of the great saint revered and respected in the valley in general but by the people of Arwanpora area in particular. There was a market place where shops had been erected in shanties. The shrine building was illuminated all around. In the evening there was a programme of lighting earthen oil lamps around the building. The local police managed the traffic and did not allow any kind of vehicles to reach nearer the shrine lest these should hinder the movement of devotees. Men, women, children young and old from various parts of the valley were present. So was Ama Ganaie and his family. The hustle and bustle around the shrine was a thing to watch. The *Darood O Azkar* was being recited on the loud speaker fitted in the shrine. A large group of people mostly attired in white *Kameez shalwar* and donning *Karakul* or skull caps over their heads participated in the process very much inside the shrine. Women engaged in the ritual of praying. Some even went towards the cave where the saint is supposed to have spent some part of his life. It was on the hillock where only a small number of physically fit people went.

On the back side of the cave area, concealing themselves from the gaze two persons sat behind a bush. One was the captain and other his love bird Ruby. The captain attired in shirt and pant looked smart and Ruby in her new dress looked elegant. The rose cheeked girl could make anybody mad. So was the captain.

"I thank you Ruby for accepting my invitation to meet personally. I will surely talk to Ama Ganaie myself and ask for wedlock with you," he caught the hand of Ruby while talking.

"But it is not possible,"

"Why . . . . what is the hurdle?"

"Not one but many,"

"You mean I am a Hindu and you a Muslim. Or I am from the army which . . . ."

"Don't you think these are bigger hurdles?"

"Yes but I have a solution," the captain beamed with confidence.

"Like?"

"I will convert to Islam,"

"Hahahahahah,"

"Why do you laugh?"

"You seem mad . . . . it is not so easy . . . . ,"

"I will surely . . . . I take oath on this holy place behind this hill I will convert for you . . . . I am really mad for you,"

The oath by the captain influenced Ruby and she went into a deep thought. She pictured the captain seated in front of a Moulana reciting '*La ilaha Ilallah, Muhamad ar Rasool lal la*' and converting to Islam. Someone, among the people present, put a copy of holy Qur'an on Captain Rajat's head who took it in his hands, kissed it three times and touched his forehead between brows. Her parents and few more neighbors cheered and congratulated the captain to have come into the fold of Islam, the religion of God and the Prophet (SAW). And she pictured herself being congratulated by her mother, sister and the women in the neighbourhood for influencing an infidel to embrace Islam. The setting sun set some crimson rays over her face which gave a more glittering effect. The captain's madness increased.

"Ruby, I hope you agree,"

"Hmmmmmm" she was woken up from the dream by Rajat who pulled her elbow. She could say nothing feeling a straw in her throat.

"Ruby, I will change my name from Captain Rajat to Rasikh Khan,"

"Rasikh . . . ."

"Yes, Rasikh was my friend in the army. During an encounter he laid his life for me. When he saw militants targeting me, he jumped in between fired at the militant but got few bullets in his chest. I must confess Muslims are very brave. They don't care for their lives. When they give their life they give with conviction and when they take life they do with firm belief. True to their word. They can't be subjugated; they have even challenged the most powerful nation on this earth. They drove Soviet forces from Afghanistan and at that point Muslims all over the globe got united to fight in unison . . . . And Rasikh, he saved me and I want him to live again . . . . in my own body,"

Ruby then rose from the spot and Rajat followed. Before reaching the spot where they had to diverge, Rajat wanted the date for next meeting. But Ruby was not able to commit any thing.

"You know waiting for one's love bird is the most difficult task . . . . There are many dreadful diseases in the world which take life out of a person. But I don't know why 'Love' becomes the dangerous of all. It alternates between life and death like a sinusoidal wave. Up and down . . . ." Captain continued with his explanation. Comparing the most dreaded diseases to waiting for someone you love, he declared that it is the most difficult task in the world.

"Hmmm . . ."

"What *hoon haan* Ruby, I am the one who loves you most. Don't waste time in counting stars lest you lose the moon,"

"So Rasikh Khan, bye and take care." Ruby smiled and took faster steps lest someone looked out for her and got suspicious.

In few minutes time they were back in the market place where they parted ways.

Through whispers, news reached far and wide in the locality that Ruby had an affair with the captain. Ama Ganaie's friends talked about it. His enemies added spice. His well wishers wanted to bury the matter. But all wanted this matter to end soon.

Affair with a Hindu army officer!

No way!

The people tossed their tongues as if it was a religious duty to develop an affair with a local Muslim boy.

Suggestions started pouring in from well wishers. Some proposed early marriage. Others reprimanded Ruby. Few tried a soft advice. But nothing took the matter to a logical conclusion. Couple of prospective grooms were threatened by the captain with dire consequences and they stepped back fearing for their lives. Reprimand and soft advice had no effect on Ruby.

Winter season had set in and November evenings had turned chilly. People in Kashmir villages had resumed use of long robes called *Pherans* in the evenings. Even the elderly people used *kangri*, the local fire pots. Winter sees more of power cuts than summer because use of power and energy consumption increases as people take to electric gadgets.

In addition, the power generation decreases due to low water level in the feeding rivers. Power department issues curtailment schedules but these are hardly adhered to. So there are more of distress power cuts in addition to scheduled ones. Due to the distress cuts special lines also get affected.

Ghost towns increase their horror!

On one such evening whole area was reeling under darkness. Ama Ganaie wore Pheran and so did his wife. A fire pot was placed in front of him. His servant was milking the cow.

'Allah o Akbar'

The Muezzin called the faithful to Isha Namaz.

Druff

A low intensity noise of few people jumping over the wall was heard which was lost in the sound emanating from mosque loud speakers. None in Ama's house paid attention thinking possibly a dog or cat had jumped. But within few moments door was knocked feebly. Ama signalled to his younger daughter Shazi to see who is there thinking possibly he had bolted the door when his servant went to milk the cow. As Shazi opened the door a volley of bullets was fired. Before anyone could react in the house the assailants ran and jumped above the brick wall and disappeared in the thick and dark cover of the night. The servant came running after hearing the gun shots fearing for his life. Ama Ganaie, his wife and daughter Ruby ran towards the door where Shazi was lying in a pool of blood. The driver came down the stairs from his room, started the vehicle. Shazi was put into the car. The chaos engulfed Ama's family. Before the car could move Major Salvan, Lt. Arti and their security persons were on the gate. The army doctor examined Shazi in the car itself. She was no more.

All in the family wept. Arti controlled her sobs. She hugged Ruby and consoled her. Ama's nephew and business partner Rashid was among the first to reach. Not much time passed when a police party reached the spot. The major had informed the local police. It was decided not to conduct post mortem at the behest of Ama Ganaie and his family. Police investigation was confined to the broader aspects of the incident. The relatives and neighbours were busy in preparations for the last rites. Nazir was informed through phone about the incident and asked to reach home immediately.

"*Badmash ladki army officer se pyar karti hai (The debauch girl indulged with an army officer),*"

This was informed by Ama Ganaie's driver to the police official as having heard while attackers left the scene.

News further spread that Farooq was seen in the area that evening.

Honour killing!

But due to mistaken identity Shazi became the victim of the assailant who had in fact come to kill Ruby.

Nazir reached his home. Arti remained in the house till late night consoling the ladies particularly Ruby. Ruby became a victim of self reprimand as she felt that she was responsible for death of Shazi.

'Had I not indulged in love affair with the army officer, my young sister would be alive' Ruby thought and wept bitterly.

"Wake up Shazi . . . . wake up my Delicion . . . ." Ama Ganaie hollered and wept himself. His wife was inconsolable. She became hysterical calling Shazi loudly to get up and serve dinner to father.

The neighbours assembled to condole the demise of young Shazi and helped in last rites. She was laid to rest during night hours.

All family members and close relatives and neighbours spent the night in Ama Ganaie's house. The mourners attended from far off places. Distant relatives, common people and acquaintances from nearby localities and others attended during next three days. On the fourth day big congregational prayers were conducted at the graveyard followed by similar function in the house. Two big *shamianas* were erected to accommodate men and women separately.

On the back side of the courtyard arrangements were made for chefs to prepare food and mutton in big containers. Since many people were expected to attend on the 4th day so arrangements had to be bigger. Kashmir that way is a peculiar place. "*Bibi Mare halwa Bibi bache halwa*" has been taken over by "*Bibi mare mutton Bibi bache mutton*". In the cases of joy or sorrow mutton makes special entry and is served even if one has to borrow money for the arrangements. But Ama Ganaie was a moneyed person having lucrative business of different kinds so big arrangement was no problem. A large number of people attended. David was one of them.

Tea and feast followed.

In the evening when relatives and neighbours left, Ruby sat in her room holding a photograph of Shazi in her lap.

"I am responsible for your death, sis. Had I not indulged in the love affair you would be safe . . . . But had these killers known the factual story they would be happy. Rajat had promised me that he will convert to Islam. It would have made them proud to celebrate the event and praise me . . . . but gun listens to none . . . . sis . . . . sis . . . ." she kept on weeping bitterly.

Although after 4th day all looked normal for others but Ama's family was inconsolable.

Was it a beginning of end for Ama Ganaie?

Was it a warning shot for Ruby which missed her narrowly?

Was it a conspiracy by the detractors of Ama?

Was somehow David involved?

Was it another secret deal fixed by Major Salvan?

Was Farooq too ashamed to listen to the stories about his sister Ruby and the captain?

Was someone against the affair between Nazir and the army girl?

Was the renegade commander taking his revenge of humiliation?

Was it a ploy by Zulqarnain, the HW militant?

Nobody had the answers.

*　　*　　*

Nobody had the answers!

The scene in the room was strange. The captain dressed in a dark blue track suit sat in his chair. Got up and brought a bottle of wine and a glass tumbler. Some soda also got space. He poured the glass tumbler full. Using the light emanating from the removable table lamp, he ran his pen on the sheet of paper. The bent up bulb holder at the top end of the table lamp concentrated the light on the paper and released very little out of the window. This was done to camouflage so that no one outside suspected him being awake late in the night. After finishing the sheet of paper he read it again and nodded his head right to left. Tore the sheet and threw the mutilated paper into the dust bin. He again sat to write. For some time he repeated the exercise, in between pressing his temple with the back of ball pen, as if struggling for right words. This page was finished and he again read it. Not satisfied with his writing he tore the page into pieces and used the dust bin. Then he again sat, lifted his unfinished wine peg and sipped the rest. Then came the turn of the pen and paper. Scrambling his pen on the page he reached its end. Played with his teeth with the pen and dropped it on the table. Filled another glass and sipped few drops with his eyes fixed on the page. Rubbed his eyes to ward off any signs of sleep and tore this page also. The exercise of writing and sipping and tearing the written pages continued till he started dozing off. A large part of night passed by. He was now in the state of uncomfortable sleep with his forehead tucked on the table top. The bottle was now empty. Glass tumbler used as peg lay on its side with the mouth pointed towards the window. It looked as empty as his life. Down on the floor stood the filled up dust bin near the table leg. The 12 inches high dust bin was overflowing with paper cuttings, some rolled, some torn into pieces and few dropped down out of the basket. Only one sheet was spread on the table over which the captain rested his head during the night. The cot arranged in one corner of the room had a printed sheet spread over it. The sheet had not been disturbed during the whole night.

Chirping birds awoke the sleepy captain. He pouted as he stared on the basket containing pell mell pages

*   *   *

Nobody had answers as to what could be the end result of two love stories running side by side. Nazir and Arti on one side, Ruby and Captain Rajat on the other side. The difference was that Nazir and Arti had been able to conceal their side of the story very efficiently. But Ruby and the captain could not keep their story under cover which finally devoured a young life. Nazir and Ruby were in mourning. Arti and the captain wanted to share the grief with their love birds.

For Nazir and Arti, it was not as big problem to meet as it was for Ruby and the captain. New development which snatched Shazi had made the things more difficult rather impossible. The news had already spread and the well wishers of Ama Ganaie kept watch over the movements of Ruby and she was emotionally and psychologically disturbed by the death of her beloved sister. In such circumstances she was not in a position to take romantic sojourn. The captain used all methods to convey to Ruby and request for a meeting but did not succeed. Ruby had almost stopped coming out of her home. Even Arti did not invite her to the camp for a routine breakfast and gossip.

The captain found all his exit routes blocked. As few more days passed, his condition turned pathetic. He in any case wanted to meet Ruby. Even just one sight would make him comparatively comfortable. One night he did not sleep well. He rolled his pen over paper and kept writing to Ruby. Though he used lot of paper but kept destroying it after jotting down few lines. Final result out of his night long activity came out in just two lines.

"Those who are responsible for your pathetic condition won't go scot free. This is my commitment to my love."

On the other hand Arti did not think it proper to invite Nazir for any outdoor meeting. She took advantage of her proximity to Ruby and directly went to their home to express her sympathies.

"Have you got some clues about who did it?" Arti asked while sitting between Ruby and Nazir in the drawing room sofa.

"No . . . . nothing," Nazir replied.

"Will you allow us to probe on our lines? Then army will take its own action,"

"In fact we don't want to escalate the situation,"

"What does that mean? Was Shazi not a human being?"

"She was our beloved sister and shall remain in our hearts. But there are many things that have to be kept in mind," Nazir replied and Ruby nodded her head.

"I can't force you to accept. But please think over,"

"No . . . . please . . . . no,"

After remaining with them for some time, Arti asked for permission to leave. She hugged both the sobbing siblings. She herself felt in the company of dear ones.

Nazir conveyed her the meeting date through a whisper.

Rivalry

War was on and took violent turns as the time passed. There were many players in the field. Army fought militants. Police fought the over ground workers and the Umbrella politicians. Skirmishes between various militant ranks raised head occasionally. Renegades had formed their own fiefdom. The participation of non resident militants, commonly called as Mehman Mujahidin (guest militants), gave new dimension to the armed struggle. Newer arsenal found way into the fighting. Militants holed up in various buildings encircled by army refused to surrender and when their weapons exhausted, army blasted the houses killing and destroying all. Militants employed new and fierce strategy of suicide bombings which culminated in deadly attacks. The suicide bomber driving explosive laden vehicle would detonate the material near his target killing himself and the people around. Army installations and political offices became prime targets.

Army and security agencies on their part tried best to counter such attacks. They tried whatever means at their hand, both moral and immoral. Among the immoral steps, they encouraged factional feuds both among militants and their supporting organizations. David, the politician was in favour of it. During his meeting with Major Salvan, he referred to some religious leaders whose support base was used by the militants as helpers and whose property was used as hide outs. The two devised a strategy so that they are annihilated and the factional feud rises making them diametrically opposite to each other. Renegade group leader was there to execute the plan. The people from different backgrounds, different castes, and different outlook had a common meeting ground.

David wanted his political opponents get weaker.

Salvan liked to see himself overpowering armed militants.

Renegade ring leader wanted his fiefdom to expand.

Maulana was in his seventies and sported a long flowing white beard. He usually wore a turban or *karakul* cap and had cultivated lots of respect being a good orator and Islamic scholar. He delivered Friday sermon in the grand mosque where more than ten thousand people prayed on Fridays. The mosques were frequently used as a political platform particularly by Umbrella politicians and religious leaders. As usual the Maulana lamented the government and the mainstream politicians for their role and got a rousing response from the crowd present. This was a routine practice for him that on all Friday congregations he rebuked those whom he thought were anti Tahreek (movement). This had irritated David and the people of his ilk.

Not many days passed when Maulana had returned home after evening prayers. He was accompanied by half a dozen people up to the house. This was a two pronged strategy. One, these people held him in high esteem and second they provided a security cover to him till he reached his home. In about half an hour couple of vehicles stopped at the gate and gun wielding masked men got down, jumped over the walls and forcibly entered the house of Maulana. Before inmates reacted and shouted at the roof tops, Maulana had been bundled in the waiting vehicle and driven away. The operation ended in such a short time that it took people in the locality some time to assemble, enquire and then raise slogans against the abduction. The police and administration authorities reached the spot on hearing about the abduction but could do nothing at the late hours. The night passed off. The day also passed off. Another night and no clues came. People continued with their protests but to no avail. However, next day the bullet ridden body of the Maulana was found in the orchard. While many bodies had been found in fields and orchards in the past also but one interesting thing about this recovery was that it was found in the orchard belonging to militant leader Zulqarnain. The idea behind this being that intra party feud needs to be got escalated.

The death of Maulana shook the valley and his ardent supporters came on the streets protesting the killing. The processions turned violent at places burning government property and clashes with the police continued for many days. However, the political leadership spearheading Azadi movement tried to control the passions which could have led to intra party clashes. They roamed from village to village and locality to locality to reinforce the idea of unity among various groups and were successful in dousing the flames of suspected sectarian clashes.

David was the first among those denouncing the dastardly act. His press release read that 'we need to fight political battles on political turf and not with gun and bullet.'

The idea was to target opponents as well as show himself as a democrat.

With the death of Maulana renegade leader became darling of the major. He had executed the plan to precision. Major Salvan now started depending upon him more for information as well as dubious deals. But he did not ignore Ama Ganaie completely. He kept Ama in good humor while continuing his equation with David also.

David, the political face.

Ama Ganaie, the public face.

Renegade, the terror face.

Though people suspected someone behind the scene but were not able to pin point the person or group responsible for the heinous crime.

"Why should Zulqaranain drop the dead body of Maulana in his own orchard?" a pertinent question was being asked.

*　　*　　*

Although November evenings remained colder, yet days were cosy when sun shone. The big leaves of Chinar with brown colour were falling and women collected and burnt these leaves to make precious charcoal for ensuing winter months.

"Why are they burning these brown leaves? They look so elegant," Arti enquired.

"These are closer to the maple leaves and you know why these are called Chinar trees?"

"How could I know? We don't have chinars in our place. So big, so huge, so enormous . . . . vow!"

"A Mughal king Jehangir came to Kashmir in autumn. He saw a pile of brown leaves. He was fascinated at the sight and felt some sort of fire was there,"

"A pile of these leaves looks like a fire,"

"Yes. He asked his people Chi-Naar. In Persian it means what sort of fire. Then people named the tree as Chinar."

"Well Chinars are majestic trees. But look at that tree. It resembles today's Kashmir. Upper half is dried up. Lower portion has extended branches and leaves. On one side, in the trunk, cave like intrusion has taken place. As if heart has been snatched out." Arti, deeply entrenched in thought process, spoke her heart out.

"You are right but we have to live with it."

At a distance from the Chinar tree, Arti and Nazir occupied a seat and they enjoyed the Dal Lake. They sat in such a position so that sunlight is received on the back and not front. Autumn sun is to be enjoyed on back lest face gets dry. Lake spread to far off distances with hills in the backdrop. On the back of these hills stood tall mountain range with recently fallen snow layer visible from distance.

Nazir had recovered from the shock of his sister's death and was now comparatively comfortable. Arti wanted him to resume the normal work so she thought to have a daylong sojourn which could help him further rejuvenate his inert feelings and energy. Although she had heard the story yet she intentionally did not touch the subject of Ruby and the captain. Neither Ruby nor the captain had talked about their love story or sought any help in the matter. Whatever came into the knowledge of Arti was heresy. May be she did not believe the story fully and if she believed she did not like to embarrass Nazir. She, therefore, touched the subjects of environment and Nazir's examination.

Being around Dal Lake and not taking a boat ride, that too by love birds, is like growing long hair but not combing and braiding it. So Nazir and Arti engaged a boat and went deep into the lake. Due to turmoil very few *shikaras* rowed in the lake. Arti kept her head on the chest of Nazir who played with her hair. And Arti herself tried to chew Nazir's fingers and palm. The duo deeply engrossed themselves in romance.

After spending quality time within Dal lake area they returned and boarded Nazir's car to take them back to their destination.

Using their usual camouflage the duo parted ways at some distance from the camp wherefrom Arti took a private bus so that nobody recognized her.

*   *   *

With the introduction and participation of foreign militants the armed struggle took new turn. One among the group became very famous and popular in certain circles. Particularly the supporters of the party, he worked with, boasted of his presence. Gul Mastan, the battle hardened mulish Afghan, was a man to watch. The six feet two inch tall, well built with long hair falling over his shoulders and thick beard looked dangerous by face. He would usually be seen walking with a bigger gun on his shoulder or else brandishing two Kalashnikovs hanging down his right and left shoulder. Usually dressed in Pathan suit and ankle high shoes he wore a wide belt over his long shirt. The members working with him remained subdued in his presence. He had couple of foreign and half a dozen local militants in his company. Additional reinforcement would be at his beck and call. Though he moved freely even during day time but usually he stayed in the upper reaches where from he could keep a close watch on the troop movement. Stories about his ability to strike at will had been woven, partly true partly concocted. It was said that even army feared him and whenever he was on a roam, the army men would make way and allow him to leave the area without coming into direct confrontation with him. The youngsters were always on lookout to have a glimpse of him as if he was a popular actor or a sportsperson.

He enamoured the striplings.

And cultivated hero worship among the youth.

Gul Mastan's foreign colleagues were ardent believers in religion and prayed with religious zeal and enthusiasm and maintained punctuality. They even recited Qur'an from small sized holy book copies always kept in their pockets. Gul prayed as a hobby and occasionally recited holy verses that too in the morning only. Nobody dared to ask him the reason behind this though being part of the 'holy war'. But at times, he intentionally touched the subject and informed that while in Jihad one can ignore certain things. It was his theory about religion. His colleagues, polite and religious, did not confront him over the issue.

Gul Mastan's huge body frame deserved similar food and he had a special liking for large quantities of mutton, veal and beef. He, in fact, had developed a penchant for barbeque around a camp fire during his days in Afghanistan war against Soviet forces. Gul's group used to roam about in the rugged terrain and mountainous regions concealing themselves behind huge rocks and in the caves as a safeguard from bombings by Soviet military planes. They would light a camp fire with around a dozen people seated nearby. A sheep, calf or a goat would be hung over a tripod and then every one of them sliced the meat with the sharp and long knives which they kept handy for meeting any eventuality where big guns may not prove helpful.

Roaming for some days in the hills of Kashmir, Gul felt a similar need and he asked his accomplices to arrange similar barbeque. His local boys helped and purchased a goat from a shepherd who tended his flock in the area. The goat bleated till the shepherd himself sliced its throat. Behind a rock a tripod was fixed and camp fire lighted. While they enjoyed the sheet thin slices, smoke from the camp fire rose. The civilians did not pay any attention towards the smoke billowing thinking that usually shepherds and the charcoal makers light such fires but it alerted the army. They immediately gathered information partly through their long range devices and some through their local sources.

One evening, he felt the presence of army had increased above the area he usually stayed in. On further investigation he was told that army was zeroing in on him and his party. A very good strategist of military actions, he took refuge in the nearby shrine. The shrine of the revered saint was in high esteem for local population who thronged there in large numbers particularly on Thursday nights and some auspicious days. The passage to the shrine included a two hundred step flight of chisel dressed stone which people young and old, men and women traversed to reach uphill to the exact location. The shrine had a green colour CGI sheet roofing with four minarets at corners. Green flags hoisted above the minarets fluttered with breeze blowing across. Downhill, near the bus stop local bakers and grocery shops had come up selling various eatables and other things for which shopping would be done by the visitors and the devotees.

Gul Mastan had enquired about the shrine and the visitors. But he was not amused with the reverence attached to it. Though occasionally he expressed his displeasure over the issue but did not take the matter too far. Now when he feared a possible attack from the army he took refuge in the same shrine.

'Army would not enter the shrine complex as they feared a backlash.' Gul was told by some local advisor. The advisor even referred to one such incident in Punjab in past when a Sikh shrine was similarly attacked and the repercussions were incredible and devastating.

During the stay of Gul Mastan in the shrine, Farooq led another militant group and reached there obviously to pay obeisance. Farooq was true believer in the spirituality of saints and he often visited various shrines. His parents were attached to the shrines more. They had told their kids the story about their attachment to the shrines.

"We did not have any child even after three years of marriage. I did not conceive so long. We tried all possible help from doctors both allopathic and homeopathic. Lots of tests were conducted and lots of medicine was consumed by us but without any result. Finally Haji Sahib (Farooq's grandfather) advised us to visit Baba Rishi and mop and paint the hearth there. I did the same and Nazir, your elder brother was born. Subsequently, Allah bestowed us with three more children."

Farooq and his small group went around the inner portion of the shrine. In one area Gul Mastan sprawled, seated leisurely with legs spread as if enjoying a picnic. Since he did not have any spiritual attachment to the shrine he had not taken his long shoes off and sat with shoe soles in the direction of most revered position in the shrine. Farooq became furious over Gul's attitude and reprimanded him. In response Gul glowered at Farooq.

"Shee . . . . be calm . . . . he is Gul Mastan," the local accomplice of Gul tried to cool tempers and informed Farooq likewise. His aim was to frighten Farooq by the name of Gul Mastan.

"So what?" asked angry Farooq.

Both Gul and Farooq cocked their guns and aimed at each other. Before situation took ugly turn Gul's foreign accomplice intervened and separated Gul and Farooq from eyeball to eyeball position. Both groups encircled their respective leaders and had hard time in cooling off the torrid situation. Farooq and his group left the scene but both kept shouting, yelling and challenging each other. Gul was asked to refrain from such acts which won't be tolerated by the locals.

*   *   *

The night passed off peacefully. But in the morning Gul Mastan and his local advisor were proved wrong. Army had closed in and the whole area around the shrine had been cordoned off during night hours. Three tier security grid had been employed with soldiers taking positions at vantage points. Even helicopter flew very low to ascertain and finalize the exact strategy. The worshippers from outside were not allowed in and those inside were not allowed out. Many vehicles and couple of ambulances remained stationed in the area surrounding the shrine.

Pretending insouciance towards the issue and careless about the development, Gul Mastan and his accomplices had a heavy breakfast and they rechecked their arsenal which was very less as compared to what the army had brought in. Not much time passed when actual fight started. Gul fired at couple of soldiers, whom he saw through one of the windows, coming uphill. The fire was returned and continued till evening. In between the army asked the group to surrender through mega phones but Gul's response was return fire. Inmates, among them mostly worshippers from far and wide, prayed for their lives and ducked every time behind walls when gun shots ricocheted. Women in particular sobbed. Pusillanimous men bowed before the grave of the saint. Children screamed and squalled with every gun shot. In the ensuing battle shrine walls were damaged. Since Gul's group was at advantageous position they did not suffer any loss of life. Some soldiers got injured from bullets coming from top.

The battle continued for full day. Then Gul's group exhausted their arms as well as their energy. By midnight they continued the fight. Accidentally, fire broke out in one corner of the shrine. Then there was mayhem. The inmates rushed to save their lives. Women clenched their babies with their breasts and ran. Even weak hearted attempted acrobats to save their lives.

They say mother is the dearest of all.

But one's life is dearer!

Till fire brigade pressed its men and machines into action the entire shrine was engulfed in fire. The tall minarets tattered. The wooden portion of the structure was mostly consumed.

BBC and Voice of America, in their morning bulletins, broadcast the news about the total destruction of the shrine. They also, quoting their sources, informed that Gul Mastan and his accomplices had escaped from the place as no corpses were found inside the shrine complex.

Army and the government issued press releases blaming Gul having set the shrine on fire to make escape. Curfew was clamped in the valley to restrict movement lest people come out on the streets to protest the desecration of the shrine.

But the people did come out!

*   *   *

Hundreds and thousands of people came out on the streets in the cities, towns and villages. The Umbrella elements received a shot in the arm with this incident. The people having reverence towards the shrine were ready to lay down their lives. The leadership did not lose any moment to take advantage of the situation and incite the public on one side and reinvigorate the Azadi sentiment that at certain times seemed dying down. The leaders attired in costly dresses which included *karakul* caps, designer suits and other clothes visited the places and led the protests. The government was forced to make arrests, and at certain places use batons and firing. The burning issue of Azadi got momentum with coverage on all major international TV channels and the print media. Sentiments ran high. Cry for Azadi became louder. Drying up lamp of demand for freedom received additional oil to burn with more ferocity. At times police used ruthless tactics to quell the street fighters who used stones and petrol bombs. The violent protests continued for many days till it died down due to repressive measures by the government and the fatigue experienced by the protestors.

*   *   *

Tragedies strike

December to February is the acute winter season in the valley. There is every apprehension of snow fall, which, if heavier becomes very troublesome for the common people. Roads get blocked and essential supply becomes scarce as well as dearer. The main 300km long highway connecting valley with rest of India gets blocked and remains cut off for days together. The blockade results in stoppage of supplies to the valley particularly cooking gas. The power supply is the second casualty which is very deficient in normal times. The top most government machinery shifts to plains and leaves the Valeyites high and dry. Over the years affluent class in the valley had raised small structures in Jammu area to spend winter months there so to save themselves from the harsh cold, frost bites and the difficult days.

Ama Ganaie was one such person who constructed a three bed room set in Jammu. 3-BHK is regarded smaller as compared to what Kashmiris build. Kashmiris have love for big houses which they construct using all possible means of income. In fact Kashmiris are said to spend their life in accomplishing two tasks on priority; build a big house and marry off their children. Ama would not leave valley during winter months because he usually used to say 'valley is alive with snowfall' and enjoyed snowfall on the window of his

Hamam the local arrangement for heating. Because of his Hamam he would never feel the onslaught of winter how much harsher it would be as heating and warm water was always available to him. He used to visit Jammu for few days and returned back in hurry. He had lot of business to look after. But now the situation had changed.

His business had expanded. PWD contracts were there. Band saw machine doing timber work was there. Orchards and grain fields and structures housing government and private establishments were to be looked after. Despite all this his heart was not as pleased this year as in previous times. Not more than one month had passed when his daughter was gunned down. The news about his other daughter being in affair with an army officer had made his head bow. Although the captain had informed Ruby that he was ready to embrace Islam but none knew about it and, as such, tongues wagged continuously. Affair with a Hindu army officer was considered a blot in the Muslim dominated valley. David had eaten up part of his power which he wielded through Major Salvan. The renegade group leader was another stumbling block in his prosperity. Killing of Rahim Dar, the HW commander's father, by supporters of David made him uneasy. Some people had talked about Ama Ganaie being in hand and glove with David as he talked in his favour when elections were on. Though he tried to clarify his position but all was not well. He also received news about his son Farooq having altercation with the dreaded foreign militant Gul Mastan. Somehow he felt certain things were going against him.

With this he decided to shift to Jammu and spend winter months there. The mission was many folds though he talked about one only. He declared he and his wife are not feeling well and as such winter chill may give more problems.

But the fact is that he wanted to keep Ruby farther from the captain's reach. The issue had become major source of embarrassment for him.

One day early in the morning his complete family consisting of his wife, son, daughter and one personal servant left for Jammu in his own car. His own driver drove the vehicle while Nazir drove his own Maruti car. Since he had lot of business so many workers worked with him and as such, it was not much bigger problem to keep watch and ward. Secondly, presence of army camp nearby and his closeness with Salvan was enough safeguard. By evening they traversed the highway to reach Jammu. In Jammu, he heaved a sigh of relief. Nazir had taken the final examination and now waited for results. Ruby's college was closed for winter months so no worries.

Ama Ganaie wanted an escape route from his worries. Jammu provided the same or at least he believed so.

With the advent of winter the forest life had become very difficult. In the upper reaches there was snow accumulation. In the lower reaches though snow was scarce but chill had increased. The nomadic population had left for warmer areas leaving their mud and log huts behind in which they spent summers with their cattle grazing in the area. During armed conflict between militants and the forces personnel life of these nomads had become hell like. The armed militants found safer heavens during summers in these forest areas and they made the nomad population their shields. They forced them to allow the comfort of their dirty and untidy living spaces and stinking beddings.

These nomads lived in small cave type sheds constructed out of mud and logs. They distributed their space in a kitchen and living space. Outside their living space they enclosed some portion with loosely arranged stones. During nights big and ferocious dogs were released by them for watch and ward of their property. Their belongings always smelt animal 'aroma'.

But fighting and saving themselves from the armed forces was a priority for the militants. Though nomads had to bear the brunt of military atrocities for harbouring the militants but they were forced by the militants also to listen to their instructions.

Double edged sword!

However, with temperature falling, the militants found it difficult to continue their stay in these forest areas and shifted towards plains. In the plains the hide-outs would be the houses of common people in the congested localities. On one side the houses became more comfortable for them to hide but on the other hand army got better and pointed information about their stay. So the raids by army increased in the winter months when space squeezed for the militants to operate in the congested localities.

It was a chilling December morning when army had laid siege to a cluster of houses on the outskirts of the village. Before people prepared for morning prayers the inmates were asked to come out of the houses. The people adhered to the instructions. Preliminary investigations revealed that militants were hiding in two houses in that particular locality. The army instructed the armed inmates to surrender but in response fire was returned from the houses. In the ensuing battle, the houses received bullets which damaged the wooden door and windows but militants continued to remain holed up and firing from their automatic weapons. The encounter prolonged till army decided to blast the houses. Major Salvan was joined by his commanding officer for a final decision. Then a unique case of army brutality was thought over. One of the middle aged persons, the owner of the house, was asked to contact the armed inmates to surrender. He was asked to place a bag near the door of the house. While he thought he may be able to convince the inmates to surrender he walked a bit freely up to the house as there was a lull from both sides. But as soon as he stepped into the house, through the main door, there was a bang.

Thadakh

Human bomb developed by the disciplined forces!

A huge blast ripped off his body and the house also. The timber pieces flew off. The dust rose like a storm. The CGI sheets were in air like flying kites. The army was now sure that all inside had been killed. They ordered the people in their custody to search inside for bodies and arms. About twenty young and middle aged persons were now engaged in clearing debris. After working for more than one hour four dead bodies and one severely injured person were recovered from the debris. Arms and ammunition with some live cartridges were also recovered.

The overall operation turned out to be a gold mine for Major Salvan. Four militants killed, one injured arrested and around half a dozen guns and some ammunition recovered. When the identity of the injured was revealed Salvan's joy knew no bounds. He could be seen cavorting while disseminating the news of prize catch to his seniors over the walkie talkie.

"Commander Zulqarnain!" he almost shouted.

He asked his juniors to do further job at spot and himself rushed to his camp with the prize catch Zulqarnain. Zulqarnain was given necessary medical help so that he regained consciousness. Salvan was least interested in his recovery but he wanted him to reveal important secrets of his plans. In the camp, Salvan entrusted the job of interrogating Zulqarnain to Arti and the MI captain.

"See we will provide you the most modern life saving treatment . . . . but you need to co-operate," captain tried to be sympathetic towards Zulqarnain.

"Co-operate . . . . shit . . . . who are you to give me life saving drugs?" Zulqarnaian responded with anger." I will prefer death than accepting your medical help . . . . I will die a martyr. I don't acknowledge any help from infidels,"

"Don't try to be foolish. First save your life. Life is a gift from God and does not come twice," Arti intervened.

"Madam, you are a lady and my religion does not allow me to ridicule or attack women. Even in this condition I can fight any army . . . . fight till death,"

"Ok, keep fighting . . . . I don't care . . . . but tell me whatever you know about the plans of your party . . . ." captain continued.

Blood oozing out of his wounds all over his body he revealed one truth which shook the interrogators. The simple mention of this episode sent shivers down the spine of the captain and Arti. He spoke and narrated the story about Farooq, Ama Ganaie's militant son.

"Ama Ganaie was not a wealthy man always. He rose from rags to riches when we people from works department helped him. And instead of remaining obliged, he boasted of his acquaintance and power. When militancy erupted, I decided to teach him a lesson but I was constrained when he sent his own son for training. Somehow, I knew he had no conviction towards the Tehreek and wanted to cash in on the sentiment. He did the same. He made friendly overtures to army officers and used his position to get people arrested and released against money. People had to sell land . . . . even cows and buffalos to get their wards released,"

"But your father was his friend,' Arti asked.

"No . . . . he feared him and wanted to keep him in good humour so that my family is not targeted,"

"Why should he target you?" captain asked.

"He is so cheap and venal, he can do anything. He used his daughter Ruby to remain friendly with army officers,"

"You bastard . . . ." the enraged captain slapped him twice "*Ruby ka naam mat le saale (Don't involve Ruby's name),*"

Arti tried to pacify the captain.

"Proceed . . . . go on," Arti said.

"His son Farooq tried to attack our guest commander Gul Mastan. When he failed, he informed army about his presence and army attacked the shrine. Gul Mastan had a miraculous escape. Then we decided to eliminate him. In three weeks time we encircled a house and abducted four militants including Farooq,"

"Then . . . . where is Farooq?" a visibly perturbed Arti asked.

"Killed all four including Farooq . . . . and dumped their bodies somewhere near the forest. We will finish off these traitors,"

Visibly depressed Arti and the captain dropped their heads in grief. They did not express to each other but they felt for Nazir and Ruby. Grief struck both of them. They remained dumbfound for some time. Plangent duo turned stupor. Then the captain recovered from the shock and tried to awaken Zulqarnain whose eyes were closed.

No movement
No response
No conviction
No commitment
No Tanzeem
No revenge
Zulqarnain was already dead.

*   *   *

Zulqarnain had become a terror in the area and his presence sent shockwaves in the ranks of armed forces. Repeated attacks, IED blasts, ambushes and the like were his frequent strikes which sent his opponents into tizzy. And when his dead body was in the custody of Major Salvan it was time for him to rejoice. The forces released press note declaring that the organization had received a setback due to his killing and that was very much true. Major Salvan expected some gallantry award for his unit over this success.

Success always has two effects rather side effects. One the successful person tries more to achieve and second he becomes arrogant. Salvan inebriated by recent success cultivated a feeling that higher ups, satisfied with his precision strikes, shall be forced to ignore his short comings or little bit of limitations.

Swagger!

He after few days arranged his men to carry out another ambush in the area on the pretext that he had specific information about militant movement. The major arranged few Kashmiri robes called Pherans and made a couple of passenger buses to remain in the camp. In the dead of night Major Salvan led the ambush himself driving his gypsy himself. On his left he made Lt. Arti to board the same vehicle. Other soldiers wearing Pherans which had been forcibly borrowed from the local people boarded the long passenger buses. The whole exercise was done to use it as a camouflage so that local population did not get the whiff of doubt. The buses travelled on the road and, whosoever saw, presumed that normal passenger buses moved on. After alighting from their vehicles, about fifty soldiers hid themselves behind bushes or the earth mounds spread in the area.

Complete silence followed. Major Salvan in fact had some satanic idea up his sleeve. Seated alone with Arti he tried to flirt with her. Accidental touch on Arti's thigh did not disturb her. But intentional touch followed, which sent a jerk through her spine. She did not expect this from her officer.

"Sir, I don't expect this from you. Please restrain yourself." Arti tried to maintain calm.

"Why should you feel irritated. All this is a biological need. Everything will remain discreet," Salvan again tried his hands.

"I again and for the last time warn you to refrain," she glowered and anger spilled from Arti's expression.

"What warn . . . . I am your officer . . . . if I want I can ruin your confidential report. I know you are intimately poised with a militant's brother," Salvan pushed her breast while threatening her on career front.

Phatak

A slap hit Salvan's right face when Arti used her left hand. In a jiffy, Arti collected her weapon and alighted from the vehicle. Fearing her agitated response, Salvan almost ran after Arti.

"Sorry . . . . sorry please," Salvan tried to pacify Arti.

Arti stopped few meters behind the outer cordon of the ambush.

"What is your opinion Arti. I think militants have got suspicious and they may have abandoned their plans,"

Major tried to divert her attention so that his soldiers did not get suspicious.

"Possible Sir. Forty minutes passed since we laid the ambush," Arti replied in a way to substantiate her officer's apprehensions.

"We better call off,"

"Your take, Sir."

In a few minutes walkie talkie buzzed and the retreat started.

*   *   *

In a few days sanction of Arti's leave was received. She had two facts to rejoice. One, she was going home after a long time and second, she wanted to meet Nazir in Jammu. She remained busy for a couple of days in shopping. She purchased from local as well as Srinagar markets certain items which would not be available in her home town. And she sought certain items for which Kashmir is known for. Saffron, dry fruits, Kashmir arts, shawls and Kashmiri lady's Pheran which had of late become a craze in rest of the country.

She travelled on the highway to reach Jammu. Since she had contacted Nazir and Ruby in advance they received her at the bus stop and took her home in their own car. She was received by Ama Ganaie and his wife with extreme warmth. Ama Ganaie's wife always called her daughter despite the fact being illiterate she was not able to convey what she desired. But Ruby would be there to translate it for Arti. Arti had learnt few Kashmiri words like *'warie' 'khush paeth'* (How are you? And Very happy) which she used whenever she talked to some Kashmiri. Ama and his family were normal in their moods through which Arti comprehended that they had no information about Farooq's abduction and subsequent killing by Zulqarnain's group. She made up her mind that she would not make them aware about the news that Zulqarnain broke to her during interrogation.

Arti remained in their house for two days. Ama's family was highly hospitable towards her.

"I know Kashmiris are hospitable towards guests but you seem to cross every limit now," Arti acknowledged while taking delicious mutton dishes.

Rista
Kabab
Yakhni
Tabakh Maaz
Gushtaba

"You are not our guest, you are my daughter," Ama's wife responded.

Arti presented a shawl to Ruby and embroidered Pheran to her mother as a gift she had bought while leaving Kashmir.

During her stay in the house Arti and Nazir did find time and chances to come closer on one pretext or other. They showered love and even found time to kiss each other.

Nazir's parents and Ruby had no reason to suspect any development between the duo. They felt that Arti in fact was friendly with Ruby only. The duo did not give any chance to suspect. Secondly, Kashmiris are very obsessive about their own race. They marry outside Kashmir in rare cases. And if someone marries outside Kashmir, people suspect that no parents were in a mood to give their daughter to such person.

Two days passed off with all enjoying each other's company. Arti was dropped at the bus stand in his car by Nazir. Ruby accompanied the duo. Arti hugged both siblings before boarding her bus. Then Arti left for her home to return after thirty days leave period.

*   *   *

In a couple of days Ama Ganaie's nephew Rashid was called by major Salvan to his office. The captain working with MI was also present in the meeting. The major wanted to convey him the news about Farooq's abduction by Zulqarnain's group but he wanted to be sure if any more information would be available. He asked him few questions about Farooq. His whereabouts and any other information, whatsoever, were possible.

"You have to believe me Sir, for many days he has not visited his home or village. I heard he had some altercation with foreign militant Gul Mastan and since then maybe he is hiding somewhere to escape the wrath of his group. The other group is powerful and dreaded also. They don't allow any body to rise. So I believe he must be hiding somewhere," Rashid tried to explain the whole position.

"You better don't tell anybody yet before you confirm yourself from your own sources. Our information is that Farooq had been abducted by Holly Warriors (HW) militants," the captain intervened.

Rashid's anxiety grew. The major got up and went into another room.

"Don't feel perturbed until you confirm yourself,"

"Sir, please tell me if you have any more information,"

"Let me be frank with you. I had promised Ruby that I won't let the person go scot free who tried to kill her and killed Shazi due to mistaken identity,"

Rashid stared at him with hollow eyes.

"I later came to know that Farooq was against my friendship with Ruby and he executed the plan. So I wanted to avenge the death myself,"

The major returned to his seat.

"But to my ill luck that Zulqarnain *behenchod* intervened," the captain related the whole story.

"This is our information. Now you confirm further. But don't tell Ama Ganaie anything unless you have exact information," Salvan advised. "Ama Ganaie and his family are disturbed due to their daughter's death so better be cautious."

Rashid got up from his chair and with elongated face and battered legs moved towards the door. He was left in lurch by the information.

The words of the captain reverberated in his mind "Let me be frank with you. I had promised Ruby that I won't let the person go scot free who tried to kill her and killed Shazi due to mistaken identity," For some time Rashid thought it may be a plan by the army to trace Farooq. And they may be seeking my overt or covert help in finding his hideouts. But he could not ignore the threat from other group as news of inter party clashes had surfaced time and again in which cadres of both parties succumbed.

Rashid, after leaving the army camp straightway drove to his home. He immediately started searching for a photograph of Farooq. Ama Ganaie had in fact removed all photographs of Farooq as soon as he left for arms training. He did not want to keep any thing that could help the army in identification of Farooq. But Rashid had concealed all photographs in which Farooq appeared. After searching his steel trunks, kept in the attic, he recovered couple of latest photographs. In one such photo Farooq held a gun near a training camp in PAK. He kept it as a souvenir and handed over to Rashid as a memoir.

For next two days Rashid went from place to place about which he had information Farooq occasionally stayed on. After hectic wandering for two days, Rashid reached the final destination. A middle aged man in a remote village identified the person in photograph.

"Yes, I myself buried this Mujahid and two others in the dead of night," he informed.

"Who brought them here?" Rashid asked.

"The fact is that some Mujahidin woke me up and three more villagers. Then, at gun point took us outside the village. Three corpses with gun shots were lying on ground,"

"You did not ask who killed them."

"They informed themselves. They said army killed them in encounter so bury them in the night itself,"

"Had you heard of any encounter going on that night?"

"No, we never had an encounter in this village,"

"So you are sure you buried this boy?" Rashid pointed to the photograph in his hand.

"*Sola aane paka* (hundred percent sure)"

Rashid left the place with moist eyes. While driving his car he wept bitterly.

For Rashid the problem became two fold. One to bear the news of Farooq's death, that too, in such tragic circumstances and second, he was now to inform his uncle and his family about the tragic incident. He was thinking about as to how he will break the news to them.

He was deficient of words.

After reaching home he consulted some well wishers and finally decided to inform Nazir in the first instance.

"Nazir, hope everybody is fine in Jammu," Rashid talked to him on phone.

"Yes . . . . all is well,"

"Will you be able to return to valley for a few days?"

"Why . . . . Is everything all right?"

"Yes, but I have to discuss something important,"

"Don't you think it is too cold there? In fact my results are out and I have to submit application form to the recruiting board. I was thinking to submit through someone but no problem I will return,"

"Better come tomorrow,"

The phone dropped.

By next day after noon Nazir was back in the valley.

*   *   *

Arti spent few days with her family describing the adventure and gory battles with the militants. The younger family members enjoyed the stories about encounters and the risk of life involved. The photographs of Kashmir were awesome. Everybody appreciated the scenic beauty.

The rousing water streams like romantic passion of love birds.

The green hill tops as if braided silken hair of a virgin.

Snow clad mountain peaks like white turbaned headgear of revered saints.

Vast Dale Lake like open arms of a compassionate mother.

Small rowing *shikaras* on the still waters of the lake like cute babies sulking boobs.

Big dwelling boats called house boats ready to accommodate all.

During the sessions some talked of Kashmir politics and the reason behind the armed insurgency and rebellion. Some suggested that India should let the part go as the people want. Others resisted leaving even an inch of Kashmir as it is the paradise though lost. In next few days news was broken to Arti that there is a good proposal for her marriage.

"The boy is an air force pilot," her mother informed.

"Have a look," her elder sister suggested.

Arti could not come out of the cocoon that Nazir's love had woven around her. She replied nothing for few days. Then pressure started building up.

"The boy wants to meet you at an earliest. Before a small ceremony is arranged both of you need to meet, see and talk to each other," her mother again caught up with her.

"Or is there anybody else who wants to steal my younger sis?" elder sister tried to pull her leg and make things humorous.

"Yes!" came blunt reply from Arti.

Everybody in the room was stunned. Silence ruled for few minutes. Mother and sister tried to read each other's eyes.

"Who is that?" Arti's elder sister broke the silence.

"A Kashmiri boy," Arti replied with confidence.

"Some more details,"

"Name Nazir Ahmad . . . . just completed engineering . . . ."

"A Muslim boy . . . . what nonsense," mother became furious. "I heard all Kashmiris are militants. How come you marry an *atankwadi*?"

"That is the problem with Kashmir and Kashmiris. None tries to listen to their woes. All want to rule through gun . . . . just suppress them into submission . . . . ridiculous!" Arti expressed her part of anger.

Before mother could speak anything more Arti's elder sister signalled her to stop.

Silence ruled for few more minutes. Then Arti rose from the place. Mother and sister followed after some time.

Now Arti's sister got suspicious about photographs. When on arrival Arti showed the photographs, her sister felt some photos were concealed intentionally by Arti. But she did not give the issue much importance thinking that may be some horrific photos of militants killed must be there which Arti did not like to show. Her doubts grew and she at any cost wanted to have a look. Same evening when all went for a roam around the market, Arti's sister intentionally remained home making some excuse.

Skeletons in the romantic cupboard of Arti started tumbling. Stunning and awesome photographs of a Kashmiri boy in different locations were there. In some Arti and Nazir stood as love birds.

"Vow . . . . Arti is not to be blamed. Any girl can lose her heart to this hero . . . ." she murmured.

After dinner when the siblings came to the common bedroom, situation looked calm.

"Any photograph of the Kashmiri Muslim boy?" Arti's sister asked.

"I know you have seen those. You stayed back for that only. I checked on my arrival from the market. The sequence had been disturbed,"

"Yes, you are right,"

"So, you with me?"

"It is not so easy. Parents will never agree. You have to choose between your family and the boy . . . . and I know you are not immature,"

"Don't you think he is worth?"

"He is so smart . . . . but his name is Nazir . . . . no one will accept,"

"Religion . . . . oonh . . . . and if he becomes a Hindu or me a Muslim?" Arti's rebellion surfaced.

"Mom thinks that all Kashmiris are terrorists,"

"Not mom only, every Indian including armed forces think on those lines. But nobody concedes that they have been pushed to the wall; forced to take up guns by non performing politicians, deceits and intrigues. Bal Ganga Dhar Tilak said *Repression is repression, if it is legal it must be resisted legally. But if it is illegal it must be illegally met.*

"If you remain few more years posted there you may become their leader and take up gun on their behalf," sister said smilingly.

"Unfortunately nobody understands their psyche,"

"You better fight elections there . . . . You may even become the Chief Minister there." Arti's sister wanted to keep her in good humour so that she controls her anger.

"Hmmm,"

"Now sleep well. Let us see what is destined," her sister ended the topic and put the lights off.

*   *   *

For the breakfast all members met at the table. The table was around 10 ft in length and half a dozen chairs placed around it. All seats were occupied and head of the family Brig. (R) Ajay Ranawat, dressed in black track suit, was seated on the oval pointed end. Sun light entered the room through a high level ventilator. One of the doors of the dining room opened in the kitchen. Various dishes were placed in chinaware bowls. Mother dressed in printed cotton Kameez shalwar, seated on the left side of her husband, pushed plates and cutlery towards the members. Arti's elder sister, dressed in a loose gown, helped the members with passing the porcelain bowls on. Their brother a businessman who did not like joining army was seated opposite to his elder sister. Intentionally, Arti was given the seat between brother and father. While all seemed or pretended to be calm Arti's mother looked tense from her face. Tension prevailed over her nerves and exhibited through wrinkles on forehead getting deeper. She had crinkling eyes. While Arti enjoyed an omelette with her fork and slicer, her mother touched the subject of Arti's marriage again. Raising the issue from nowhere all got stunned and Arti's part slice got almost stuck between her teeth in the corner of her mouth. Ajay, his elder daughter and son continued chewing whatever was in their mouth. Mother had already stopped taking anything. This infuriated Arti, who pushed her plate, got up and dropped her leftover from her mouth into the dust bin and left the room. As she went upstairs, her sister objected to her mother for raking up the issue.

"What use Mom. You denied her the breakfast. Can't you wait for some time?"

"Let her not eat anything. But I won't allow what she demands," Mother expressed her anger in full quantum.

All members now lost interest in the breakfast. Arti's sister picked the plate left there by her sister and rushed towards the room of Arti.

*   *   *

Days passed by. Morning sun shone like glittering gold. Arti followed her daily routine of morning drill and exercise while her sister continued sleeping late. At breakfast all family members met and the topic continued to be touched by one or the other person. The discussion about the topic became hot sometimes and was cooled down by one or the other member of the family. Though father and sister tried to control passions with their soft approach but mother was up in arms against the proposal put by Arti. She was in no mood to concede. Till Arti's leave period expired and she decided to return to valley, the topic remained burning with each side giving one or the other explanation. Even at the bus stop mother and sister tried to convince Arti against the proposal.

Arti left for the valley.

Mother and sister waved to her.

Arti was happy for a chance to meet Nazir.

Her mother and sister feared these meetings.

*   *   *

The tragedies had ruined Ama Ganaie's family. Their one daughter was already dead. Now confirmed news about the abduction of their son shattered them. Despite cold climate in the valley they had returned from Jammu to mourn the death of their beloved son. And in spite of the captain being in the neighbourhood they were forced by circumstances to come back. Ama Ganaie had never comprehended that while he dispatched his son for arms training to safeguard his family and financial interests, he was in the grave before him. News about son's coffin lowered into the grave is the worst news for any parent. And Ama was forced by circumstances to accept it. And the grave was confirmed by a person through the photograph only. He often thought may be the man made a mistake while recognizing the photo.

"May be, one day Farooq lands up in my courtyard hale and hearty. I will embrace him. Kiss him on his forehead. His mother will hug him tight and they will remain like that for long." Ama often thought and continued with his self concocted script. This gave him some solace in loneliness. Some respite from scorching internal heat. The worst hit by the tragedy was Ama's wife. She almost became a mental wreck. She would often go upstairs to the attic which she used as a watch tower to look at the road expecting Farooq to return. The tragedy with the family was that they knew about the grave of their young daughter but nothing was known to them about their son's grave. Only Rashid and Nazir visited the place identified by a villager.

Un-identified.

Un-named.

Grave without a tombstone.

Grave without any proper identification.

Grave or a grave mistake!

The rituals after the death had ended when Arti joined the duty. She came to know about the whole episode. First of all she decided to join the family for mourning. She hugged them one by one and the family members wept bitterly again. Plangent Arti could not control her emotions but her army duty had taught her to be strong in most tragic situations.

Control.

Control.

*   *   *

Winter in Kashmir ended. Snow had disappeared from the villages and towns and was visible in the higher reaches only. The mustard flowers blossomed all round and gave a very pleasant look. In other fields green grass had elongated out of the seeds sown before winter set in. This large quantity grass would be used for the domestic animals. Schools and colleges reopened. There was good news for Nazir and his family. All rejoiced over the news. Arti was one among the lot. She brought sweets for the family and a costly neck tie for Nazir. Nazir had been selected in the engineering department as an engineer. Though Ama Ganaie did not need any employment for his son because he had lots of business establishment but a government job is always an attraction and place of pride and privilege in Kashmir. All were happy but Ama's wife wept again.

Why not?

She remembered her son and daughter and wanted them to be part of the celebration.

But that was not to be.

With Nazir posted in the works department, Ama Ganaie and his nephew Rashid were happier expecting some help in allotment of contracts and other support from him. Arti herself was also happy as she could now present a better picture of Nazir in addition to his looks.

Adonis the adroit!

He was a gazetted officer in the state government. She felt that her parents will now accept Nazir and her courtship.

Ruby also resumed her college. Leaving behind the tragedies attached to the gruesome murder of her siblings she thought to move on in life.

There is definitely no alternative.

Early spring is pleasant in Kashmir. Sun rays reflecting from the freshly fallen snow over mountains give elegance to the peaks. Yellow mustard flowers are so attractive. Only drawback with this part of the season is that fluffy cotton like pollen fall from the hybrid poplars and cause nasal infections. Ama Ganaie had become victim of the fluffy substance. He remained confined to home for a couple of days.

On a sunny afternoon Ruby roamed with the captain in a tourist spot a usual meeting place for the youngsters.

"Kashmir is so beautiful . . . . so are its people Ruby," the captain pointed towards the mountain peaks.

"You are right, Rasikh Khan Sahib," Ruby smiled.

"Are you sarcastically calling me Rasikh? I swear any time you ask me to convert I am ready to take up the new name . . . . Rasikh Khan."

Not many non local tourists were present. However, some picnickers were enjoying the environment. Young and old, men and women all were there to come out of the stifling security restrictions and the choked atmosphere due to gun fights, killings and nocturnal raids.

Ruby and the captain could not conceal their identities. Ruby, the rose cheeked Kashmiri girl, and the tall but dark complexioned young man made a varied combination. There had been such occasions when couples of different complexions were suspected. Same happened here. Two young boys spotted the difference and came forward.

"Could you please reveal your identity?" asked one. Suspicion gave birth to belligerence.

"Why?" the captain tried to be more confident. Dreaded law AFSPA invoked in the trouble torn state encouraged him to be over confident.

"I am asking who you are and who this girl is. How is she roaming with you?" The boy became a bit rude.

"His name is Rakish Khan." Sensing trouble Ruby tried to intervene to save the situation.

"Don't talk . . . . we understand," one among the group shouted at Ruby.

"First tell me who you are . . . . a police officer?" Captain Rajat paid in same coin.

Before conversation could move further half a dozen people got attentive and encircled the duo. The scene was engulfed by a torrid exchange.

"Yes, he is asking relevant question. Reveal your identity," another person among the group asked.

Ruby, sensing trouble tried to sneak away but was prevented by the people who assembled around.

Since the captain had no reply, the young man slapped him.

"*Kashmiri ladki ke saath ghoomta hai. Behan hai teri* (You are roaming with a Kashmir girl. Is she your sister?)"

Before the captain could react the men around pounced upon him and thrashed him. His clothes were torn. Sensing some trouble policemen around intervened, took charge of the issue, saved the captain from the onslaught and took him to the police station. Ruby had to follow. Some youngsters even abused Ruby.

"It is a matter of shame for us. She is roaming with a non local. Had she been my sister I would kill her," one among the group of people behind the duo said. Shenanigans followed.

Embarrassed by the development, Ruby got blushed and her face shone more. But she shivered over the idea of this news going to her parents. She yearned that a crater is formed beneath and the earth swallows her.

However there was no way out.

She had to follow.

In the police station the real identities of both were revealed. While the police officers too got angry with Ruby but a face saving act was done by on elderly police man.

"She has made a mistake but she is like our daughter. Don't embarrass her anymore," the elderly policeman took her from the room where many people had assembled. He offered her a glass of water. She wept bitterly.

"Daughter, don't weep. I will see to the issue,"

In other room the captain was rebuked by the police officer.

"Are you on duty or have come to enjoy here. I will register a case of abduction against you. I will make sure you lose your job and get jailed,"

"Yes sir, we will depose before the court against him. They think they can do anything under the garb of AFSPA, "the angry young man shouted.

"Now please be assured I will frame the necessary case against him. You can leave now," the police officer tried to pacify the crowd which had gathered outside and some of them had entered the police officer's office room.

On getting assurance from the police officer the people dispersed and left to enjoy the scenic beauty.

*   *   *

After passage of around one and half hour, Major Salvan reached the police station. Half a dozen vehicles were part of his caravan. In one vehicle Lt. Arti was seated. Rashid came in his own car. Just after entry Arti enquired about Ruby and went into the room where she was seated. "Be at ease. I am here," Arti hugged her and massaged her head and tried to console her as she wept.

Rashid also entered the room. Although he was not happy with her but he said nothing to Ruby. He remained standing on one side.

"I have not filed an FIR as I came to know he is an officer. But I can't release him now as people outside are agitated and they may raise hue and cry," the police officer talked to Salvan who was seated like a warlord.

"I understand,"

"People have left on my persuasion and promise that case shall be slapped against him,"

'I thank you for that, but I hope he is not injured seriously,"

"No, nothing to worry. I got him examined by the local doctors. Some bruises are there,"

"So?"

"Send someone in the evening. I will send the captain with him. Rest be assured. But ask your people to abstain from such practice,"

"Yes,"

"It is a sensitive issue here and can snowball into a major controversy."

After doing some formalities Ruby went along with Arti and Rashid. Rashid drove the vehicle and Arti and Ruby sat in the rear seat. They did not want that back home any controversy should crop up.

Major Salvan also left.

*   *   *

Back home Arti's family were on tenterhooks. They wanted a suitable resolution of the issue but the way Arti expressed her resentment, it looked far from settlement. Suggestions came from all. Mother, sister, brother, father, brother in law all looked helpless.

"Better get her transferred from the valley. You are a retired brigadier. You must have so much influence," Arti's mother said.

"But what is the guarantee that after transfer the issue will settle," sister intervened.

"I don't know but if it happens I will commit suicide. I can't show the face to my neighbours and relatives,"

"Don't talk like that. Some solution will come out," retired brigadier tried to soften his wife's attitude.

"In this age these things do take place. And her intimacy with that Kashmiri family has added to her softness towards Kashmir and Kashmiris. She says Kashmiris have been maltreated," sister justified.

"Why are you not saying anything?" Arti's mother turned to her son.

"If no solution comes out then I will think over something. I am also not in favour of her marriage to a Kashmiri Muslim boy," the brother declared.

"When will you start thinking over? After she has married?" mother turned a bit furious.

"That will not happen, mom. Don't worry," Arti's brother declared with firm conviction.

*   *   *

In the dead of night when all people were asleep, the silence was broken by the movement of vehicles. Around half a dozen vehicles passed by and stopped in the newly developed locality outside the main town. Dogs barked as gun wielding soldiers marched on the inner road. They were joined by few masked men who carried firearms. The soldiers and their companions zeroed in on two houses encircling them from all sides. Main doors of these encircled two houses were knocked. The inmates got anxious. Neighbours also had their sleep broken and they peeped through the glass panes to see what the matter was. Seeing the soldiers in combat positions was enough to sweat them from top to bottom.

Nocturnal raids and then arrest was as bad as death during the circumstances. There would be no guarantee as to the safe return of the arrestees. Anybody picked up could disappear or his corpse could be found lying in some remote area. Lucky would be those who could be identified through their faces, if not mutilated, or those carrying identity cards in their pockets. Such people could at least get a systematic burial according to religious rites. And their relatives would also be lucky to know that their relatives have not died unnamed.

Unnamed!

Unidentified!

Like Shadows beyond the ghost town!

The inmates were asked to come out. Following the orders all men and women, young and old assembled in the courtyard. A search operation was conducted and valuables

TV, fridge, car wind shields and the like damaged with gun butts. The end result was that two youngsters were bundled in the army vehicles. The inmates tried to block the exit routes of the vehicles but they were pushed back, beaten up, showered with choicest abuse and those who laid on the road surface dragged away.

Women screamed.

Children wept.

The small convoy left the spot leaving behind a trail of smoke and dust.

The arrested persons were blindfolded and pushed in separate vehicles. Made to lay prostrate on the floor of the vehicles the arrestees were burdened with heavy shoes on their shoulders, back, buttocks and calf muscles by the soldiers seated on either side of the one tonner vehicles. In between they were abused and threatened with death as they called them "active *atankwadis*". The arrestees were in such a position that they could neither reply nor refute the allegations levelled against them. They only screamed when they felt pain due to the burden above their back.

One of the soldiers pointed his gun on the rectum of the arrested youngster. Then he tried to pierce his gun into his anus.

"It will take us around one hour still. I better ease out. See he is in proper position. What do you think?" one of the soldiers asked his companion.

All present in the vehicle laughed except the one lying on his belly at the mercy of soldiers.

"It is better to shoot this bastard and throw his dead body in some *nallah*. Why take so much trouble?" a soldier in other vehicle frightened the arrested young boy.

The vehicles traversed the distance on various roads. The arrestees could not judge the area they were travelling but felt as if they travelled in the same area again and again. After the vehicles stopped they were pushed down the vehicle and they fell on the ground experiencing slight bruises due to the fall. They were made to walk the distance which they could not see due to the blindfold. Pushed into a big room which had high level ventilators, the frightened pigeons recognized each other as their blindfolds were removed. But they could not judge where they had been brought. Left to sleep on the unfurnished floor, without any cot or mattresses, the duo were given a bottle of water. They remained tight lipped for some time till they realized that nobody was outside or nearby. They first made signals followed by whispers.

"Why do you think we are arrested?"

"No idea,"

"May be some mistaken identity,"

"God knows"

"What should we do?"

"Allah Allah . . . . nothing else can save,"

While they talked in whispers for some time, they soon fell asleep with one of them snoring at high pitch.

* * *

The close relatives could not sleep for rest of the night. Parents, siblings, relatives and close neighbours remained assembled in the courtyard till morning. In the morning residents came out in larger numbers on the street to protest against the arrest. The media attention was invited. But no response was available in the first instance. However, as crowds began to swell district administration woke up to the development. The collector and the police chief reached the spot themselves promising action. The political heat also increased. Meanwhile, some of the relatives started their search through friends and acquaintances in the security establishments. With media attention growing on the protest demonstration the Umbrella leadership also plunged into the fray. Some of them even reached the spot to lead. Some were arrested on way to the spot lest things may go out of control.

But no definite information about the duo was forthcoming. And no substantial progress in the search operation materialized.

Protest demonstrations continued.

*   *   *

The duo was woken up by the soldiers and taken to separate rooms. It was time for interrogation. Interrogation in local parlance does not mean questioning but results in extracting such information which may not be relevant or even about the offences which have never been committed. The duo in separate rooms was first asked about their links with the militants. Supplying and transport of arms, planting IEDs, killing of prominent politicians and the logistic support to armed militants was attributed to them. They naturally declined to accept anything. The interrogation then changed to third degree torture.

"Have you ever enjoyed an aeroplane ride?" asked one soldier.

"No sir," he believed to be truthful thinking that the interrogator was purposefully asking about his aeroplane ride. He never knew that the soldiers were extracting sadistic pleasure out of his pain.

Schadenfreude!

Next moment two of the soldiers tied the fellow both at wrists and ankles and made him to hang in air in horizontal position. The pain at back, wrists and ankles made him scream. As he writhed in pain, his wrists experienced deeper bruise due to rope when he twisted it to get some relief. Near his ankles he felt some fire was burning. He experienced so much pain in his back that he felt his backbone may get fractured. Simple words can't elaborate the description.

"What were you doing in Pahalgam area? Surveying to plant IEDs to blow up holy cave devotees?"

"Sir, I am not a militant," he replied screaming and weeping loudly.

In response he was stripped naked, tied to a chair and electric current given to his penis. The pain could be gauged by his loud shrieks only.

"How many boys have you sent for arms training across the LOC and how many times you crossed yourself?"

"None sir . . . . never Sir,"

He was then laid prostrate. Some combustible liquid was inserted into his rectum through a pipe. Match stick lighted and was left to burn.

"Please kill me . . . . for God's sake kill me . . . . shoot me once for all," he kept on shouting. He yearned for death as pain became unbearable.

Death is the remedy for all pains of life when it becomes too hot to handle!

The interrogators left the room and the tortured rolled on the ground with hands and legs tied waiting for the apostle of death to rid him of all miseries.

After about half an hour, the duo was pushed into same room and kept tied at a distance from each other so that they could not help each other in removing the knots. Little water and one snack to each was served. Now two persons entered the room. One of them was wearing civvies and other in military uniform.

"You bastards recognize this officer . . . . do you?" the uniformed person asked.

"No sir, "he replied with squinted eyes. His eyes were partly closed due to acute pain all over his body.

"*Tumhara jheeja hai yeh salo.* (He is your brother in law)" The man kicked and slapped vociferously the youngster who declined to recognize.

"Sir, Sir, I recognize him," the other boy replied hastily fearing torture.

"*Haan . . . . dekha apne behan ke pati ko jaldi pehchana* (See he recognized his sister's husband)" uniformed man spewed filth. "The other day he was with your sister when you attacked him and incited others also."

"Sir, please forgive us . . . . please sir . . . . ," the duo pleaded.

"I will forgive you . . . . but you have to get your sisters for two days to this camp . . . . ready?" the uniformed man continued his choicest abuse.

"*Behen chod* . . . . they will die in an encounter." The uniformed officer left and the man in civvies followed him.

"What do you think? Will they kill us in a fake encounter?" one boy asked his companion in whispers.

Both were writhing in pain, adjusting themselves in one or the other direction; sometimes on their haunches alternately and then on their foot soles as if in a bowling movement over Indian type commode.

"So what . . . . more than fifty thousand people died here? But we can't tolerate the behaviour of these bastards. Do you think we will allow them to flirt with our women in the garb of stringent laws like AFSPA?"

"No never . . . . that will be on our dead bodies . . . . let them burn our property, kill us all . . . . but our respect has to last!"

The assertion was there.
Confidence of higher degree.
And of course the anger.
Visible wrath against such injustice!

*　　*　　*

Three days passed and there was no trace of the duo. No information was coming. The district administration was at tenterhooks. The police chief tried to get information from all sources at his disposal. On third day the police officer who had arrested the MI captain with a girl about a week ago shared the proceedings of the event with his boss.

"Sir, these two boys are the same who had spotted the MI man with a local girl. The man was, subsequently, thrashed by the crowd and my men saved him with great difficulty,"

"How you think these are the boys,"

"Sir, they promised to testify in the court of law. So army knew their names and addresses,"

"Hmmmm . . . . it could be the revenge,"

The police chief received further information regarding the unit and the place with which the MI officer was associated. He then proceeded further with his information and corroborated with other inputs available. The police chief then zeroed in on the particular army unit where the duo could be kept.

The political temperature had already risen and there was danger of fallout which could spell out of hands and would result in mass agitation. David joined in seeking whereabouts and immediate release of the young duo. By evening, the local minister declared that the duo are safe and shall return very soon. While the people in general did not believe and presumed that the politicians do talk for public consumption and raise hopes to thwart any public outburst but hope was rekindled in the hearts of their families.

One more night passed. The parents, siblings and the relatives assembled in the two houses spent this night also in fear and despair. Some consoled others pacified. Some advised to have faith in Allah; others raised some hopes due to minister's assurances.

"He would not say unless he has some concrete information,"

"They say anything for public consumption,"

Hope, despair.

Prayers, consolation.

Anger.

The night was not passing off for the family. It elongated to many nights. It spread over too many hours. It equalled to days, stretched to months and years. Groping in dark and waiting is the most difficult thing

People at other places came out of the mosques after morning prayers. At two different places in far flung areas two youngsters tied with ropes were rolling on the dusty road to invite attention of the public. Some people went nearer and listened to the pleas of the boys pleading for clearing their stuffed mouths and removing the cotton. They were, subsequently, released from the ropes tied to their hands and legs. They were served water and tea. The information was disseminated to their homes through various channels. Their family members reached the spot in vehicles and lifted them to the hospitals first. Nursing their injuries and recovering from the shock of severe torture they spent few days in the hospitals.

Despite the third degree torture they were satisfied.

They returned homes safely.

Something uncommon in such situations in the burning paradise!

*　　*　　*

The incident took an ugly turn with more people joining the protest. The Umbrella leadership was released from detentions but the emotions ran high as news spread about the severe torture inflicted upon the young duo. Government was forced to order an enquiry and police on its part pursued the case further. The first axe fell on the police officer who had taken the case lightly and did not register the FIR when the captain was apprehended with the girl. It was presumed that had he taken the case forward and not taken a lenient view, the situation would not turn so ugly. Army on its part was also forced to order internal enquiry. The enquiry report, both by civil as well as military establishment, found the MI captain guilty of misconduct and as a first step he was immediately transferred out of the valley. The transfer or redeployment of a particular unit or person was something which used to be done after any incident of misconduct or human rights abuse and was sarcastically called a 'big punishment' by the locals.

The captain was forced to leave without maintaining any communication with Ruby who remained house trapped after the incident. Though Rashid and Arti had not leaked the information about the incident to Ama Ganaie and Nazir still, Ruby felt harassed and stayed mostly indoors and did not visit her college after the incident. Her communication with the captain was broken. Despite the fact she narrated the whole story of proposed conversion by the captain to Islam, Rashid had reprimanded her for the act. Arti tried to console her when she wept later.

*   *   *

Not many days passed when a group of other soldiers was also ordered out of the valley. This group included Lt. Arti. Nobody suspected anything and thought of it as a routine affair and deployment strategy within the institution. Before leaving the place Arti came to Ama's house. The family had invited her for a dinner. Ruby and her mother, though broken by the events, tried their best to serve sumptuous dinner amid Kashmiri hospitality. Some gifts like dry fruits, apples, handicrafts etc were packed for the lady. Arti accepted all with gratitude and humility. She was overwhelmed by the love showered on her by the Ganaie family. Before leaving, she spent few minutes with Nazir who kissed her passionately.

Love birds at the peak of emotions.

All the family members walked along her up to the main gate where her army guards waited for her. Waving hands, she left for her camp nearby.

*   *   *

All seemed to go normal and usual. However, there were two exceptions. One Ruby and the captain separated by circumstances craved to see and talk to each other. Second, Arti and Nazir with their hearts bursting for each other were now separated by distance. Nobody could analyze the fire raging inside them.

Abida Parveen's melodious voice was heard from a radio. She sang famous Urdu poet Ibn Insha's Ghazal;

Hain lakhoon rog zamane main kyon ishq hai ruswa bechara

Hain aur bhi wajhain wahshat ki insaan ko rakhte dukhiyara

Haan bekal bekal rahta hai wo preet main jis ne ji hara
Par sham sey lekar subh talak youn kon phire ga awara

(There are many diseases in the world why should love only get a bad name.

There are many reasons for fear which keep a person in despair.

Yes, anybody who lost one's heart in the love stays abnormal Otherwise who should roam dawn to dusk without a goal)

They also did not express to anyone. But one day the telephone rang. Ruby and the captain talked for a long time.

Expressed themselves.

And so talked Arti and Nazir.

Expression of love though far from each other.

Walking alone is not difficult. But when we walk a mile with someone, then coming back alone is difficult.

Barriers don't stop expression of love. Fragrance and love can't be concealed, can't be arrested. These come out of its own. Same happened with the love birds. Despite repeated attempts by Ama Ganaie and his family, Ruby declined to marry. Although pressure mounted on Arti to accept the air force officer, she categorically negated the offer. What followed was some threatening to Nazir on phone to refrain from the act.

Days went by till one day the captain disseminated the news to Ruby that he had been posted on active duty in north east region of the country, infested by militants. She could do nothing except pray for his safety.

And days passed when one day Arti's brother and her 'would be' met for a secret meeting. Subsequently, some telephonic conversation followed with an army officer posted in some area in the valley.

*   *   *

Nazir, the engineer, was on tour inspecting works to be started or going on. He had a hectic schedule. He visited two bridge sites and gave instructions to his junior staff to be more attentive as this involved the big structure and could endanger life and property if not executed to proper specifications. He then visited a building site where he lost temper and got a portion of brick work demolished because of poor specifications. The contractor at site had an exchange of hot words as he felt Assistant Sahib exaggerated about the poor quality of work and went out of way to get the work demolished. The contractor had a feeling of embarrassment and accused Nazir of jeopardizing his reputation, though he being a renowned contractor in the area.

"This is much better work than what your father used to execute during militancy," the contractor referred to his father's works. This was sarcastic reference

"Why should you get my father into the issue? Do good work and that is all I want," Nazir responded in anger.

Before things would take ugly turn, the junior staff at site intervened and brought things under control.

Nazir had few more sites to visit which took him lot of time. Evening fell and Muezzin called the faithful for Namaz. Nazir was now on his way to home. Driving his own car, he looked exhausted, yawning at intervals. After he had crossed some distance he reached a lonely spot which had been turned into a more frightening one by the presence of various trees. Darkness added more to its frightening scenario. The residential houses were few and far between. Hardly any light, from these houses at a distance, reached nearer.

Ghost town presented horror!

Nazir was signalled to stop. His car came to a screeching halt when he saw couple of men standing in the centre of the road and waving hands to stop. He then saw three vehicles parked on the road edge. The head lights of these vehicles were off and so were the inner lights. He could not see the number plates which were either under the thick mud layer or not visible in the dark. The vehicles were like demons of old ghost stories ready to engulf the whole earth and turn everything into dross stone.

Silent and listless!

The gun wielding men came near his car window and asked him to park the vehicle on the road edge. Nazir quietly followed the instructions.

No arguments.

"Get down from the car," orders were issued.

"What is the matter?" Nazir enquired politely.

"We have reports militants are driving an explosive laden vehicle to blow up an army camp . . . . you know suicide attacks,"

"But I am an officer in the government. You can check my I-card,"

"We have to check many things. Your car, your papers and something more,"

Nazir tried to take out his purse from back pant pocket. Purse contained his I-card.

I-card, the most precious commodity which one could not afford to forget to take it along.

I-card, the thin line between life and death!

"I know you own a government identity card. Keep it in your pocket," the person did not allow him to take his I card out.

Two more gun wielding masked men appeared from the scene and bundled Nazir into the waiting vehicle.

Blindfolded, he was made to sit in the back of a closed vehicle so that he did not make noise and attract attention. The vehicles sped fast to the unknown destination.

Night fell and Ama Ganaie and his family got anxious. Ama rang up his nephew Rashid who came to the house with some known persons. Numbers were dialled to get some information but all they could gather was that Nazir had left for his home a bit late in the evening. Perturbed by the event Rashid and a couple of neighbours went in search of Nazir in a car. After travelling for about half an hour they spotted Nazir's car near the blind curve on the road. They stopped, searched here and there and tried to contact someone nearby. None could provide any clues.

Having returned from the scene empty handed, the discussion wrapped up at the lodging up of an FIR. Though late in the night, Ama Ganaie rang up Major Salvan to enquire if he could provide some help or clues in the matter. Major Salvan was gracious enough to visit Ama's home and seek further details and promised help.

Next day police lodged an FIR and started investigation. The first finger was pointed towards the contractor who had some altercation with Nazir during day time about poor specifications adopted for the work. But nothing yielded except some money for the police. The issue snowballed into a major controversy with newspapers highlighting the case. The Umbrella elements pointed fingers on the armed forces and the renegades working under them. Government promised enquiry and police assured thorough investigation. Few more days passed and no clues were available. Even the national press reported the news.

Arti received the news through some Delhi based newspaper. She rang up to enquire from Ruby.

The result was a blind no.

As days passed Ama Ganaie lost hope. His wife started losing mental balance. His daughter struggled to carry on. All turned psychos almost.

No foods, no work.

The visitors kept enquiring if any news was forthcoming. The family felt tired answering same questions day in and day out. The process continued for few more days.

*　　*　　*

One evening, a taxi stopped near Ama Ganaie's home and Arti alighted with a small bag in her hand. She had taken leave for few days after she learnt about the disappearance of Nazir. She was welcomed by Ruby and on her part Arti tried to console Ruby and her mother who sobbed intermittently. After getting all information about the case including copy of an FIR, she tried to convince the family that something will come out. All had a disturbed sleep but Arti's presence had given the family a new lease of life expecting that Arti's connections within the army will help them trace Nazir.

Arti decided to keep Ruby and her cousin Rashid with her to try out further in the case. Next morning their struggle of tracing Nazir started. She first met Major Salvan in whose office it was made clear that nothing had been done in the jurisdiction of the major. Possibly someone else was responsible. Nothing substantial came out of the enquiries around the site of occurrence of the crime. Either the people living at some distance did not know anything or they feared enough to reveal anything. None could even give any clues about the vehicles parked that evening there.

No recognition, no number plates. The people in the conflict zone had experienced bad days. Any credible information about the misdeeds of soldiers had invited wrath and people were made to suffer. Possibly no one wanted to get stuck in the thistle.

It became daily routine for Arti and her group to leave early in the morning and return in the evening. She used her influence in the army on one hand and her intelligence and expertise of interrogation of various people who could in some way be helpful with any clues. They searched in the police stations, army camps, Para military area and even tried their contacts in the militant ranks who were opposed to his brother and slain militant Farooq's Tanzeem. The daily routine made them tired but they did not express their helplessness or exertion.

One day Arti got a novel idea. She decided to travel in a local passenger bus that travelled on the same route where Nazir had been abducted and his empty car was found. Nobody suspected the lady as she wore local dress and even covered her face like local Muslim girls. When the passenger vehicle reached the spot two women seated behind Arti talked in whispers.

"Ama Ganaie's son was abducted here. His car was found here only,"

"They have found no clues yet,"

"May be he has been killed. Here thousands have disappeared like this,"

"Yes,"

"Renegades have done that,"

"I also heard but no names are mentioned,"

"People fear renegades. They work for army. Nobody likes to make himself a target,"

"Rumour is that Aamir Ikhwani did it. He works for the army camp near highway,"

"Yes . . . . I also heard,"

Over the years Arti had learnt to understand some Kashmiri language though she could not speak fluently. She gathered the information and recorded it in her mental computer. She understood what the highway camp meant and looking for Aamir was not any problem. The process continued for a week or so when she finally zeroed in on the renegade. Arti invited Aamir for a cup of coffee. He did not suspect anything fishy when he heard that the girl was an army officer herself. He felt overwhelmed by the invitation and gave his consent to attend. In a day or two he was seated in a posh restaurant on the banks of Dal Lake in Srinagar. And across her sat Arti the army officer.

Aamir was dressed in blue jeans and matching shirt. He was of good height and sported stubble which was arranged nicely. He had concealed a revolver in a small bag which he carried along. So was Arti carrying a small weapon in her hand bag. Arti wore flower print Kameez Shalwar like Kashmiri girls. Here and there, this and that Arti made Aamir to speak out. He gave the broader details of the operation and people behind the case.

During soft interrogation and a couple of friendly smiles he did mention name of an officer on whose directions the abduction had taken place. Ironically, she somehow connected the officer with her own brother and the proposed 'would be'. This infuriated Arti but she kept her cool and did not disclose any thing to Ruby and her family lest they may hate her for being a source of inconvenience to them. Next day, she directly went on to meet the commanding officer, the suspected officer was associated with. The CO was categorical in his reply and straightaway declined to buy the argument of involvement of any of his subordinates in such crime. He trashed the statement declaring it heresy and calumny. Blunt in his replies, he rebuked Arti and advised her not to exceed her limits being herself an army officer. But Arti, assiduous as always, was explicit in her discussion to convey that she will follow the case and lead it to its logical end.

*　　*　　*

The people rose to the horror of couple of corpses lying across the river. The dead bodies were dumped in two jute sacks tied around with ropes. The bodies were spotted by those going for their early work in their paddy fields. As soon as news about the bodies spread, people from adjoining villages reached the spot to identify and confirm if any known person or an acquaintance had been killed and dumped there. The news reached Ama Ganiae's home also. Already shocked by the sudden disappearance of Nazir, they got goose pimps. In such situations very bad thoughts engulf the mind and same happened to the inmates including Arti. They thought, God forbid Nazir has been killed and the body thrown there. Without waiting for anything, Arti and Ruby rushed towards the river bank to find out the truth. By the time police had reached the spot.

When police officials opened the sacks they found the bodies with their throats slit. They took the dead bodies in their control and sent the same for post mortem. However, Arti recognized one of the bodies. It belonged to the renegade namely Aamir who worked for army and had a conversation with Arti the other day. This man had given a pointed reference to Arti about involvement of a particular army officer whose name she mentioned to the CO. So the officer wanted to remove all traces of any doubt which may raise its head and finally nail him. Fangs of suspicion had to be trimmed.

Arti understood the whole game.

In a few days time the dust settled over the dead bodies which had been found stuffed in jute sacks. The newspaper story, subsequently, was relegated to the inner pages with a minor reference about police investigation being carried on.

Arti left for her home.

*   *   *

This year 15th August celebration was comparatively well organized with some civilians attending on their own. The participation by political leaders had encouraged commoners to visit the venues and enjoy some cultural programmes and few dare devil acrobats by the uniformed men. The stadia and the function spots had been decorated with buntings. The arrangements for the general public were also there. Plastic chairs had been fixed in spaces reserved for the public. The spots were covered with *shamianas* and some coverings provided by the security establishment. Civil administration had made elaborate arrangements for a successful function. VIP area and podium space had been barricaded to provide extra security cover to the minister, political leaders and the senior officers.

The march past was main attraction for the visitors. The soldiers of various contingents in tidy dresses passed in front of the podium where VIP took salute. The security contingents were followed by school children. Neat and cute school children, both boys and girls, took part in the parade. After the parade cultural show was organized. Some patriotic songs, some mimicry, some skits depicting local culture was part of the function. Then the VIP spoke.

David was one such VIP at a similar function.

He talked of development, road building, and school up gradation, medical facilities and a resolve to sustainable peaceful atmosphere.

Peaceful atmosphere! Huhhhhh

A government officer disappears and there is no trace.

People are asked to get down near army establishments and walk.

The uniformed man is the master. He can enter any home anywhere and at any point of time.

The arrested person has to prove he is innocent in the court of law.

The arrestee released on court orders is rearrested outside the court itself and has to spend another year or so till again released and rearrested.

Peaceful atmosphere . . . . my foot!

The function closed after distribution of prizes.

Prizes to those who contributed for the society.

Contribution to the society! . . . . damn it.

The engineer, the doctor, the policeman, the teacher, the journalist, the this, the that . . . . and so on.

The engineer who shared the booty with people like Ama Ganaie.

The doctor who prescribed spurious drugs.

The policeman who tortured hapless people.

The teacher who encouraged private tuitions.

The forest officer who colluded with Ama Ganaies of society to deprive the landscape of forest cover.

The journalist who highlighted the news item proposed by the district magistrate and the police chief.

The consumer department official who consumed midway whatever meant for the poor people.

Those who contributed . . . . hilarious!

The functions culminated in all places and the people at the helm of affairs had a sigh of relief. No incident of any consequence happened. All patted their own backs.

Similar function was the star attraction in the national capital where biggest function took place. The Prime Minister was the chief guest. He addressed the nation from the ramparts of Red Fort. He boasted of economic growth, security system, military strength and democracy. He praised the soldiers for their daring deeds and resilience in the conflict zones. He assured peace.

Peace! Peace under the barrel of gun.

Peace or wild rape of peace.

Democracy or broad day molestation of democracy.

Military strength which results in forced disappearance of an officer.

Security system which forbids a young officer to marry with her own choice.

This function also culminated in the declaration of awards for bravery. The show was live. And Ruby watched it.

"Captain Rajat Sharma . . . . he laid down his life just one week back fighting militants in north east," was declared at the stage.

Ruby's heart beat vociferously. She felt her heart may fall out of her chest. Then a middle aged lady holding captain's photograph walked to the podium. Ruby cried and cried loudly. She recognized the photograph of the slain captain carried by his mother. The captain had died. Rasikh Khan was no more!

Ruby's emotions ran high. Sobbing Ruby pictured Rajat in her wedding ceremony. And then the Moulvi announced that Rajat is ready to embrace Islam and his name changed to Rasikh Khan. The Moulvi made him to recite verses and then congratulated all. Subsequently, Nikah ceremony was performed in presence of near and dear ones. Ruby was now wife of Rasikh Khan.

After sometime her eyes ran dry.

Rasikh Khan died a second time!

*   *   *

"Government employee and renegade murder; Army officer accuses senior officer."

Newspaper story had this caption and the details referred to the letter written by a lady army officer, Lt. Arti to the army top brass. The letter leaked to the media accused the army officer of abduction and subsequent enforced disappearance of Nazir, the engineer. The accusation followed by the alleged murder of two renegades who could have been involved in the whole game. There was clear reference of one having disclosed a part story about the abduction. The letter also accused the commanding officer of attempts to save the officer.

The news story created furore in the media and the army top brass decided to investigate. But what followed was summoning of Arti and pressurizing her to take back the accusations.

"You are part of the institution and you can't level baseless accusations. If you have to fight then leave the institution," the coercion was clear. They impugned the truth.

While she tried to explain her position but nobody was ready to listen.

"Simply take back the letter. Don't be imbecile!" the orders were clear cut.

A day after another letter reached the head office written by Arti seeking premature superannuation from the army.

The action stunned many. The news reached her family where her parents and siblings received the news with shock and they were awe struck. They had never expected that Arti would take such a drastic action. But whatever had to happen, happened.

What next?

This was the most important issue for the family.

But Arti had decided already.

*   *   *

A week later Arti reached the valley and straightway drove to Ama Ganaie's house. The family was perplexed over her sudden arrival but all felt happy. Arti was a source of unflinching support. Though all were happy but Ruby was more than that. She now got a companion; presumably a permanent one. Arti proved herself as Ruby's brothers and sister all combined in one. Army had taught her to be firm and fearless and she exhibited same traits in normal life also. Next week Arti filed a petition in the state high court through her lawyer seeking justice for the Ganaie family.

Justice for Ganaie family or herself?

God knows.

The honourable court issued notices to all concerned including the government and the army. The battle was long drawn.

Affidavits.

Counter affidavits

Arguments

Counter arguments.

The issue stopped finally at the tables of ministry of defence and home. Both proved a stumbling block in the carriage of justice. The necessary approval needed for prosecution did not come by.

Arti, Ruby and Ama Ganaie waited for justice.

Ama's wife did not wait. She, after losing mental balance due to repeated tragedies, did not know meaning of justice any more. Her day started with a loud call to Shazi, Farooq and Nazir for the morning tea. Then she would invariably run towards the main gate of the courtyard declaring that Shazi was leaving for the school. Occasionally, she ran upstairs and in her day dreams watched from her watch tower, Nazir leaving for the engineering college. When to eat and what to eat had no semblance for her now. Who comes and who leaves had no meaning for her. The day break and sun set had stopped meaning the rotation of sun and the earth. The cow mows or the birds chirp had lost the essence. Scorching sun and the chilling snow fall was without any attraction.

The days passed.

The nights fell.

The winds blew.

The sun shone.

Justice eluded. All, but Ama's wife understood.

*   *   *

Justice eluded all in the hapless state. And if there was any semblance of justice it was selective one. But the government felt conditions had improved.

"There is more of peace visible on the streets than bloodshed, bullets, mayhem . . . . we need to give the people a sense of it. Our government has improved the situation," the politicians boasted of their achievements. The fruits of peace and normalcy were reflective in abandonment of some security camps. One army camp established in the part of Ama Ganaie's orchard was also made defunct. The soldiers loaded their belongings in the trucks and prepared to leave. The unit had been relocated somewhere outside the valley.

In the evening Major Salvan came to Ama's house. Dressed in full army uniform, the major had ankle high military boots which have long laces and it takes time to bind. Secondly, army men stay in alert positions particularly in the conflict zone, and so do not like to put their shoes off. But Kashmiris have a custom of not entering their homes with foot wear on. Since they have furnishings placed in their rooms they put their shoes off before entering a home. However, here the major entered the drawing room with boots on and Ama Ganaie did not think it proper to object to it. Major Salvan sat with him for around twenty minutes. They had tea together. He remembered some of the precious moments. He talked about the chemistry both enjoyed. He thanked him for his cooperation. Before leaving, he apologized for any inconvenience caused due to him and his men. Then both hugged each other.

Next morning the long convoy left the spot.

*   *   *

The news about the unmarked graves caused a splash in the media. The journalists, civil society members, human rights watchers made a beeline to the spot. News about long lines of graves, without any epitaphs, created ripples. First the government refused to acknowledge but then under pressure from world bodies and its own human rights commission accepted to investigate. The police remained in denial mode claiming that these graves belonged to the unidentified non local militants who were killed in encounters with the soldiers. But intervention at various levels forced it to accept that may be some others are buried in these graves also. This raised a hope in the minds of those whose loved ones had disappeared without any information. Media reports had suggested that some local persons who buried these men in the graves could prove helpful. May be they remembered the faces of the corpses or some clues related to them.

One such person was Arti who had complete information that her love bird Nazir had been subjected to enforced disappearance at the behest of her family members by one army officer. Though her petition was in consideration before the honourable court but there was nothing in sight for an immediate solution.

On hearing about the news of unmarked graves she decided to visit the spot herself. She wanted some clues. The reports about these unmarked graves rekindled a ray of hope. One morning Arti filled her pouch with all relevant information papers about Nazir and boarded the car. Ruby accompanied her. The travel was cumbersome as they had to cross over more than hundred Kilometres to reach the spot. It took them more than three hours to travel on the traffic jammed portions of the long stretch and at places the road was in bad condition. Since they had started their journey very early it proved of help.

Although very few people came forward to help the duo, about providing any information, but they managed to lay hands on the person who had first hand information. After about forty five minutes the person was contacted who had gone to his fields for some work.

Jum Khan was a middle aged man with grey long beard. He wore Khan Suit which had streaks of dirt at spots. Skull cap on his head, he had sharp thin nose and deep eyes. His fingers trembled while talking.

"*Beti, main kya help kar sakta hoon* (Daughter, what help can I do?" He asked.

"*Hum ko jo bhi information de sakte ho wo day do* (Whatever information you can, give to us),"

"*Tum kya akhbar wale ho* (Are you journalists?),"

"*Nahi . . . . mera bhaie gum ho gaya* (No, my brother disappeared)," Ruby intervened.

"*Jab se yeh news phaili hai police aur army mere peche hai ki koi information mat de do . . . . is liye main savere khet par chala jata hoo. Main budha wahan kya kaam kar sakta hoon . . . . bus bachao ke liye bhag jata hoon savere* (Since this news appeared police and army are after me not to divulge any information. So I attend my fields in the morning. What work can this old man do? I just leave early to save myself),"

"*Hum ko tumhari halat ka andaza hai lekin hum bhi desperate hain information ke liye.* (We understand your position but we are desperate for any information you can give)" Arti tried to gain his confidence.

"*Tumhare bhaie ki koi foto* (Any photographs)?" He asked Ruby.

Arti took no time to open her pouch and take couple of photographs and showed anxiously to Jum Khan. Jum Khan had a thorough inquest into the photographs, as if, he tried to unearth some deep story behind. After few minutes he got up and asked the duo to follow him. In between the passers-by gazed at the duo. Girls from city area attracted attention. They walked the ups and downs of the village interior till they reached the mud brick single story house. The hut had steep sloped CGI sheeted roof.

"*Yahan baraf zyada girti hai is liye tez chhat lagani padti hai* (We experience heavy snow so we use steep roofs)"

Jum Khan entered the room and made some space for the guests. The floor was covered with the *Pataj*, a sheet made of strings woven out of grass. He raised his right hand up to the lips and turned it a bit signalling his wife to prepare tea who peeped from a small opening in the wall. The portion where Jum Khan's wife stood was the kitchen area. A hearth constructed out of mud stood there. Few utensils of aluminium were kept on a timber seat. Spoons, big and small, hung through nails projecting out of the pierced hole in the tail of the spoon. One earthen pot and one plastic bucket contained water.

A wooden stair took flight to the attic cum second story of the hut.

"Daughters, be at ease. I will return just now," Jum Khan said lifting himself from the floor and headed towards the stair. Taking support of wooden railing he went upstairs. In the attic some rejection wood was spread in bundles which are used for preparation of food in the hearths. Grass and hay was stacked on one side. Jum Khan lifted few bundles of grass and couple of bundles of rejection wood and took out a small wooden box. He came down with the box and put it in front of Arti and Ruby. His wife brought tea and corn flour bread and couple of china cups.

"Why should you take so much of trouble? We have some eatables in the car," Arti expressed gratitude.

"Daughter, you are our guests. You must be from city but in this far flung area we can't provide much to your liking,"

"Uncle, don't say like that. I know you have taken a risk to talk to us,"

"Never mind. I don't care for life. I am sixty years old and have buried as young as twenty years with my own hands," Jum Khan raised his hands. "I buried around forty people in the graves with no identification. Some had bruised faces. Some bullet ridden heads. But I managed to keep whatever identification was available in their pockets. I kept the items in this box and have concealed it till now. Nobody knows it. Don't disclose to anyone,"

"We won't tell anybody . . . . be assured," Arti tried to assure Jum Khan.

"With these items at least three people so far have been recognized by their relatives. I feel satisfied at least I could provide some relief to them. Allah will help me on the day of resurrection . . . ."

"Insha Allah," Ruby and Arti responded.

"Please take tea . . . . this will cool off . . . . cold tea has no taste,"

The duo took sips of tea and few pieces of bread.

After finishing the tea Ruby lifted the Samovar, cups and small basket to carry it to the kitchen area but Jum Khan's wife didn't allow her to do so.

Jum Khan opened the box and lifted out the belongings one by one. These included few papers, wallets, half a dozen photographs and couple of handkerchiefs with some initials over them.

One of the wallets made Arti's and Ruby's heart beat fast. They recognized it. They almost snatched it from Jum Khan's hand. Curiously Arti opened it. Two photographs in the space were visible. In one photo Arti and Nazir stood side by side in romantic pose. Other one belonged to Shazi, his slain sister. Arti and Ruby wept bitterly. They hugged each other screamed, cried and sobbed. Jum Khan's wife came forward and cried with them.

"Don't cry daughters . . . . have patience. You at least have an address now. Many people don't have even the information about their loved ones," Jum Khan consoled them.

Jum Khan's wife brought a jug of water and a plastic bucket and made the duo wash their faces.

Arti now scanned the wallet fully. Few hundred rupees and Nazir's I card was inside it.

"*Chacha (uncle)*, if you are sure it belongs to one who is buried by you, can you identify where is he?" Arti asked.

"Yes, I can give you the information. It is a case of around two years back so I remember vividly. It is third from right end,"

"Can we go there?"

"Yes, but I will show from far off. I can't come closer,"

"Yes, no problem. You can just point out from a distance. We don't want any trouble for you,"

Arti took out a small bundle of cash from her pouch and secretly tried to put it in Jum Khan's hand but he refused.

"My life is simple. I can't handle this cash etc."

Though Arti and Ruby tried to persuade him to accept but he remained adamant. In few minutes time Jum Khan led the duo to a secluded place. He signalled towards the spot. Arti and Ruby moved forward and Jum Khan kept an eye over them.

Ruby and Arti now stood in front of a long stretch of land with elevated mounds of earth. In between sharp edged stones had been erected to distinguish between the graves. Arti and Ruby stopped near the mound, third from right and looked around. Jum Khan signalled with his right index finger. Arti took out her camera and took few photographs to keep identification of the spot. In one photograph a 3ft by 2ft blue background board read the name of Rural Development Department with few more lines about the work executed.

'This board can provide a clue and identify the spot if needed in future.' She thought while clicking the camera.

Spending some time there, they left the village in their car.

*   *   *

Kashmir is on the crossroads. Kashmiris are on the crossroads. Kashmir deserves a political solution. Kashmiris yearn for a lasting solution so that the repeated revolutions don't devour their own children. The Umbrella leadership is on the cross roads not knowing what to do next. Arti is on the cross roads. Her love bird Nazir disappeared as if vanished in thin air like thousands whose whereabouts are not known. Ruby is at the cross roads not able to make a decision of her life after the captain fell to bullets in the North East. David is at the cross roads thinking whether his political decision is correct or something else need to be done. Major Salvan is at the crossroads pondering why his many men were killed and why his men killed so many. Ama Ganaie is at the crossroads. Whether his decision to send Farooq across was right or wrong.

Ama Ganaie grew frail. He lost strength to withstand. He hardly had few morsels of food. He almost lost taste buds. And one day he stopped walking. He was supported on a walking stick. Doctors at the hospital tried very hard but Ama did not respond much to the medication. He himself felt the days were numbered. Few more days and he called Arti and Ruby. He was on his bed with his belly facing the ceiling. He asked Ruby and Arti to help him sit in his bed. The duo kept couple of pillows behind and made a comfortable back support. The duo, while helping him, threw their arms under his arm pits and lifted him somewhat to drag him backwards. The arms felt like the wings of a chicken; frail and thin. They supported Ama to sit with back against the pillows. Arti offered him some water which he sipped. He rolled his hands over the heads of both girls as they sat on either side on his wooden cot.

"You know Ruby is my daughter but I have placed you Arti as other one. I know what you desired. I also know what Ruby desired. Both things were out of my control and authority and I could not help you. I know where your heart beat but I could not help your union.

I have done so many sins in my life. I collected so much of property and land estates but nobody is alive to enjoy the fruits. None is here to look after. I sinned and many others sinned with me. I have been punished by Allah. But, why me only? . . . . Major Salvan was my partner. David, the politician did the same. Rahim Dar contributed his bit . . . . Now my daughters, I leave it to your wisdom. I have framed a will that you both will look after my whole property. You will decide as to what should be its proper usage and correct expenditure. We all are orphans. I am one as I don't have my young sons and my beloved daughter. You both are orphans as you don't have the loved ones with you. Your mother is an orphan as she does not have sense to differentiate as to who belongs to her . . . . the people who deserve must get their share,"

Both ladies sobbed. Rehman the servant entered with Qur'an in hand. Tears rolling down his cheeks he sat in one corner of the room and recited *Sura Yasin* bit loudly.

"Don't weep daughters. Just decide how to make best use,"

"What is your suggestion, father?" Arti asked.

"We have many orphans . . . ." Ama Ganaie could not complete the sentence and his head dropped to one side.

Zam Zam

The holy water from Makah.

Few spoons of holy water were poured into his mouth by Arti and Ruby. Ama breathed his last.

His funeral was a low key affair. Close relatives and neighbours joined in. Arti and Ruby wept bitterly hugging each other. After some time they consoled each other. The corpse was bathed in one corner of the big compound covered temporarily with a big sheet of tarpaulin spread over big logs, held high on one end over the brick wall, and rested on ground on other end, by the locals who assembled after hearing the news. The shroud clad dead body was kept in the wooden coffin brought from the local mosque. The coffin was covered with white cloth and in between black colour cloth, having Qur'anic verses inscribed in gold, was placed. As the coffin was taken away from the compound towards the local graveyard carried by six people who changed shoulders at intervals, the women assembled in the house wept and screamed loudly. Some consoled Arti and Ruby. But Ama's wife had strange effects of this whole situation. She intermittently asked other women as to why they wept. She did not stay at one place for long.

Sat, stood up, walked and ran faster.

She finally used her watch tower to see the whole scene.

In next four days few people attended. Salvan was posted out of the valley. David did not think it proper to visit due to time constraint. Few people had tea on the fourth day of his death. Still fewer people recited Qur'an and had feast.

It was no match to Shazi's funeral and fourth day function.

*   *   *

Unnatural justice

Arti and Ruby periodically took Ama's wife to a psychiatrist who managed her with some medicines. In order to save her from night walking due to less sleep which could have endangered her life, if she ventured out, she was prescribed with sleeping pills and sedatives. Arti and Ruby administered her scheduled drugs under their close supervision and would wait till she had some sleep. This night they repeated the daily routine and after feeling satisfied that she was in deep slumber they set her bedding right. They pulled the bed sheet here and there, spread another blanket over her and went to bed themselves.

Calm and composed Ama's wife lay in the bed. This medically induced calm and relief was no match to the quietitude which she felt when she was a poor farmer's wife living in a shack.

Ama Ganaie was dressed nicely with a Pathan suit and a black short coat. He wore black polished leather chappals. His wife, dressed in superior Shalwar Kameez, looked elegant. The local robe Pheran with golden work around throat and neck and near the arm openings added to her grandeur. They walked hand in hand and Ama tried to flirt with her by pressing the hand.

"What are you doing? Don't try to be shameless. Your son and daughter in law are looking," she managed an artificial anger.

"Where . . . . who . . . . ?" Ama asked in astonishment.

"What happened to you? Can't you see beyond that apple tree in the corner, "his wife elongated her arm to point out to the far off corner in the orchard?

"Your eyesight is really stronger than me. I could not locate Nazir and Arti in the corner. Actually this year we have good apple crop and the trees are fully laden with fruit. The sight is partially blocked," Ama tried his explanation.

Both walked freely till they reached the corner where Arti and Nazir stood.

"*Kysa chukh gobra karan* (What are you doing daughter?)" Ama asked his daughter in law.

"*Ba chus seb peti manz barnawan, wuchhan* (I am getting apples packed in boxes)" Arti replied in Kashmiri with a non Kashmiri accent and wording

"*Hati wouni hi kadakh leke. Yuth koshur nai chu me hajat* (I don't need your Kashmir language. Now you will start abusing)" Nazir cracked a joke and all laughed.

"*Ma wanus kenh. Me na chana wata yiwan kuni aohund koshur boznas* (Don't rebuke her. I feel on stars while listening to her Kashmiri speak)" Nazir's mother reprimanded her son.

Ama Ganaie and his wife remained there for some time and happily left the spot.

"*Ada sa gobra kariw tohi paneni kaem* (Ok, dears carry on)"

As they walked few steps more, Ama Ganaie took a turn towards his left and kept on moving. His wife was perplexed by his sudden movement farther from her.

"*Tse kot oor gatchan. Andar atch karmas manz* (Where are you going. Come inside the room)," she almost shouted to make him listen.

"*Tse pakh be gatche Major Salvan saebus nish* (You go inside I am going to meet Major Salvan,"

"*Magar su kati chu. Dapaan hi su go transfer* (Where is he. They say he is transferred)

"*Tus wana mey saeti khe bata* (I will ask him to have food with me),"

"*Kya bata khe su. khabar kati chu* (What food shall he take. Don't know where is he),"

"*Ba tchandan te khyawan panas seiti bata* (I will look for him and make him have food with me),"

Ama almost jumped over the fence which made his wife perturbed lest he should injure himself.

"*War war hasa . . . .* (Easy, easy)" she shouted.

Her voice was heard by Arti and Ruby whose sleep was disturbed due to her shout. They jumped from their beds and went near her.

"*Mouji mouji* (Mom, mom)" Arti and Ruby shouted simultaneously.

"*Kihe daleel* (what is the matter?)" They tried to awaken her and ascertain the reason of her shout.

"*Yehi aosu mol ami ditchi dosi peth woth dapan Salvan khyawan bata panas seiti* (It was your father. He jumped over the fence. He was saying I will ask Salvan to have food)"

Drivel ran down her lip corners.

"*O, datur khyawes* (Hush . . . . let him offer poison)," Arti used Kashmiri accent and said with utmost anger.

They then tried to make her sleep again.

*　　*　　*

Around a week passed when Arti contacted her lawyer again to file an application before the court. She now wanted exhumation of remains in a particular grave. She wanted the

DNA profile to ascertain the identity of the person buried there. Since she had lost faith in the police hierarchy so she took support of the judiciary. All people pinned hopes on judicial system only. She also wanted to keep the happenings a secret as Jum Khan had advised.

The court issued notices to the government and police who, already under pressure, agreed to DNA profiling. On the orders of the court district magistrate deputed a senior officer to supervise the exhumation and sample collection from the remains of the dead body. On the particular day the police presence on the outskirts of the village was heavy. Three tier security arrangements were in place. One ring was formed around the village so that outsiders do not enter and reach the spot. Even media was barred not to talk of human rights activists. The activists were enthusiastic as they felt one battle had been won. But the known activists were stopped and prevented to travel forward. Lesser known were stopped outside the village area. Second ring was formed around one hundred meters from the actual site. Whereas some thirty meter wide area was covered by erecting coarse cloth covers so that nobody can peep through. A white sheet was placed on top to prevent any birds flying above. Arti and Ruby had permission from the court as well as the district magistrate and they watched the proceedings amid intermittent sobs. As the grave was being dug out, in-between tears rolled down their cheeks. Seeing their plight some officials requested them to leave the spot but they gathered courage and remained alert. They wanted to authenticate the sample collection lest someone tried to fudge the process as had been done in some other case few years back. Both ladies were then offered two plastic chairs by the officer in charge.

"Keep it for these ladies. I requested them to move away as it will be a pathetic and heart rendering scene," the officer told his worker who brought chairs.

"Sir, they won't agree. You don't know possibly she is the army officer who removed lid of this whole issue. She fought her own officers and department. *Darwo kaemi pathwukh pan ni paeni.* I heard she was in love with this boy," the worker informed the officer in whispers.

Diamond cuts diamond!

As the digging was complete and the body exhumed, Arti and Ruby hugged each other and wept bitterly.

The sample collection was done and the packed samples were signed among others by Arti and Ruby. The two ladies did not want to leave anything to chance.

While expert advice was sought from concerned, the samples were taken under requisite norms and sent to couple of laboratories for ascertaining the identity of the buried person. It was established through samples taken from Ruby and her mother that the slain person was actually Nazir and belonged to the Ganaie family. The DNA profile report came handy for Arti who pursued the case vigorously for punishment to the culprits. She was joined by some human rights activists in the process.

In Kashmir people say'*Darwa keim phatwukh* . . . . *paneni peni*' which loosely translated reads as "Who broke the ceiling beam and the reply is its own wedge". Something similar happened to the army establishment. Arti acted like a Trojan horse against her own establishment.

Diamond cuts diamond!

An officer among its own ranks was able to crack the hegemony and arrogance as the establishment was forced to order an enquiry. Swaggers had to part away with their ego. Though very few believed in the customary probes like that but here the situation became different through the connections used by Arti herself. As time passed and enquiry progressed it became evident that a major was directly involved in the case. Arti's own enquiry had indicted her own brother. Pressure mounted on Arti from her own family not to pursue the case so vigorously but she refused. New development had given her more energy and she at all costs wanted punishment to the culprits. Commission of Inquiry (COI) by the army established that the army officer involved had received inputs about Nazir through Major Salvan who loathed him over the issue of being in romance with an army officer, that too from his own camp. It was further informed that he himself had an eye over Arti and even at couple of times tried to flirt with her. But her snub created animosity in his heart towards Nazir and when he found a chance to strike, he did.

Not only was the officer's promotion stalled in the first place but further enquiry opened a Pandora's Box. Major Salvan became another prime target. He already had an FIR registered against him in the fake encounter of Master Abdullah's son Rizwan but the misconduct in case of Arti added fuel to the fire. The results created havoc in the lives of both Salvan and the other officer.

*   *   *

Major Salvan had left the valley and was posted somewhere else. Arti continued her relentless struggle to get the culprits involved in Nazir's abduction and subsequent murder punished. She was part of the various organizations fighting for justice to the victims of HR abuse. The fight continued on various fronts. The courts were agitated. The international human rights bodies provided their support.

The human rights activists, writers, lawyers, journalists fighting the cause within the country came forward to help. The governments both at centre and state were under pressure. The State Human rights commission became active in view of continued newspaper reports. This forced the government to order enquiries. One such enquiry zeroed in at Nazir's abduction, killing and subsequent murder of some renegades. These renegades had been identified by Arti as being involved in Nazir's abduction and had possibly been killed to suppress truth about Nazir. Enquiries did not stop at this abduction case only. It spread to murder of Rizwan, Master Abdullah's son. This murder with a bomb blast, some misappropriations and reports of grabbing money against release of militants surfaced like a series of crime. Even smaller cases like illegal timber smuggling also came to fore. Salvan's further promotions were stopped in the first instance and he was repeatedly asked to explain his position.

Army decided to launch a court martial on its own to decide the fate of the case. During the Court Martial proceedings, Salvan was served the charge sheet. One evening all the cases unfolded before Salvan as if a film rolling and being shown on a projector. He was nervous and continued to drink late in the night. He tried to get some solace from few more pegs. His wife repeatedly asked him to stop.

"Have dinner and sleep, "she yelled after confronting irritating behaviour of her husband.

"Sleep has left Salvan for good. I can have eternal sleep only which will shove away the miseries from my life,"

Repeated assertions by his wife irritated Salvan who had lost his senses now due to over drink. The army officer swilled and turned muzzy.

"I am asking you to stop. Or I will sleep in other room,"

"Yes, you will sleep . . . . I know I indulged in misdeeds for you and your children only. You can sleep but I can't. You lived like a princess and your children are studying in the best colleges in England and US. But I suffer alone. But why should I only suffer . . . ." he continued in his stammering voice, inebriated. "I robbed during my service career to provide you and your children best facilities in life. This big house. On its ceiling the Kashmir manufactured Khutumband. This is manufactured with human hands in Kashmir only. You know golden hands of Kashmiris. See that silken hand knitted Kashmir carpet . . . . it costs half a million rupees. Ama Ganaie arranged it for me . . . ."

Before Salvan's wife could comprehend what was in store from the insane, drunkard Salvan whipped out his service revolver.

Khattak

Khattak

One

Two

Three

Four

Five

Six

The bullet sounds ricocheted in the room. His wife fell in the middle of the room drenched in her own blood. Blood was oozing out of wounds at four spots. She dropped her arms in different directions with back on floor. Empty eyed, motionless, she stared at the ceiling which she once cherished to enjoy and boast of this heart rejoicing selection. The Kashmir silken carpet sent by Ama Ganaie some years back looked fresh in the middle of the room. Now, she had no interest in the interior designing of the rooms of her 4-bed penthouse. The cupboards, dining table, modular kitchen, costly cutlery and crockery, expensive saris and other boutique were of no value to her. She was on the floor covered with high density timber flooring which she had got fixed with attention in detail. Her eyes fixed open but motionless on the *Khatumbund* Kashmir ceiling.

Just she and her blood making serpentine movement on the silken carpet flowing on to the HD flooring!

Salvan's head dropped towards left side. Although muzzy few minutes before he was seated calm on the rocking chair. Blood was flowing down his left shoulder. Drops of blood falling from some height on the same HD flooring.

Tup

Tip

Tup

Tip

The service revolver, he just used to finish off his wife first and then himself, got stuck in his hand. Hand held revolver rested then on his right thigh.

Calm

In peace

No allegations

No enquiries

No court cases

No Court Martial

Glass pegs and tumblers of various shapes stood on the side table kept on right side of the rocking chair just below the huge chandelier hanging down the ceiling. Few empty and few filled wine bottles now remained as silent as the person who used them few minutes before.

Everything and every person in the room were now motionless!

Salvan lost all hopes to get promoted. Fearing more punishment and humiliation, he one night used his service revolver to end his life. The news was splashed in the newspapers and the electronic media. Hearing the news Arti did not like it.

"I wanted him to face the law in this fake encounter, "she told Ruby. "The punishment through court would have been natural justice. Had it been so, all others would repent their misdeeds and take a lesson so that no innocents are harmed in future."

Both could do nothing except weep bitterly.

*   *   *

The natural justice

The school is spread over a vast chunk of land with apple trees. A straight path has been connected to the main road outside. The main road is black topped with bituminous macadam. Although the school is a residential one and students hardly come out of the premises, yet on both sides of the school gate at some distance speed breakers were erected so that vehicle owners don't ply fast and cause danger to the life of these children. The school wall has been reconstructed with more height so that nobody is able to jump over. A black colour steel gate is wide enough to accommodate the school bus nicely. Over the gate a big and high rise semi circular board reads in bold letters;

'Amsons Residential School Arwanpora'. A smaller plaque reads 'For Orphans'.

On entry through the gate on the left side stands the huge house constructed many years back where Ama's family lived. Now Arti, Ruby and her mother live here. Although the house has big fifteen rooms yet the three ladies sleep in one room. Ruby and Arti are friends so they don't want to live in separate rooms. Ruby's mother is a mental wreck and can't be allowed to sleep in separate room. One male member Rehman, the servant, also lives in one room in the ground floor. He has grown old but he still continues to work in the household. He had promised Ama Ganaie, before his death, that he won't leave till he is alive and he keeps his promise.

On the right side of the main gate is servant's room where Chowkidar (guard) and couple of vehicle drivers live. Around 200 meters inside the land estate stands a tall three storey building which houses class rooms. The brick work has been plastered with cement plaster. The building is roofed with timber trusses and CGI sheets fixed over. The building is painted from outside. 'Academic Block' reads the plaque painted on the front side.

On either side of the academic block are two hostel buildings. One for male students and one for female students. In these separate buildings few rooms have been reserved for the few male and female teachers who serve as school wardens. Such teachers stay in the hostels for the night also. The hostel blocks are segregated by brick walls. A good area has been kept as playground.

Cute children wearing tidy uniforms play in the school ground. A small group of them are playing cricket. They have set their own rules. Since their pitch is near the wall the ball can fly off the bat over the wall and fall in the hostel area. Normally it should be a six but, to retrieve it, the fielder has to traverse long distance. So their rule says whosoever makes the ball fly across the wall he has to get it back himself. The fielders are less in number and small children are roaming here and there, so a powerful shot can send the ball far away and there is apprehension that small children may get hurt so only 'stop the ball' is allowed. A powerful shot across the boundary will invite punishment like 'out' or getting the ball back from the boundary.

The teachers, mostly females, are from nearby localities and belong to the families whose men folk became targets during militancy. Some were murdered by army for being sympathizers to militants. Others lost their lives to the accusation of being Mukhbirs (informers). Few were caught in the cross fire while others were consumed by IED blasts. These female teachers are compassionate towards these children. Some have their own children studying in the same school.

Arti and Ruby are now in mid and early thirties respectively. They have grown small streaks of grey hair starting from forehead to the crown. They don't like to colour the white streaks. They feel they look graceful with these streaks which is quite true. Their full day and most part of evening is spent taking care of the studies and other requirements of these students. These students had none to look after when they became orphans. They were either sent as domestic helps in some homes or asked to do menial jobs in automobile workshops. But with Ama Ganaie's advice, Arti and Ruby collected over two hundred children to be taught and fed nicely.

All living in the premises are now happy. They tend to forget previous tragedies and cope up with the miseries of life. But one person in the premises can't be analyzed as being happy or sad. Sadness and happiness is miles away from her. She is widow of Ama Ganaie. As children play, she rushes above to the attic, her watch tower. Due to her frequent visits to the attic the windows have been provided with steel grills to prevent her fall. A caretaker lady always remains with her, particularly during day time, when Arti and Ruby are busy in the school.

A young girl playing in the school ground is cute and chubby.

"See Shazi is playing . . . . Shazi don't run fast lest you fall down," Ruby's mother cries out. She then refers to two kids.

"You know that boy is Farooq's son. He was born to his Pakistani wife. He went to become Mujahid. He was married off to a Pakistani girl. I brought that *bahu* (daughter in law) with me. And the other boy, he is the son of Nazir and Arti. Arti, the military officer, married my son Nazir. He is their baby. I love watching them play . . . . so cute . . . . so happy."

From the watch tower can be seen the grave of Ama Ganaie who is buried under an apple tree in one corner of the land. He had himself selected the spot for his grave. It is visible from the watch tower.

"Ama Ganaie sleeps there. I wish he was alive to see his daughter Shazi and the offspring of his sons," the lady, Ama's widow, continues.

Continues with her self expression.

Continues with her concocted stories.

Continues with the hell she does not feel.

Shadows beyond the ghost town continue to spread.

As the volcano simmers, the burning paradise continues to deflagrate!

*　　*　　*

Post Script

(Indian Express 21-08-2011)

For the first time in Jammu and Kashmir, an official inquiry has said that it is "beyond doubt" that there are scores of unidentified bodies in unmarked graves in the Valley—as many as 2156 bodies buried at 38 sites since militancy began in 1990. The report says that of the bodies, a few were defaced, 20 were charred, five only have skulls remaining and there are at least 18 graves with more than one body each.

Report released by Association of Parents of Disappeared Persons (APDP)

Through our research work we have documented the existence of 7000 unmarked graves and mass graves in 5 districts (Kupwara, Bandipora, Baramulla, Poonch and Rajouri) out of the 22 districts of Jammu and Kashmir

Glossary

DEE	The divisional engineer
Assistant	The Assistant engineer
Khutumbandh	Ceiling in floral and other patterns jointed out of small timber pieces by Kashmiri craftsmen.
Dastarkhwan	A cloth sheet spread, over which crockery/utensils etc are kept and food taken.
Halal	Animals slaughtered as per Islamic rituals.
Pakoras	
Muthi	
Samosa	Indian snacks.
Salaat	Arabic word for Namaz
Dhabas	Indian roadside food outlets
Abhaya	Long robe worn by Muslim women
Iftar	Breaking of daylong fast during Ramadan